Medieval History and Culture

Edited by
Francis G. Gentry
Pennsylvania State University

A Routledge Series

Medieval History

Francis G. Gentry, General Editor

The Literal Sense and the Gospel of John in Late Medieval Commentary and Literature
Mark Hazard

The Reproductive Unconscious in Late Medieval and Early Modern England
Jennifer Wynne Hellwarth

Mystical Language of Sense in the Later Middle Ages
Gordon Rudy

Fair and Varies Forms
Visual Textuality in Medieval Illustrated Manuscripts
Mary C. Olson

Queens in the Cult of the French Renaissance Monarchy
Public Law, Royal Ceremonial, and Political Discourse in the History of Regency Government, 1484–1610
Elizabeth A. Mccartney

The Contested Theological Authority of Thomas Aquinas
The Controversies between Hervaeus Natalis and Durandis of St. Pourçain
Elizabeth Lowe

Body and Sacred Place in Medieval Europe, 1100–1389
Dawn Marie Hayes

Women of the Humiliati
A Lay Religious Order in Medieval Civic Life
Sally Mayall Brasher

Consuming Passions
The Uses of Cannibalism in Late Medieval and Early Modern Europe
Merrall Llewelyn Price

Literary Hybrids
Crossdressing, Shapeshifting, and Indeterminacy in Medieval and Modern French Narrative
Erika E. Hess

Pestilence in Medieval and Early Modern English Literature
Bryon Lee Grigsby

Race and Ethnicity in Anglo-Saxon Literature
Stephen J. Harris

Aspects of Love in John Gower's Confessio Amantis
Ellen Shaw Bakalian

The King's Two Maps
Cartography and Culture in Thirteenth-Century England
Daniel Birkholz

The Medieval Tradition of Thebes
History and Narrative in the OF Roman de Thèbes, Boccaccio, Cahucer, and Lydgate
Dominique Battles

Worlds Made Flesh
Reading Medieval Manuscript Culture
Lauryn S. Mayer

Empowering Collaborations
Writing Partnerships between Religious Women and Scribes in the Middle Ages
Kimberly M. Benedict

The Epistemology of the Monstrous in the Middle Ages
Lisa Verner

THE EPISTEMOLOGY OF THE MONSTROUS IN THE MIDDLE AGES

Lisa Verner

LONDON AND NEW YORK

Published in 2005 by
Routledge
711 Third Avenue
New York, NY 10017
www.routledge.com

Published in Great Britain by
Routledge
2 Park Square, Milton Park
Abingdon, Oxfordshire
OX14 4RN
www.routledge.com

First issued in paperback 2014

Routledge is an imprint of the Taylor & Francis Group, an informa business

Library of Congress Cataloging-in-Publication Data

Verner, Lisa, 1966–

The epistemology of the monstrous in the Middle Ages / by Lisa Verner.

p. cm.—(Studies in medieval history and culture ; v. 33)

ISBN 978-0-415-97243-7 (hbk)

ISBN 978-0-415-76275-5 (pbk)

1. English literature—Middle English, 1100–1500—History and criticism. 2. Monsters in literature. 3. English literature—Old English, ca. 450–1100—History and criticism. 4. Mandeville, John, Sir. Itinerarium. 5. Bestiaries—History and criticism. 6. Animals, Mythical, in literature. 7. Monsters—History—To 1500. 8. Travel, Medieval. I. Title. II. Series.

PR275.M625V47 2005

820.9'37'0902—dc22 2005018259

In memory of
Charles Wilson Verner
(1972–1989)

Excerpts from Pliny, Vol I, Loeb Classical Library Vol. 330, translated by H. Rackham, Cambridge, Mass., Harvard University Press (1938), reprinted by permission of the publishers and trustees of the Loeb Classical Library. The Loeb Classical Library is a registered trademark of the President and Fellows of Harvard College.

Excerpts from Pliny, Vol. II, Loeb Classical Library Vol. 352, translated by H. Rackham, Cambridge, Mass., Harvard University Press (1942), reprinted by permission of the publishers and trustees of the Loeb Classical Library. The Loeb Classical Library is a registered trademark of the President and Fellows of Harvard College.

Excerpts from Pliny, Vol. III, Loeb Classical Library Vol. 353, translated H. Rackham, Cambridge, Mass., Harvard University Press (1940), reprinted by permission of the publishers and trustees of the Loeb Classical Library. The Loeb Classical Library is a registered trademark of the President and Fellows of Harvard College.

Excerpts from Pliny, Vol. X, Loeb Classical Library Vol. 419, translated by D.E. Eicholz, Cambridge, Mass., Harvard University Press (1962), reprinted by permission of the publishers and trustees of the Loeb Classical Library. The Loeb Classical Library is a registered trademark of the President and Fellows of Harvard College.

Excerpts from St. Augustine, Vol. V, Loeb Classical Library Vol. 415, translated by Eva Matthews and William McAllen Green, Cambridge, Mass., Harvard University Press (1965), reprinted by permission of the publishers and trustees of the Loeb Classical Library. The Loeb Classical Library is a registered trademark of the President and Fellows of Harvard College.

Contents

Series Editor's Foreword

Far from providing just a musty whiff of yesteryear, research in Medieval Studies enters the new century as fresh and vigorous as never before. Scholars representing all disciplines and generations are consistently producing works of research of the highest caliber, utilizing new approaches and methodologies. Volumes in the Medieval History and Culture series include studies on individual works and authors of Latin and vernacular literatures, historical personalities and events, theological and philosophical issues, and new critical approaches to medieval literature and culture.

Momentous changes have occurred in Medieval Studies in the past thirty years, in teaching as well as in scholarship. The Medieval History and Culture series enhances research in the field by providing an outlet for monographs by scholars in the early stages of their careers on all topics related to the broad scope of Medieval Studies, while at the same time pointing to and highlighting new directions that will shape and define scholarly discourse in the future.

Francis G. Gentry

Acknowledgments

I would like to thank those teachers and scholars who read and commented on every draft of my work and provided helpful direction and suggestions: Roy Liuzza, Michael Kuczynski, and Gerald Snare. I also owe a debt of gratitude to additional teachers and mentors who have influenced and assisted me over the years: Betty Candler, Charles Knight, Richard Rambuss, and Molly Travis. Colleagues at the University of New Orleans who have been particularly encouraging and supportive include Nancy Easterlin and Bonnie Noonan.

I am indebted to the staff at Tulane University's Howard Tilton Library, especially Patti Windham, Jennifer Cella, Annie Bullock, Thelma Osbey, Anquienetta Dickerson, and Graciela Alejos.

I am grateful to Andy Orchard for permission to quote from *Pride and Prodigies: Studies in the Monsters of the Beowulf Manuscript,* and to University of Aberdeen, Scotland, for permission to quote from the *Aberdeen Bestiary Project.*

My friends provided both intellectual and emotional support throughout this project. Special thanks are due Martha Tanner, John Halbrooks, Shelby Richardson, Robin Stead, and Sidney Lambert.

Lastly, I owe an enormous debt to my family for their patience and encouragement: my husband, Michael DeMocker; my son, Charlie DeMocker; my parents, Charles and Bonnie Verner; Bonnie Anne Verner; Brad and Valerie Yearta; and John and Janice DeMocker.

Introduction

The uninitiated generally believe medieval literature to be populated by Arthurian knights fighting fire-breathing dragons, bloodthirsty giants, or some other malevolent monster. Such a belief of course greatly oversimplifies the subject matter of medieval literature, and yet one cannot ignore the presence of the monstrous throughout the Old and Middle English periods. The hero must battle three *aglæcean* in *Beowulf* alone, and the remainder of the *Beowulf* manuscript may constitute, as Sisam suggested, a treatise on monsters (66–7). Monsters are ubiquitous in the copious material on Alexander the Great, in the Arthuriad, and in medieval romances generally. To the medieval mind monsters clearly constituted, if not an obsession, at least a preoccupation, for one can find them not only in literature but also sculpted in the walls of churches and religious houses, incorporated into heraldry, and worked into the decorations on sword hilts, drinking cups, and jewelry (Thompson 120–1).

The appeal of the monster seems obvious, much like that of the modern freak show: the grotesque simultaneously repels and fascinates. Scandalized, even horrified, the observer (or reader) still cannot look away. However, as with any obvious answer, one should be suspicious, for the analogy I have made here is clearly temporally biased. It assumes medieval people would have had the same visceral and intellectual responses to a monster as a "modern" (or even a "post-modern") would. Such an assumption not only misrepresents the thought of the Middle Ages but also prevents one from ascertaining anything true or useful about the medieval mindset and the changes it underwent over the course of a millennium. One must instead look at what medieval writers actually said about monsters in order to observe what, if anything, the literary use of the monstrous reveals about the medieval way of making sense of the world. Such a project can best be termed, in the words of R. Howard Bloch, a "literary anthropology" (1).

What follows is a chronological survey of the medieval monster, its symbolic value, and the increasing variety of kinds of didactic meaning the monster accumulated from its foundations in ancient thought through the later Middle Ages. In order to chart such a trajectory, one must first determine what constitutes a monster, a task made difficult not only by the 1300-year span of primary sources under consideration, but also by the fact that the definition of a monster is inexorably tied to its function. One is tempted to declare in exasperation that a monster, like art, is indefinable but that, also much like art, one knows it when one sees it. While pithy, such a declaration does not help the reader toward any understanding of the subject, so I will instead attempt a brief survey of the definitions offered by pertinent sources in order to construct a useful working definition of the word *monster* that reflects the intent of medieval writers when they use the word.

St. Augustine, serving as Christianity's and therefore medieval Europe's moral compass, is a good place to start, but St. Augustine does not define *monster.* He does, however, go to great pains to define *human,* "animal rational mortale" ("a rational mortal creature") (my translation) in *City of God,* and to include the possibility for the existence of entire races of monstrous humans—"monstrosa hominum genera"—as well as individual monstrous humans among our own race—"monstrosis apud nos hominum partubus" (16.8). He gives numerous examples of the former, such as sciopods and pygmies, and well as a few examples of the latter, such as hermaphrodites and polydactyls. He comes closest to a definition when he admits that "Apparet tamen quid in pluribus natura obtinuerit et quid sit ipsa raritate mirabile" ("there is a clear distinction between what has by nature persisted in the majority, and what is marvellous by its very rarity") (16.8; trans. Sanford). Yet St. Augustine for all his examples seems far more interested the function of the monster than in giving a definition or enumerating sensationalist occurrences of it:

> Deus enim creator est omnium, qui ubi et quando creari quid oporteat vel oportuerit, ipse novit, sciens universitatis pulchritudinem quarum partium vel similitudine vel diversitate contexat. (16.8)
>
> God is the creator of all things, and he himself knows at what place and time a given creature should be created, or have been created, selecting in his wisdom the various elements from whose likenesses and diversities he contrives the beautiful fabric of the universe. (trans. Sanford)

Whatever a monster may in fact be, its function for St. Augustine is quite clear: it demonstrates the beauty of the superabundance of God's creation. Beyond this, he seems to imply, one need not inquire.

Isidore of Seville goes into more detailed categories of monsters in his *Etymologies* than St. Augustine did in *The City of God.* He divides single monsters into human-animal hybrids; overly large and overly small examples of their species; monsters having a single body part that is overly large or small; monsters having an abundance or a lack of body parts (such as fingers or legs); the lack of or presence of only a body part; the mislocation of a body part; transformations (e.g., a woman gives birth to a calf or snake); and the mixture of genders in a single specimen. Isidore also records entire races having one or more of these deformities, and, like St. Augustine, he apparently sees little or no important distinction between the races and the individuals (11.3.7–27). He does, however, give a definition of *monster,* yet the definition seems mostly concerned with the etymology of *monstrare* (Latin, "to show"): "Monstra vero a monitu dicta, quod aliquid significando demonstrent, sive quod statim monstrent quid appareat" ("Monsters, in fact, are so called as warnings, because they explain something of meaning, or because they make known at once what is to become visible") (11.3.3; my translation). Considering the title of the work, such etymological bias comes as no surprise, but of more interest is the fact that the function of the monster, *to show,* is not only inherent within the word, but also that the very beginning of the section on monsters links the monster to God's divine plan: "non sunt contra naturam, quia divina voluntate fiunt, cum voluntas Creatoris cuiusque conditae rei natura sit" ("they are not contrary to nature, because they come by the divine will, since the will of the creator is the nature of each thing that is created") (11.3.1; trans. Brehaut). Thus, once again the function of the monster, its ability to show humankind something about divinity, becomes more important than, but inseparable from, the monster itself.

The title of the *Liber Monstrorum* would lead one to believe that this would be the best source in which to find a clear definition of *monster* or at least a clear delineation between monster and human/animal. The *Liber Monstrorum* fails to offer any kind of definition of *monster,* but it appears to distinguish between monster and beast and serpent in its general prologue when the author writes that he will speak of "monstruosis hominum partibus . . . et de ferarum horribilibus innumerosisque bestiarum formis et draconum dirissimis serpentiumque ac uiperarum generibus" ("the monstrous births of men, and the horrible and innumerable forms of wild beasts, and the most dreadful kinds of dragons, and serpents, and vipers") (trans. Orchard). Indeed, the epilogue to book one appears to indicate that the author is leaving the realm of monsters proper and moving on to other creatures: "Haec sunt inmania monstra de quibus me fluctus tuae postulationis tundebat" ("These are the huge monsters concerning which the wave of your request buffeted me") (trans. Orchard); and the prologue to book two seems to distinguish *beast* from *monster:* "Belua nuncupari potest quidquid in terris aut in gurgite in horrendi corporis ignota et metuenda reperitur forma" ("Whatever is found on land or in the sea of unknown and fearsome form of terrible bodily appearance can be called a beast") (trans. Orchard). However, the author almost immediately confuses his newly established categories by equating "sea-beasts" ("marinarum genera beluarum") with "monsters" ("monstrorum") (2.prologue; trans. Orchard). He confuses the categories of *monstrum, belua,* and *bestia* at intervals throughout his treatise (2.20,21; 3.1,20). Such crossover implies that a beast or serpent can also be a monster if sufficiently fierce or unusual, but this unfortunately does not help the reader toward any clear definition of *monster.*

While it may appear that the religious intent has been lost in the function of the monster in the *Liber Monstrorum,* such appearance is deceiving. Without ever mentioning God or the religiously symbolic value of the monster—indeed, the author repeatedly implies that the monsters and beasts and serpents he is describing have no purpose or value whatsoever—the treatise is actually a theological study whose intent is to communicate something about religion and reliability. In this way, the *Liber Monstrorum* actually does resemble the work of Augustine and Isidore in that the subject matter itself is secondary, in fact, almost incidental, to the single-minded theological intent of the work as a whole.

The *Bestiary* or book of beasts is also surprisingly coy about what constitutes a *monstrum* or *belua* or even a *bestia* as opposed to a mere animal. After recounting the creation story, the *Aberdeen Bestiary* divides the category *animalia* into several subcategories: *quadrupedia* are animals like deer that are "neque bestie . . . neque iumenta" ("neither wild beasts . . . nor beasts of burden") (trans. McLaren); *pecus* refers to "omne quod humana lingua et effigie caret" ("anything which lacks human speech or appearance") (trans. McLaren), but generally means edible animals like cattle and pigs; *iumenta* are, simply enough, beasts of burden; *armenta* are *animalia* suitable for use in war, such as horses; and finally *greges* are "caprarum et ovium" ("flocks of goats and sheep") (trans. McLaren). These appear to be rather minute distinctions, yet nowhere does the *Bestiary* describe the criteria for a *monstrum* or indicate that it is a subcategory of *animalia.* Three entries specifically use the word *monstrum* to refer to the animal under consideration: the bonnacon, an Indian bull with a horse's mane and the peculiar ability to defend itself with flaming excrement; the monoceros or unicorn; and the crocote, the offspring of a union between a hyena and a lioness. *Belua,* a slightly more ambiguous word that can be synonymous with monster, is used in reference to three other animals: the whale; the flying fish; and the hyena, whose monstrosity probably derives both from its hermaphroditic physique and its diet of human corpses (*Aberdeen Bestiary*).

Despite the *Bestiary*'s use of these terms and its insistence on defining the subcategories of *animalia,* the necessary conditions for being categorized as a monster remain elusive and seemingly arbitrary; the bestiarist apparently just knew a monster when he saw it. The function of the beasts, monsters, and animals of the *Bestiary,* a work that has often been described as a source book for sermons, clearly relates to the "morals" to be derived from the behaviors described. Once again, the *monstrum monstrat,* but, as chapter three will demonstrate, unlike the monsters found in Isidore's *Etymologies,* for example, the monsters and mere animals of the *Bestiary* do not "show" only in the religious realm; by this point their potential moralities have branched out into areas I would designate secular morality.

Ironically, the *Travels of Sir John Mandeville,* a fourteenth-century work that was rewritten, abridged, emended, and expanded dozens of times over the following centuries, offers the first really useful definition of *monster:* "a monstre is a Þing difformed aȝen kynde bothe of man or of best or of ony Þing elles" (30). "Deformed against kind" is the best, most concise definition of *monster* offered by any of the primary sources I consulted for this study, but even so, the phrase "aȝen kynde" presents some difficulties. In Middle English "kind" often means "nature," and such a definition would put the late medieval definition in direct opposition to Isidore's insistence that nothing can be against nature. This would underscore how far the monstrous signification of the later Middle Ages has moved away from a direct correspondence with divinity, and such a dynamic may in part be at work here, but "kind" does not necessarily mean "nature" in this case. According to the *Middle English Dictionary,* "kinde" can also correspond approximately to what we mean by that word: "A class of creatures; human beings, birds, reptiles, etc." More pointedly, the phrase "aȝen kynde" can mean "contrary to the nature of a bird, animal, planet etc." or "abnormal, monstrous, unusual; pathogenic; abnormally." In this light, "deformed against kind" may mean not "deformed against nature itself" but rather "deformed against the nature of the general category of creature under consideration."

In order for "deformed against kind" to function as a suitable working definition, the reader must agree to interpret it broadly. For example, one might argue that races of unusual men, such as sciopods, cannot be classified as monstrous because they are not actually deformed against their own kind. To such an objection I would reply that "kind" is to be broadly interpreted as humankind with the medieval European representing the standard form; accordingly, sciopods, a single-footed hopping race of men, are clearly monstrous.

A broad interpretation of "deformed" would include behavior as well as appearance. Surprisingly, this corresponds nicely to the late medieval definition of "kind" as a form of moral feeling, for "aȝen kynde" can also mean "morally perverted" (*Middle English Dictionary*). Thus a race of cannibals can be designated "monsters" because the consumption of human flesh is a deformed and unusual kind of behavior. Other less offensive but equally unusual behaviors that would qualify as monstrous include unusual maturation rates and life expectancy, as reported of pygmies who achieve sexual maturity at six months and rarely live beyond their seventh year (*Mandeville's Travels* 138), and unusual methods of sustenance, such as the race that subsists on the smell of apples without ingesting them (*Mandeville's Travels* 198). Non-procreative forms of reproduction also qualify as monstrous, as in, for example, the barnacle geese that come to life from fruit that falls in the water (*Mandeville's Travels* 176), or as in the phoenix that self-immolates and then comes back to life as a worm that grows into a bird (*Mandeville's Travels* 30). Since only one phoenix ever exists, it might appear that it cannot be "deformed against kind" since it comprises the entire kind; but, broadly interpreted as a kind of bird, the phoenix can clearly be considered a monster.

The *Travels* departs from earlier works most obviously by giving a clear and concise definition of *monster*, but it also departs from Augustine, Isidore, and even the *Bestiary* by seeming much less concerned with the monster's function on the moral symbolic level than were previous works. Of course, the *Travels* is a narrative and not a list nor an explicitly religious treatise, but the differences between the treatment given monsters in the *Travels* and in earlier works go beyond a difference in genre. Whereas very early works confine the monster's significance to the strictly religious realm and the *Bestiary* introduces the possibility of practical morality as well, in the *Travels* monsters signify on the spiritual, moral, political and mercantile planes, sometimes simultaneously but almost always independently.

Each avenue of signification in the monster exists autonomously and possesses its own epistemological limits. The monster always "shows," but what it shows, the variation of meanings it is allowed to express symbolically, does change. What begins in Christian Europe as direct access to God's intentions (as when Augustine claims He put monsters here to show His superabundance) becomes increasing detached from God yet still representative of religious truth in the Anglo-Saxon age. In the twelfth century the *Bestiary* expands monstrous signification into areas of truth and morality that are not strictly speaking religious, although if true they must naturally reflect something of the divine. The change takes place in the increasing distance from a direct encounter with Divinity, and what the monster shows may be true in a secular sense, a religious sense, or both senses. Finally, by the later Middle Ages, *Mandeville's Travels* presents an apparently infinite variety of arbitrary symbolic functions for the monster, many of which are religious, but some of which appear areligious or even anti-Christian.

Observations such as I have made here are not particularly earth shattering or even difficult to understand, yet they surpass the treatment given to medieval monsters in most critical works until quite recently. Critics have often focused on medieval monsters as evidence of scientific decline during the "Dark Ages" or simply as sensationalist narrative failures. For example, the editor of one version of the *Marvels of the East,* a virtual map of Anglo-Saxon literary monsters, has this to say about his subject: "The fabulous element in classical literature was apparently seized upon, wherever found, by the author of *Wonders of the East,* and put together by him, in no very artistic fashion, to make what is rather a compilation than a work of literary merit" (Rypins xlv). The great M.R. James, in his introduction to a facsimile of the three surviving manuscripts of the *Marvels,* which he assembled, studied, and transcribed, refers to the object of his labor as "the collection of absurdities which I am rescuing from a perhaps merited oblivion" (James 9).

Other texts dealing with monsters receive equally disdainful treatment. Editorial opinion of the Old English *Alexander the Great's Letter to Aristotle,* bound with the *Marvels* in the *Beowulf* manuscript, is that "[h]istorically, as well as geographically, it has obvious shortcomings which make it rather a curiosity than a reliable tract" (Rypins xxxviii). Concerning the *Liber Monstrorum,* one critic writes, "[o]n its own merits it scarcely deserves more than a small niche in the voluminous literature of superstitions, fables, and marvels" (Whitbread 434). Another scholar, while disagreeing with her predecessors, accurately sums up previous critical opinion of the *Physiologus,* the late-antique basis for the medieval *Bestiary:* "Naive and unartistic, fantastical, romantic, and magical, the *Physiologus* was responsible virtually singlehandedly for blotting out the bright light of Aristotelian science for nearly a thousand years" (Cox 433). Similarly, the *Bestiary* "has usually been assumed by scholars" to be "an ignorant collection of moralities and old wives' tales" (George and Yapp 1). And the *Travels of Sir John Mandeville* never fully recovered from "the disconcerting nineteenth-century discovery that the text is a 'fraud' and the author a 'mendacious' missing person" (Higgins 8). Wittkower in his highly influential study characterizes the entire Middle Ages as a period suffering under the "unscientific approach" of Pliny, during which "sound judgment and exact knowledge" were "replaced by imagination and fanciful stories, curiosities and marvels" (166–7). In short, outside the world of the romance, medieval monsters are scientific mistakes and narrative blunders; they are an embarrassment.

I believe a great deal of this embarrassment derives from mistaken notions of genre and purpose. If one considers, for example, the *Marvels* as ethnography, one must naturally regard it as very bad ethnography, for it tells the reader nothing objective or true about Indian and Asian people, their way of life, their religion, or their marriage and child-rearing practices. Likewise, if one considers the *Physiologus* as biology, one notes with disappointment that it explains nothing about the behavior of the lion or the salamander or the pelican in the wild and nothing about biological make-up, food, reproduction or place in the ecosystem. But to the medieval reader knowledge of the salamander's reproductive habits was not the purpose of inquiry into the salamander. Knowles, discussing Hugh of St. Victor's (b. circa 1100) attitude toward earthly knowledge, can help explain the role of natural history and the monstrous in the medieval mindset:

> Far from being hostile to reason and science, Hugh welcomes all knowledge: "Learn all you can," he writes, with a rare reference to his own experience as a beginner, "you will find later that nothing is wasted"; and again: "all human learning can serve the student of theology." This last sentence, perhaps, so quintessentially medieval in its implications, supplies a reason for the modern neglect of Hugh, for his two chief postulates, that all arts and sciences can be acquired from books in the cloister, and that all natural knowledge is an introduction to theology, are so foreign to all our ways of thought as almost to deter us from the attempt to understand one who uttered them. (130)

I believe this lack of understanding has at least to some extent given rise to the abuse and the neglect of medieval monsters. The insistence on seeing them as "real," and therefore scientific mistakes, or as purely literary metaphors, and therefore narrative blunders, can hinder the reader's attempt to understand them in their medieval functions: "learning was intended to lead up to the crown of all, the study of Scripture" (Knowles 68).

While keeping this in mind, the reader can also not ignore the changes that monsters undergo from the Anglo-Saxon age through the late Middle Ages. Monsters may have begun their medieval tenure as foot soldiers in the battle to establish Christianity as the universal metanarrative, but once the war was won, they were free to branch out in, shall we say, civilian enterprises, provided they maintained their loyalty to the Christian state. That is, monsters no longer represented only divine wisdom and spirituality; they could also represent individual virtues and vices within autonomous and sometime non-religious systems as long as they did not conflict with divine truth. Knowles again, in his discussion of Albert the Great as representative of his age, the late twelfth and early thirteenth centuries, explains how the development of true but non-religious systems of thought developed:

> To us his importance is that of the thinker who marked an epoch, not so much by the force and originality of his own thought as by his definition and steadfast recognition of natural human knowledge, and in particular philosophy, as a valid and useful perception of truth, and hence as a discipline of value, autonomous within its own sphere. Hitherto, to Christian thinkers of the West, the true philosophy had been the divine message of the Old and New Testaments, illuminated by meditation and contemplation, using the bankrupt and largely erroneous wisdom of the pagans to assist and explain on the human level. Now, Albert accepted philosophy as the Arabs and Jews had accepted it, as a vision of truth on the natural level, valid within certain agreed limits and therefore to be sought for its own sake as a part of the knowledge of creation given to man as his birthright and heritage. (228)

Knowles here speaks of philosophy, but he could just as easily be discussing politics, mercantile economy, or human relationships; all these subjects become areas of inquiry with rules and advice "valid within certain agreed limits" and "autonomous within [their] own sphere[s]," as he says. For example, while Albert the Great "saw the hand of the Creator imprinted indelibly on all of the universe—mineral, vegetable, animal, rational" (Scanlan 51), yet he also "was free to compose an independent work, organized according to his perceptions of the animal kingdom" (Scanlan 16). So while various disciplines still partook of the divine on some level, they also operated according to their own rules that made sense without the imposition of any higher spiritual meaning. As I hope to make clear, the use of the monstrous in the later Middle Ages also demonstrates the development of these autonomous spheres, some of which may exist simultaneously within a single monster.

Bloch's work, *Etymologies and Genealogies,* provides a kind of parallel version of the present project, and a brief review of his method may prove helpful in understanding the use I hope to make here of monsters. As its title indicates, Bloch believes medieval grammar and lineage, as forms of "cultural superstructure" (91), are the most promising metaphors by which one can comprehend medieval thought patterns. Grammar and lineage "participate in a common representational paradigm characterized by linearity, temporality, verticality, fixity, continuity, and the inherence of semantic social value" (93). Isidore's *Etymologies,* for example, shows how words and their referents indicate an "ontologically fixed origin," i.e., God, rather than a system wherein "the creation of meaning" (Bloch 85) responds to individual circumstances and needs. In my view, the monsters of the *Etymologies* work in this way, deriving their meaning and their importance from what they indicate about their Creator.

Bloch charts shifts and changes in medieval thought patterns by examining the changing roles of language and family in the particular "cultural superstructure" of imaginative literature, and uncovers literature's participation in the rise of the monarchy and demise of the feudal state within the development of the increasingly individualized medieval romance at the expense of the earlier communal epic (92–127). Through his study of words and families, Bloch outlines a change from a stable, originary referentiality that always goes back to a root meaning or founding father in the pursuit of order, to a more fluid system less concerned with origins ("being made") than with movements, formulations, and fashionings ("growing"); the speculative gives way to the operative. This study does not claim such scope or ambition, but it does aim to chart the ways in which the depiction of medieval monsters corresponds to Bloch's theory. An examination of the monster from its classical origins through the later Middle Ages will show how a system in which the monster functioned only to indicate the presence of and do the bidding of its Creator through its ontological stability gave way to "a system of value in which worth is created not so much by origin as by relative position within a more fluid whole" (Bloch 172).

Chapter one will examine the classical monster that the medieval world inherited from Pliny the Elder's *Natural History* as well as the adjustments made by Isidore of Seville in his *Etymologies* and by the author of the *Physiologus* to make the monster not only acceptable but also useful to early Christianity. Chapter two will document how the early patristic attitude carried over and was put to even more sophisticated, if occasionally tedious, use in the Anglo-Saxon age's "monster tracts"—*Marvels of the East, Alexander the Great's Letter to Aristotle,* and the *Liber Monstrorum*—as well as in Aldhelm's *Enigmata.* Chapter three will scrutinize what I have termed a transitional text between the originary and the fluid methods of signification: the ubiquitous and problematic *Bestiary* whose contents include not just ordinary animals but extraordinary and monstrous ones as well. The final chapter will examine the much maligned *Travels of Sir John Mandeville* as a text in which the potential meanings of monsters, and of everything else of which Mandeville speaks, have become so fluid and diverse as to have virtually eliminated the possibility of any stable, originary referent; here monsters are purely situational. My hope is that this study will in some small way contribute to the recent larger project of rescuing monsters from their "(un)merited oblivion."

Chapter One
The Ancients

The Middle Ages inherited from the classical world not only a tradition of monsters and marvels, but also a culture of knowledge that relied heavily on authority and the ability to catalogue and organize all things. While accepting the general principles of *auctoritas* and organization, the early Middle Ages, from around the fall of Rome in 410 A.D. until the early twelfth century, replaced or adjusted the specific authorities and methods of organization they used in order to reflect the Christian, instead of the pagan, perspective. This change is manifested particularly in the categories of the monstrous and the marvelous where changes in their functions, sources and organizing principles in early encyclopedic, pseudo-zoological, and geographical writings can be traced. These changes do not necessarily represent a shift in fundamental ways of thinking, since reliance on authority and a compulsion to catalogue and organize this world remain primary concerns from the age of Pliny (A.D. 23–79) until the Norman Conquest and the subsequent intellectual revolution of the twelfth century. But these changes do demonstrate authoritative and organizational replacements of the pagan by the Christian, and these replacements will later become modified themselves in the allegorized monsters and marvels of late medieval narratives.

This chapter will focus on the journey from Pliny's *Natural History* (A.D. 77) through the analogic reconstruction of nature in the *Physiologus* (second century A.D.) and into the early encyclopedic tradition as epitomized by Isidore of Seville's *Etymologies* (circa A.D. 636). The focus on Pliny will provide the reader with a pagan encyclopedic background with which to contrast the early Christian encyclopedic works, which often drew on the *Natural History.* In many ways the exhausting attention to details and the slavish reliance on *auctoritas* in both Christian and pagan works point to profound similarities between the two ages under consideration. However, the changes that do take place—the new religious significance given to apparently meaningless details and the transfer of authority from human agents to God in the emerging Christian tradition—set the course for the trajectory of thought that will dominate consideration of the monstrous until at least the twelfth-century renaissance.

Pliny the Elder's *Natural History* functioned as "a standard work of reference among the English" (Ogilvy 222) and also on the continent (Healy xxxvii) during the early Middle Ages and beyond. Although "the *Natural History* was a big book to copy, and complete manuscripts are not numerous" (Haskins 112), one might say the same of the Bible, and yet the dissemination of its separate books did not lessen the influence exerted by its complete form. While it is true that the Middle Ages saw the fragmentation of the books of the *Natural History* and their subsequent independent circulation, the reader should bear in mind that, according to the *Dictionary of the Middle Ages*' entry on encyclopedias and dictionaries, "[o]f the three encyclopedists of ancient Rome—Varro, Celsus, and Pliny—only the work of Pliny has survived whole to modern times, and . . . only he had an influence on medieval encyclopedists." Pliny "survived whole" sometimes in complete manuscripts as well as fragments, and some fragments are actually very large sections. Bede, for example, had about half of the books of the *Natural History*, yet he at least partially "derived his conception of an ordered universe from Pliny"(Chibnall 61). By the eighth century complete or mostly complete copies had made it to Ireland (Chibnall 61), and complete manuscripts were "readily available" (Chibnall 74) in the later Middle Ages, arguing for the survival of copy texts from earlier periods. In this way Pliny influenced later encyclopedists, such as Isidore of Seville, Cassiodorus, and Hrabanus Maurus, on both the microcosmic and macrocosmic levels: "they not only drew details from it but also imitated its organization, beginning with the heavens, then moving to earth, man and other animals, plants, and minerals—that is, down the chain of being" (*Dictionary of the Middle Ages*). So popular did Pliny become that by "the end of the ninth century" he could be counted among those authors "so well entrenched in the literary and educational tradition and so thick on the shelves of the libraries that their survival was no longer in question" (Reynolds and Wilson 100–1).

On the microcosmic level, the monstrous material, because it "appealed powerfully to the mediaeval love of the marvellous" (Haskins 112), comprised some of the most popular excerpts and served as the source for many of the monsters and marvels that so fascinated later Christian writers. Wittkower comments that "[o]ne of the main sources for the mediaeval lore of monsters was Pliny's *Historia naturalis* (finished 77 A.D.)" (166). Pliny's influence was thus felt in specific areas, such as the study of monsters and marvels, as well as in the overall structure of medieval encyclopedias, and this specific monstrous knowledge directly affected both Isidore (Brehaut) and the author of the *Physiologus* (Curley, Notes 68–92).

The title *Natural History* could mislead the reader if s/he adheres to modern assumptions about this term, including its implication of objective scientific observation. Although Pliny "had a naturally scientific mind," he "had no considerable first-hand knowledge of the sciences and was not himself a systematic observer" (Rackham ix). If Pliny did not observe systematically, he did compile and arrange the observations, both faithfully recorded and shamelessly fabricated, of others, and it is this arrangement with which this study is interested. Pliny's subject matter is, in his own words, "sterilis materia, rerum natura, hoc est vita" ("a barren one—the world of nature, or in other words life") (pref. 13; trans. Rackham). Referring to the intended audience of the *Natural History,* Pliny says "humili vulgo scripta sunt, agricolarum, opificum turbae, denique studiorum otiosis" ("it was written for the common herd, the mob of farmers and of artizans [sic], and after them for students who have nothing else to occupy their time") (pref. 6; trans. Rackham). In spite of such a modest assertion, Pliny dedicated the *Natural History* to the emperor Titus (Healy xiii), and his great work, "a systematic account of all the material objects that are not the product of man's manufacture" (Rackham viii-ix), was something never attempted before, as he admits: "nemo apud nos qui idem temptaverit invenitur, nemo apud Graecos qui unus omnia ea tractaverit" ("there is not one person to be found among us who has made the same venture, nor yet one among the Greeks who has tackled single-handed all departments of the subject") (pref. 14; trans. Rackham). In embracing a task of this magnitude, Pliny consciously rejects specialization, abstraction and artistry in favor of a wide scope of inquiry, concreteness and the natural world in which most people spent the majority of their time (pref. 14–16; Healy xix).

So Pliny composed an encyclopedia, one that would remain popular and influential for over a thousand years, possibly because of its underlying but unstated principle: all things on earth are knowable and can be catalogued. This principle operates through the *Natural History* on the levels of organization and authority. Pliny's method of organization can be described as, for lack of a better term, encyclopedic. That is, Pliny observes the earth from above, as it were, and sees the material world as a series of concentric circles. Moving from the outermost circle to the innermost, the reader travels from the largest material thing to the smallest and least important in the material hierarchy. Pliny reduces these circles to a linear progression in the

Natural History's table of contents, which Healy has usefully and mostly accurately divided into five categories of decreasing scope (Healy vii-viii). Healy has titled the first section "The Universe and the World," and this section includes books 2–6, referred to respectively as "Astronomy," "Spain and Italy," "Europe and Britain," "The Continents of Africa and Asia," and "The Black Sea, India and the Far East." Book 2, "Astronomy," could perhaps be more accurately titled "Space, the Planets, and the Earth," for Pliny begins by demarcating his subject matter as the knowable material of the universe:

> Mundum et hoc—quocumque nomine alio caelum appellare libuit cuius circumflexu teguntur cuncta, numen esse credi par est, aeternum, inmensum, neque genitum neque interiturum umquam. huius extera indagare nec interest hominum nec capit humanae coniectura mentis. (2.1)
>
> The world and this—whatever other name men have chosen to designate the sky whose vaulted roof encircles the universe, is fitly believed to be a deity, eternal, immeasurable, a being that never began to exist and never will perish. What is outside it does not concern men to explore and is not within the grasp of the human mind to guess. (trans. Rackham)

Having thus limited his scope, Pliny works his way down, so to speak, from the planets and stars to the earth itself, its size, its shape, and the influence of celestial bodies upon it. Once firmly earthbound, he then explores the surface of the earth, this time working outward from the areas most familiar to him, Spain and Italy, to those farthest away from Roman civilization, Africa, Asia, India and the Far East.

After disposing of geography, Pliny moves on to consider what Healy calls "Zoology" in books 7–11: "Man," "Land Animals," "Creatures of the Sea," "Birds," and "Insects." Very generally speaking, Pliny organizes animals in terms of their decreasing importance or position in his human-centered hierarchy of living things: "Principium iure tribuetur homini, cuius causa videtur cuncta alia genuisse natura magna" ("The first place will rightly be assigned to man, for whose sake great Nature appears to have created all other things") (7.1; trans. Rackham). He then moves on to the area of "Botany" in books 12–18, which includes trees, fruits, viticulture and agriculture. The section Healy titles "Materia Medica" (books 20–32) might easily have fallen under the category of botany as well, since this section includes chapters on flowers, herbs and wild plants. However, Pliny spends a great deal of time discussing the medical uses to which plants can be put and also discusses medicine in general, the medical uses of aquatic creatures, magic, and superstition. Still, such subjects remain well within the realm of the material world. Healy's final division, "Mining and Minerals," treats only the inanimate world of stones and metal and the uses to which they can be put, such as sculpture, painting and architecture. For Pliny, the physical world exists to provide humankind with material to make human life possible and enjoyable, whether it be animals for food, plants for medicine, or stones for building and art. Pliny's universe is human-centered, in a very literal way: the humans are foremost among living things on the earth, and anything beyond the earth is not to be considered. Moreover, no relationship is posited between the things in and on the earth and the celestial world above.

The concentric organization of the material universe, rendered here in a written and thus linear format, encloses and contains all physical knowledge; it is encyclopedic. The knowledge contained in such an encyclopedia, however, does not derive from Pliny's own observations. The copious amount of material found with the *Natural History* could not possibly come from the experience of any single individual, so Pliny has naturally relied on outside authorities for his information. He goes to great lengths to document the authorities he uses in his exhaustive table of contents, which comprises all of the *Natural History*'s first book. In his table of contents, Pliny first provides a summary of the material to be found in each book by subsection and refers to this summary as "continentur" (1). Then, having broken up each book into sections, he provides a list of sources for each book, designating this list as "ex auctoribus" (1). These extensive lists contain the names of virtually every ancient historian, scientist, and poet whose work remains extant, as well as the names of many whose work is lost. Pliny himself claims to have consulted "voluminum . . . duorum milium" ("two thousand volumes") (pref. 17; trans. Rackham). From these, he has collected 20,000 facts from a hundred authorities into thirty-six volumes (pref. 17). Healy notes that this is "a rather conservative estimate since no fewer than 146 Roman and 327 foreign authors are quoted" (xvii). Ironically, this encyclopedic table of contents, which provides the reader with both a model for the known universe and the means of accessing comprehensive knowledge of all parts of the universe, makes it possible for the reader to ignore every subject except the one s/he is seeking, as Pliny explained to Titus in the closing of his introduction (pref. 33). Having collected, catalogued and organized the most important facts about the physical and knowable universe, Pliny fashions a system whereby the reader will not actually have to read all these facts. This method "fixes" knowledge in its proper place from which small bits can be extracted, used, and returned to their places as needed. In a final bow to authority, Pliny completes the preface itself with these words: "hoc ante me fecit in litteris nostris Valerius Soranus in libris quos ἐποπτίδων inscripsit" ("This plan has been adopted previously in Roman literature, by Valerius Soranus in his books entitled *Lady Initiates*") (pref. 33; trans. Rackham). Even concepts of organization have sources that must be acknowledged in order for knowledge itself to be comprehensive and reliable.

Pliny's comprehensive and "reliable" collection includes a myriad of material on both monsters and marvels, which was later used by St. Augustine (Orchard 105), Isidore of Seville (Brehaut 47), Aldhelm (Lapidge and Rosier, Notes 247), and the author of the *Liber Monstrorum* (Orchard 87), among others. Observe what Pliny says about a few of the more popular and recurring monsters and marvels of the Middle Ages, beginning with the Blemmyae. In book five on Africa and Asia, Pliny includes them in a description of races found in the African interior, where they are simply one strange race among many: "quidam solitudinibus interposuerunt Atlantas eosque iuxta Aegipanas semiferos et Blemmyas et Gemphasantas et Satyros et Himantopodas" ("In the middle of the desert some place the Atlas tribe, and next to them the half-animal Goat-Pans and the Blemmyae and Gemphasantes and Satyrs and Strapfoots") (5.8.44; trans. Rackham). Pliny then describes the Blemmyae in a single sentence: "Blemmyis traduntur capita abesse ore et oculis pectori adfixis" ("The Blemmyae are reported to have no heads, their mouth and eyes being attached to their chests") (5.8.46; trans. Rackham). Pliny does not comment on the Blemmyae except to note their physical peculiarity and apparently feels no need to interpret their deformity in any way; they simply exist, and he has assigned them to their proper place in the African interior.

Pliny also locates Pygmies but records their existence in two places in book six on India and the Far East. Near the river Indus, "Pygmaei traduntur" ("there is said to be a race of Pygmies") (6.22.70; trans. Rackham), and also "quidam et Pygmaeorum gentem prodiderunt inter paludis ex quibus Nilus oriretur" ("some writers have actually reported a race of pygmies living among the marshes in which the Nile rises") (6.35.188; trans. Rackham). Once again Pliny fails to comment on the monstrous race in question, and in this case he does not even describe them. Like the Blemmyae, they are fitted into place and made part of the known world, becoming accessible to all who can read. However, in another section, book seven on human beings and their varieties, Pliny goes into more detail about this diminutive race:

> . . . quos a gruibus infestari Homerus quoque prodidit. fama est insidentes arietum caprarumque dorsis armatos sagittis veris tempore universo agmine ad mare descendere et ova pullosque earum alitum consumere, ternis expeditionem eam mensibus confici, aliter futuris gregibus non resisti; casas eorum luto pinnisque et ovorum putaminibus construi. Aristoteles in cavernis vivere Pygmaeos tradit, cetera de his ut reliqui. (7.2.26–7)

> [T]his tribe Homer has also recorded as being beset by cranes. It is reported that in springtime their entire band, mounted on the backs of rams and she-goats and armed with arrows, goes in a body down to the sea and eats the cranes' eggs and chickens, and that this outing occupies three months; and that otherwise they could not protect themselves against the flocks of cranes that would grow up; and that their houses are made of mud and feathers and egg-shells. Aristotle says that the Pygmies live in caves, but in the rest of his statement about them he agrees with the other authorities. (trans. Rackham)

Pliny does not comment on these details, as curious as they might be; he merely records them and refers to the authority of Homer and Aristotle. The astute reader will note that, while referring to authorities, Pliny refrains from stating definitively whether or not he believes in the existence of Blemmyae or Pygmies; "it is reported," "some claim," and even "Aristotle says" allow him to sidestep the issue of veracity, although I do not believe that this maneuver necessarily implies that Pliny does not believe in such races. So common an animal as the owl, whose behavior is undoubtedly observable, warranted the same sort of verbal sidestepping: "noctuae paucis diebus latere traduntur" ("it is stated that even night-owls go into retreat for a few days") (10.41.76; trans. Rackham). Likewise the description of the viper employs similar language: "Serpentium vipera sola terra dicitur condi" ("It is said that the viper is the only snake that hides in the ground") (8.59.139; trans. Rackham). Pliny seems to use phrases like "it is said" and "others report" not as gauges of truth, but as a method of attributing knowledge to sources other than his own observations. And, as will be seen shortly, he is not above calling a lie a lie.

The Pygmies' unusual way of life appears where it does and not earlier because the chapters on geography did not require such a minute survey; those chapters were designed only to map locations, which was crucial in establishing the reader's point of view. Having established this view, Pliny provides the reader with information s/he will need in order to understand the world in its entirety, for despite what the preface says about one not needing to read the entire *Natural History*, "naturae vero rerum vis atque maiestas in omnibus momentis fide caret si quis modo partes eius ac non totam conplectatur animo" ("the power and majesty of the nature of the universe at every turn lacks credence if one's mind embraces parts of it only and not the whole") (7.1.7; trans. Rackham). The author's goal, and by extension the reader's as well, is comprehensive knowledge within a specific and individualizing framework—a true encyclopedia.

The sirens, a rather confusing group of monsters, appear in three different places in the *Natural History*. In book three on the geography of Spain and

Italy, Pliny merely uses them to demarcate a geographical area, "Surrentum cum promunturio Minervae Sirenum quondam sede" ("Sorrento with the promontory of Minerva that once was the abode of the Sirens") (3.5.62; trans. Rackham). The sirens themselves are not under discussion and serve only to map out the physical world. Later, in book ten on birds, Pliny dismisses the bird-monster sirens as "fabulous" or untrue, along with the griffin and Pegasus-bird, but accompanying this dismissal is a very interesting aside: "adfirmet . . . Dinon Clitarchi celebrati auctoris pater in India esse mulcerique earum cantu quos gravatos somno lacerent" ("Dinon the father of the celebrated authority Clitarchus declares that they exist in India and that they charm people with their song and then when they are sunk in a heavy sleep tear them in pieces") (10.70.136; trans. Rackham). Even when he declares a thing a fabulous lie, Pliny continues to give credit to the authority for the lie; even imaginary physical beings can find a place in a map of encyclopedic knowledge. Later in his book on magic, which he mostly devotes to discrediting his subject matter, Pliny mentions sea-nymph sirens as an example of a magical theme in the *Odyssey* (30.2.6). Once again, he cites authority, Homer himself, for that which he marks as a lie. But even lies—or more charitably literary fictions that have been taken too literally by some misguided souls—apparently have their place in Pliny's map of the universe.

The reader can observe an even more perverse insistence on documenting fabrications in Pliny's description of the phoenix in book ten on birds. Pliny notes that "haut scio an fabulose" ("though perhaps it is fabulous") (10.2.3; trans. Rackham), he will document the story of the phoenix:

> aquilae narratur magnitudine, auri fulgore circa colla, cetero purpureus caeruleam roseis caudam pinnis distinguentibus, cristis fauces, caputque plumeo apice honestante. primus atque diligentissime togatorum de eo prodidit Manilius senator ille maximis nobilis doctrinis doctore nullo: neminem exstitisse qui viderit vescentem sacrum in Arabia Soli esse, vivere annis DXL, senescentem cassiae turisque surculis construere nidum, replere odoribus et superemori; ex ossibus deinde et medullis eius nasci primo ceu vermiculum, inde fieri pullum, principioque iusta funera priori reddere et totum deferre nidum prope Panchaiam in Solis urbem et in ara ibi deponere. . . . Cornelius Valerianus phoenicem devolavisse in Aegyptum tradit Q. Plautio Sexto Papinio coss.; allatus est et in urbem Claudii principis censura anno urbis DCCC et in comitio propositus, quod actis testatum est, sed quem falsum esse nemo dubitaret. (10.2.3–5)
>
> The story is that it is as large as an eagle, and has a gleam of gold round its neck and all the rest of it is purple, but the tail blue picked out with rose-coloured feathers and the throat picked out with tufts, and a feathered crest

> adorning its head. The first and the most detailed Roman account of it was given by Manilius, the eminent senator famed for his extreme and varied learning acquired without a teacher: he stated that nobody has ever existed that has seen one feeding, that in Arabia it is sacred to the Sun-god, that it lives 540 years, that when it is growing old it constructs a nest with sprigs of wild cinnamon and frankincense, fills it with scents and lies on it till it dies: that subsequently from its bones and marrow is born first a sort of maggot, and this grows into a chicken, and that this begins by paying due funeral rites to the former bird and carrying the whole nest down to the City of the Sun near Panchaia and depositing it upon an altar there. . . . Cornelius Valerianus reports that a phoenix flew down into Egypt in the consulship of Quintus Plautius and Sextus Papinius; it was even brought to Rome in the Censorship of the Emperor Claudius, A.U.C. 800 and displayed in the Comitium, a fact attested by the Records, although nobody would doubt that this phoenix was a fabrication. (trans. Rackham)

Pliny spends a great deal of time documenting the history of an animal that does not exist. In spite of his doubts, however, he provides the reader with famous authorities and authoritative records attesting to the marvelous bird and its place in the scheme of the world. One may conclude from this that a marvelous bird has its place within the larger category of birds in general; that it may not exist is just another documented fact to be placed neatly amidst other information about the phoenix.

Lastly, the adamas rock, which possesses some marvelous properties, deserves some scrutiny. This stone, found in the *Natural History*'s final book on precious stones, is "[m]aximum in rebus humanis . . . diu non nisi regibus et iis admodum paucis cognitus" ("the most highly valued of human possessions . . . which for long was known only to kings, and to few of them") (37.15.55; trans. Eichholz). Its value resides in its imperviousness to force or heat: "duritia est inenarrabilis, simulque ignium victrix natura et numquam incalescens" ("the hardness of 'adamas' is indescribable, and so too that property whereby it conquers fire and never becomes heated") (37.15.57; trans. Eichholz). Pliny does not dwell overmuch on adamas' remarkable properties but rather mentions it in its properly appointed place in the material hierarchy and moves on, much as he has done with the other monstrous and marvelous phenomena mentioned here. Indeed, Pliny does not provide a classification of marvels or monsters, nor does he devote a book to them as a subject. He does say, in book seven on humankind, that "[p]raecipue India Aethiopumque tractus miraculis scatent" ("India and parts of Ethiopia especially teem with marvels") (7.2.21; trans. Rackham), but he does not confine his discussion of marvelous things or monstrous animals and humans to one area, as the number of chapters referred to in this analysis attests. From this dispersion the reader can conclude that, for Pliny, the monstrous and the marvelous were not categories of organization. His encyclopedic view did not exclude monsters and marvels, but he also did not consider the category of the monstrous part of the framework by which knowledge was classified and organized.

As for the popular conception of monsters and marvels as portents, an idea upon which the early Middle Ages vigorously seized, Pliny shows, as one might expect, some skepticism. In the introduction to his discussion of foreign and unfamiliar races which might appear monstrous to his reader, he states that he will describe "in quibus prodigiosa aliqua et incredibilia multis visum iri haud dubito" ("some things among which I doubt not will appear portentous and incredible to many") (7.1.6; trans. Rackham), implying that reality in fact differs from such appearance. Later he rejects the portentousness of "monstrous" Eastern races: "Haec atque talia ex hominum genere ludibria sibi, nobis miracula, ingeniosa fecit natura," ("These and similar varieties of the human race have been made by the ingenuity of Nature as toys for herself and marvels for us") (7.2.32; trans. Rackham). And while accepting that on occasion monstrous and multiple births may be portentous, he limits the possibilities for prodigious interpretation, noting for example that "quos Hermaphroditos vocamus, olim androgynos vocatos et in prodigiis habitos, nunc vero in deliciis" ("what we call Hermaphrodites, formerly called androgyni and considered as portents, but now as entertainments") (7.3.34; trans. Rackham). Pliny makes a systematic effort to limit the interpretive possibilities of both races of monsters and individual monsters, preferring to see them as foreign species of humans or as "toys" and "entertainments" without any meaning.

Locher has divided Pliny's sources of information into three categories: *res,* facts that simply exist, having no specific source of information; *historiae,* facts attested by *auctores;* and *observationes,* Pliny's own eyewitness accounts (22–3). He then observes that monsters and marvels—"the curiosum or mirabile, the amazing or grotesque" (23)—range over every variety of source and "can be attributed to one or the other type" (24). Such dispersal, along with the curious insistence on reporting what he knows to be lies, argues for the supremacy of comprehensiveness over truth, as well as for the absence of the monstrous or "curiosum" as an organizational category. Pliny's monsters and marvels occur throughout the physical world and provide physical beings with merely one of their components: the Pygmies' stature is of no more importance than the debate over whether they live in huts or caves.

Whether or not Pliny marvels at his subject matter, and whether or not he actually believes it, he consistently and exhaustively catalogues not just information but also his source for that information. The table of contents and the extensive in-text citations indicate a reliance on authority of some sort for all the information he reports. The early Middle Ages will inherit this devotion to sources and also the tendency to catalogue and organize; however, both these impulses will have to adjust to a new authority and, consequently, a new organizational principle: Christianity. Authority and organization remain essential criteria, and the early Christian Middle Ages maintained a belief in the knowability of the physical world, much as the ancients did. However, the Christian Middle Ages rejected Pliny's assertion that what was beyond the physical realm was unknowable and none of humankind's business. For early Christianity, the world beyond the physical was in fact the only world of any importance, and one only studied the physical world in order to acquire access to and understanding of the spiritual world beyond. Christianity also placed greater import on the idea of truth, not necessarily of the physical or literal variety, but of the spiritual sort. Such truth, especially concerning the monstrous and the marvelous, comes to be seen as worthwhile not only when literal, but also when symbolic or literary, provided the "truth" is properly Christian.

One of the first texts both to attempt this readjustment and to use monsters and marvels to do so is the *Physiologus*. An anonymous author composed the *Physiologus* in Greek around A.D. 200, and a Latin translation was circulating at least by the sixth century and possibly as early as the fourth century (Curley, Introduction xvii-xxi). The earliest surviving Latin manuscript dates from the eighth century (Curley, Introduction xx), after which the *Physiologus* became "one of the most popular and widely read books of the Middle Ages" (Curley, Introduction ix), with "well over 250 MSS in Latin, Romance and Germanic languages copied between 1100 and 1400" (Carmody, Introduction 95). The y-version is considered to be closest to the Greek original (Curley, Introduction xxxiii), but the b-version gave rise to the *Bestiary*, the subject of a later chapter, and will therefore be used here (McCulloch 25). It consists of thirty-six entries on a variety of creatures and phenomena, some of which are monstrous or marvelous, but many of which are perfectly ordinary, or merely exotic. Each entry consists of a description of a creature or thing and/or its habits and a spiritual interpretation, usually accompanied by scripture.

The sources for the material in the *Physiologus* include Aristotle, Plutarch, Aelian, Herodotus, Ovid, Homer, and even Cicero (Curley, Notes 68–92). Pliny also makes quite a contribution, but Pliny never provided his monsters or marvels with any kind of spiritual commentary or much commentary at all. The introduction of such commentary can be explained to a great extent by the new ostensible authority for this information. The word *physiologus* refers to a person, supposedly the authority for the descriptions and interpretations found in the book that takes his name, and importantly does not mean "naturalist," as is commonly believed (Curley, Introduction xv). Curley explains that "Physiologus, no doubt, was originally understood to be a person, not the title of a book. The formulae *Physiologus dicit* and *Bene Physiologus dixit* show that a person is meant. Who was he?. . . . to have merited his name, he must have written about the natural world in the spirit of what we know ψυσιολογια to have meant" (Introduction xv–xvi). Curley tells us that to Aristotle ψυσιολογια meant "philosophers whose theories about natural phenomena were grounded in observation of the sensible world" (Introduction xi), but that later, "under the influence of Neoplatonic currents during the first two centuries A.D., Christian writers conceived of a more systematic ψυσιολογια with a mystical dimension nowhere to be found among the ancients" (Introduction xiii). This mystical component involved accessing the divine through the material world. Living beings and even inanimate objects possessed enough remnants of their divine Creator that the careful observer could puzzle out a spiritual message by studying the nature of nature. Clearly, such a view shows strong Neoplatonic influence, but despite Neoplatonism's official anti-Christian slant, according to the *Dictionary of the Middle Ages*' entry on "neoplatonism," it still "had a strong influence on Christianity in both the Eastern and Western churches" during the patristic period, and evidence of such influence can be found in writers even more ubiquitous and more orthodox than the author of the *Physiologus,* such as Boethius and Augustine. Thus, a physiologus interpreted nature in order "to bridge the otherwise impassable intellectual gulf between the *visibilia* of this world and the *invisibilia* of the other" (Curley, Introduction xiv-xv). Nature itself becomes "a symbolic language, a theological text" (Cox 436), and the physiologus "mak[es] manifest the nature of God himself by unveiling the vestiges of the creator in creation" (Curley, Introduction xv). Such a project contrasts sharply with that of Pliny, for whom "there is no simplistic direct line from God to man" (Beagon 101).

Observe what *Physiologus* does with some of the material he borrows from Pliny in order to see any new authoritative or organizational principles in this Christian rendering of pagan lore. The entry on "Sirenae et Onocentauri" begins with a scriptural reference and Physiologus' description of the siren:

> Isaias propheta dicit: Sirena et daemonia saltabunt in Babylonia, et herinacii et onocentauri habitabunt in domibus eorum [Esai. 13.22]. Unius

> cuiusque natura Physiologus disseruit: sirenae (inquit) animalia sunt mortifera; quae a capite usque ad umbilicum figuram hominis habent, extrema uero pars usque ad pedes uolatilis habent figuram; et musicum quoddam ac dulcissimum melodiae carmen canunt . . . (*Physiologus* 12 [versio B])
>
> The prophet Isaiah said: Sirens and demons will dance in Babylon, and hedgehogs and onocentaurs will live in their homes [Is. 13.22]. Physiologus discusses the nature of each: the sirens, he says, are deadly animals, which have the figure of a human from the head to the navel while having the figure similar to a bird to the feet; thus they sing a song with music and sweet voices . . . (my translation)

Physiologus then describes how sirens lull sailors to sleep and then kill them. It concludes with a simile:

> Sic igitur et illi decipiuntur qui deliciis huius saeculi et pompis et theatralibus uoluptatibus delectantur, tragediis ac diuersis musicis melodiis dissoluti, et uelut grauati somno sopiti efficiuntur aduersariorum praeda. (12 [versio B])
>
> And thus are they deceived who take delight in worldly allurements and ostentations and theatrical pleasures, [who are made] dissolute by tragedies and various melodious songs, and just as they are unwillingly lulled to sleep, it is brought to pass that they fall prey to enemies. (my translation)

Physiologus then discusses the onocentaur and concludes thus: "Hi tales siue syrene siue onocentauri figuram ostendunt aduersariorum" ("Such beasts, sirens or ass-centaurs, represent the figures of devils") (15 [versio Y]; trans. Curley). According to the *Dictionary of Medieval Latin from British Sources,* Curley translates the most likely meaning of "aduersariorum," which makes clear the mystical nature of the entry. In this case *Physiologus* does not access the divine through nature, but rather the diabolical; however, the principle remains the same, and the spiritual message (that the Christian soul must maintain diligence and not be seduced by devils disguised as pleasure), not the monstrous creature itself, becomes the focus of *Physiologus*' and the reader's attention.

Physiologus' phoenix bears some resemblance to Pliny's, but the former's adjustments are quite telling. *Physiologus*' entry on the phoenix begins by clearly equating the bird with the savior and presenting the scriptural authority for doing so: "[H]uius figuram gerit dominus noster Iesus Christus, qui dicit in euangelio suo: Potestatem habeo ponendi animam meam et iterum sumendi eam [Ioh. 10.18]" ("Its figure bears our lord Jesus Christ, who said in his gospel: 'I have the power of laying aside my life and of possessing it again' [John 10:18]") (*Physiologus* 9 [versio B]; my translation). The description that follows adjusts Pliny's description by having the bird immolate itself, instead of simply dying, and by having it go through three stages (worm, chick, and eagle) until it resumes its former place of glory on the third day after its death. Pliny's scented nest for the phoenix has been transformed into the bird's two scented wings. *Physiologus* concludes this entry with comparison between the phoenix and Christ:

> Ergo sicut iam supra diximus, personam accipit saluatoris nostri, qui de caelo descendens utrasque alas suas repleuit suauissimis odoribus, id est noui ac ueteris testamenti sermones, dicens: Non ueni soluere legem, sed adimplere [Matt. 5.17]. Et iterum: Sic erit omnis scriba doctus in regno caelorum, qui profert de thesauro suo noua et uetera [Matt. 13.52]. (*Physiologus* 9 [versio B])

> Thus we say now, just as we did earlier, it explains the person of our savior, who, descending from the heavens, filled his two wings with fragrant odors, that is, the words of the old and new testaments, saying: 'I come not to dissolve the law, but to fulfill it' [Matt. 5.17]. And again: 'Thus every scribe learned in the kingdom of heaven, he brings forth from his treasure the new and the old' [Matt. 13.52]. (my translation)

The spiritual significance here seems almost too obvious. Like Christ, the phoenix dies and rises again after three days; like Christ, the phoenix brings great solace to mankind in the form of the "fragrant odors" of the old and new testaments. Moreover, the phoenix entry ends here by linking the symbolism of the bird directly to scriptural authority, which is also how the entry begins, thereby forming a sort of circle of scripture within which all significance lies. Such a circle is, I believe, quite deliberate exactly because the spiritual symbolism seems so obvious and the author did not have to refer to scripture at all in order for the reader to grasp the symbolism; therefore, the inclusion of the two verses from the book of Matthew must serve a non-explanatory purpose—to reinforce the transcendent and encompassing nature of scriptural authority.

Perhaps even more interesting is the final line of the y-version, "Physiologus, therefore, speaks well of the phoenix" (*Physiologus* 9 [versio Y]; trans. Curley), in which I detect some ambiguity. It is unclear from where the authority for speaking well derives. Is Physiologus the authority for the phoenix's goodness, or does Physiologus speak well precisely because the creature he describes tells the reader something about the Savior? This ambiguity makes Physiologus both an authority figure and a servant to a more important authority—the omnipresent Savior, the third component of the God who is the unifying factor, not only of the material under consideration, but of all creation as well.

The b-version of the *Physiologus* constructs a quite lengthy entry on the adamant stone, Pliny's valuable and durable adamas.[1] Pliny's stress on the stone's material value and its association with kings has vanished, to be replaced by scriptural and spiritual explications of its durability. *Physiologus* begins:

> The adamant-stone is found in the regions of the East, where it does not shine during the day but is found at night. It is called adamant because it "dominates" all things, but no one can "dominate" it.
>
> My Lord and Savior judges all men and is judged by no one. The Prophet says in Amos, "I saw an adamant-stone" [cf. Am. 7:7]. (*Physiologus* 49 [versio B]; trans. Curley)

Physiologus also has a spiritual explanation for the stone's nighttime appearance:

> The stone is found at night since he [Christ] came down into the darkness of this world and illumined this entire race which sits in darkness and in the place of the shadow of death, as the prophet David, representing the entire human race, "Yea, Lord, thou dost light my lamp; my God lightens my darkness" [Ps. 18:28]. Hence our Lord came down and, taking on to himself the lamp which the devil extinguished (that is, the soul and body), he lighted it with the splendor of his glory, giving it life and openly taking it back with him. (*Physiologus* 49 [versio B]; trans. Curley)

The explanation of the stone's durability shows a similar pattern of interpretation:

> Furthermore, Physiologus says of the stone that iron does not prevail against it, that is, death does not rule it. He destroyed death and trampled it under foot as the Apostle bore witness, saying, "Death is swallowed up in victory. Where is thy struggle, Death? Where is thy sting?" [I Cor. 15:55] . . . No other stone harms it, that is, no man at all nor any creature can stand against him. "All things were made through him, and without him nothing was made" [John 1:3]. (*Physiologus* 49 [versio B]; trans. Curley)

Pliny would hardly recognize in this passage the valuable little rock he had filed away in its proper category of the *Natural History*. In fact, the rock itself seems to have become lost amidst its allegorical possibilities, and undoubtedly the physical rock as such is much less important to humankind ultimately than the spiritual truths one can extract from it.

The most important assumption with which the author of the *Physiologus* begins and which governs all the interpretations he gives is not only that a wise man can see divinity in the material world, but also that God designed the universe the way He did precisely to serve this purpose. Curley explains that "these *imagines* and *similitudines* were deliberately fashioned by God to lead man's weakened intelligence to a knowledge of things hidden and spiritual" (Curley, Introduction xiv). Thus the *Physiologus* extends, but does not necessarily negate, Pliny's concept of the entirely knowable, orderly and organized physical world. That world is still present in the *Physiologus,* but it is no longer of primary importance and is not the ultimate goal of this list of animals, monsters, and things. The goal has become spiritual truth (*invisibilia*) accessed through material substance (*visibilia*).

By extension, the concept of *auctoritas* has also changed. Whereas for Pliny the ultimate authority was the author from whom he had gotten his information, whether truthful or bogus, *Physiologus* shows no interest in making reference to Herodotus or Aristotle or even Pliny himself, even when these are the sources for the author's information. Eyewitnesses, compilers, historians, scientists and poets have been replaced as authorities by Physiologus himself, but even Physiologus is not the ultimate authority; he merely interprets, albeit "well." The ultimate authority for these truths about the natural world is, of course, God who gave humankind scripture as an aid to interpretation of the world He created. As Baxter tells us, "the real teacher is Christ. His explicit teachings are reiterated throughout the text, and the typological weighting of the work allows him to subsume the teachings of the prophets too" (62). By using that scripture and the natural world around him, the Physiologus constructs an allegory to reveal to man's intellect "the nature of the Creator" through "explicit correspondence" (Baxter 62) between Creator and created. The Physiologus' own authority to do this derives directly from the God who was the subject matter of his work.

Organization does not appear to have played a major role in the author's vision for his work, for he has mixed together, apparently at random, fish, birds, land animals, insects, and rocks; nor has he distinguished categorically between the ordinary, the exotic and the fanciful. As in Pliny, monsters and marvels are not singled out, but there the organizational similarity ends. Indeed, the only hint of any kind of order at all comes at the very beginning of the *Physiologus,* which in the y-version begins with the heading, "Incipimus loqui leone primum, rege omnium bestiarum" ("We begin first of all by speaking of the Lion, the king of all the beasts") (*Physiologus* 1 [versio Y]; trans. Curley). *Physiologus* then explains the lion's tripartite nature in spiritual terms, equating the lion with Christ, the king of beasts with the King of Kings

(*Physiologus* 1 [versio B]). The correspondence is obvious, as is the logic of beginning a spiritual treatise in this way, but of more interest are the first two scriptural references in this first entry. The entry begins after the heading just quoted: "Etenim Iacob, benedicens filium suum Iudam, ait: 'Catulus leonis Iudas, filius de germine meo, quis suscitabit eum?' [Gen. 49.9]" ("For Jacob, blessing his son Judah, said, 'Judah is a lion's whelp, son of my seed, who has awakened him?' [Gen. 49:9]") (*Physiologus* 1 [versio B]; my translation). *Physiologus* then explains how the lion covers his tracks with his tail to avoid detection and concludes, "Sic et saluator noster—spiritalis leo de tribu Iuda, radix Iesse, filius Dauid [Apoc. 5:5]—missus a superno patre, cooperuit intelligentibus uestigia deitatis suae . . ." ("And thus our savior—the spiritual lion of the tribe of Judah, the root of Jesse, the son of David [Apoc. 5.5]—sent from the celestial Father, covered the perceptible tracks of his divinity . . .") (*Physiologus* 1 [versio B]; my translation). The first two scriptural references come, respectively, from Genesis and Revelations, the beginning and the end; that they appear here in *Physiologus*' very first description of the lion, i.e., Christ, tells us that *Physiologus*' organizing principle will correspond not to the perceivable patterns of the natural world as in Pliny, but to the comprehensive spiritual truth found within scripture, from Genesis to Revelations. This truth can be found within the nature of Christ, just as all scripture is here symbolically found within the lion.

The completeness of this cycle is reinforced by the end of the entry on the lion, when *Physiologus* repeats, "Dormitabit tamquam leo, et sicut catulus leonis, quis suscitabit eum? [Gen. 49.9]" ("So the lion will sleep, just as the lion's whelp, who will awaken him? [Gen. 49.9]") (*Physiologus* 1 [versio B]; my translation). Concerning this same entry, Baxter has noted that "[t]he importance of the opening and closing of a text cannot be overemphasized" (98). In a way, such circularity makes *Physiologus*' organization profoundly unimportant, for each entry will refer the reader to the same referent: God Himself. Since every physical thing ultimately refers to the same spiritual thing, it does not matter in what order the physical things appear. In fact, spiritual reality contains so much more significance than does physical reality that whether or not the physical is real or not at some point becomes an almost trivial distinction. Le Goff also noticed this tendency in the *Physiologus* when he wrote that its "later versions incorporate so much moral symbolism that the marvelous intent is all but lost" (*Medieval Imagination* 34). Just as the accuracy of information in Pliny is secondary to the organization of that information, so in the *Physiologus* are physical realities secondary to the one spiritual reality—God—to which they point the reader. What the works purport overtly to be about is subordinated to and supportive of their real subjects: the truth of the reported facts is less important than the encyclopedic organization and material comprehensiveness in Pliny and far less significant than the metaphysical source of all knowledge in the *Physiologus.* The next text under consideration, the widely disseminated *Etymologies* of Isidore of Seville, combines the preoccupation with the celestial source and the stress on organization in possibly the most influential encyclopedia of the Middle Ages in which the organizing principle, words themselves, reflects the divine organization of the Creator.

Isidore of Seville's *Etymologies* is considered the "standard encyclopedic work of the early Middle Ages" (Ogilvy 167), for "by 850, something more than two centuries after its composition, fifty-four complete copies and more than one hundred manuscripts of extracts had passed from Seville beyond the Pyrenees" (Haskins 82). As the title implies, Isidore saw language as the ultimate organizing principle for the physical world; he believed "that the road to knowledge was by way of words, and further, that they were to be elucidated by reference to their origin rather than to the things they stood for" (Brehaut 33). In this way, Isidore actually resembles *Physiologus* somewhat, in that the origin or originator outweighs the thing itself in importance. Isidore, however, definitely believes in making categorical distinctions. His encyclopedia, for that, as Lewis notes, is really what it is (91), is divided into twenty books; the first two books, "De Grammatica et Partibus eius" and "De Rhetorica et Dialectica," certainly indicate what significance Isidore placed on the trivium and on words themselves, although "the frontier between explaining the meaning of words and describing the nature of things is easily violated" (Lewis 91). His third book covers the quadrivium, and Isidore's inclusion of the seven liberal arts indicates that in his *Etymologies* he set out to combine the encyclopedic tradition with the educational tradition begun by Martianus Capella and Cassiodorus (Brehaut 44). The remaining seventeen books cover a variety of topics, from law (book five) to stones and metals (book sixteen) to war and amusements (book eighteen). Isidore, however, did not make these divisions, having died before the completion of his great work; he "made no division except that by subjects" (Brehaut 34). Isidore's friend Braulio, bishop of Saragossa, at whose request Isidore undertook the composition of the *Etymologies,* made the divisions, composed the chapter headings, and was most likely responsible for grouping man and monsters together as a single chapter (Brehaut 34).

A comparison of the categories of Isidore's subject matter with those of Roman encyclopedists, such as Varro, Pliny and Suetonius, has led Brehaut to conclude that Isidore has continued a tradition of encyclopedic learning inherited almost unchanged from the ancients:

> The literary and philological flavor, the stress on word history and derivation, the pseudo-science based on authority, the conspicuous tendency to confusion and feebleness of thought, the habit of heedless copying that we find in an aggravated form in the *Etymologies,* all these are inherited characteristics that betray the origin of the work. (42–3)

As one might surmise from Brehaut's tone, he has very little respect for the Roman encyclopedic tradition of which the *Etymologies* is an extension. The Roman encyclopedists "gave their attention to compiling and arranging the whole body of knowledge rather than to extending it at any point," and this "epitomizing tendency . . . permeated Roman thought and . . . evidenced its decline" (Brehaut 39). Whereas I agree with this assessment of the *Etymologies*' generic origins, I find Brehaut's tone antagonistic and not at all constructive, for his tendency to evaluate the work based on what he would like it to be—the term "pseudo-science" betrays him—as opposed to what it actually is prevents him from seeing Isidore's most significant accomplishment: the union of concrete physical fact with abstract celestial authority through the medium of words themselves. The widespread popularity of the work that expresses this union testifies to its acceptance as a worldview in the early Middle Ages. The reader, then, instead of criticizing it for not reflecting our own "scientific" leanings sufficiently, ought to scrutinize this view for what it reveals about the era under consideration.

Isidore's *Etymologies* reflects the organization of, for example, Pliny's *Natural History* with the addition of the seven liberal arts. The comprehensiveness of the encyclopedic tradition gives rise to "a mass of confusion and incoherence" in Isidore, along with "an increasing indifference to incoherence and even inability to perceive it" in the medieval world Isidore helped shape (Brehaut 48). The comprehensiveness of the encyclopedic tradition necessitated, as seen in Pliny, a science that relied on "books and was of an authoritative character" (Brehaut 40). But this same encyclopedic urge and this same bookish reliance on authority actually allowed ancient Roman thought to be assimilated into Christian scholarship and thereby preserved, as Brehaut acknowledges:

> Since its [the encyclopedia's] science was a science of authority, it was easy for the Christian writers to modify it by substituting the authority of the Scriptures for that of pagan writers. In fact, the encyclopedias furnished to the church fathers secular knowledge in a particularly convenient and unobjectionable form. . . . It can be seen that this literary form was better adapted than any other to pass with unbroken continuity from ancient into medieval literature. (41)

Of course, this process of modification would have subordinated the material world depicted in the encyclopedias to a supporting role in the religious hierarchy, and Isidore's job in this process would have included explaining how one might access the spiritual world through the material world, much as the *Physiologus* does. Brehaut explains this process:

> The works of Pliny and Suetonius were surveys of what was known; that of Isidore was a survey of "what ought to be known." For his age secular knowledge was valuable, not for itself, but for edification. (45)

Brehaut here has unfortunately omitted an important adjustment that could perhaps explain the apparent "incoherence" and bookishness of which he complains. Isidore not only reconfigured the purpose of secular knowledge but also the method at which one arrived at that knowledge: "Isidore rewrites the pagan encyclopedia within the frame of Christian etymological grammar and so articulates a verbal ontology whereby the knowledge of things derives from the knowledge of words" (Amsler 134). To criticize a discourse for relying on the authority of books makes sense only if the relevant knowledge could and should be attained some other way, through direct observation, for example. However, if one's "metanarrative" is, as Amsler puts it, a "verbal ontology," one is thus compelled to look to books, for books contain words; the material world contains only the physical manifestations of words, a phenomenon which is clearly secondary if true significance is to be found in words and not in things.

Isidore's process of modifying secular, pagan learning to coincide with the Christian scheme of the world in which *invisibilia* outranked *visibilia* in importance involved delineating the category of the monstrous from other categories of living things. Pliny and the author of *Physiologus* did not do this. The form in which the *Etymologies* has come down to us designates chapter XI as "De Homine et Partibus eius, de Aetatibus Hominum, de Portentis et Transformatis" (Isidore, *Etymologies* praemissa), but the name by which the chapter is more commonly known, "On Man and Monsters" (Brehaut 13) is somewhat deceiving since Isidore never indicated that he meant these materials to be united under one chapter heading and also never titled his chapters in this way. Isidore did, however, divide his material by subjects, and he clearly considered "[p]ortenta autem et ostenta, monstra atque prodigia" ("portents and prodigies, monsters and freaks") (*Etymologies* 11.3.2; my translation) to be a special category to be collected together and pondered as such in a single area of his work.

Before looking at a few of Isidore's monsters and seeing what function the physically grotesque served in the scheme of Christian history, for "Isidore was interested in nothing else but the theological aspects of teratology" (Wigginton and Stephens 69), one should observe the issue of Isidore's interpretation of the physical world in his *Etymologies,* or rather the lack thereof. Whereas "[i]n *De Natura Rerum* Isidore makes a regular practice of first giving the explanation of natural phenomena and following this with the 'higher meaning' . . . [i]n the *Etymologies* this 'higher meaning' of natural objects is rarely given" (Brehaut 66–7). Three objections to this assertion should be made before proceeding to the text itself. First, "rarely" does not quite describe the frequence of occurrence of explanations of the monstrous in the *Etymologies;* Isidore does analyze the spiritual significance of quite a few monsters. Secondly, the fact that Isidore refers to monsters as "portenta" (11.3.1) indicates that they are meant to be interpreted, as Isidore makes clear:

> Portenta autem et ostenta, monstra atque prodigia ideo nuncupantur, quod portendere atque ostendere, monstrare ac praedicare aliqua futura videntur.
>
> Monstra vero a monitu dicta, quod aliquid significando demonstrent, sive quod statim monstrent quid appareat. (11.3.2–3)
>
> But portents and prodigies, monsters and freaks therefore proclaim publicly, because something of the future is seen to be foretold and exposed, made known and reported.
>
> Monsters, in fact, are so called as warnings, because they explain something of meaning, or because they make known at once what they reveal. (my translation)

Just because Isidore does not interpret every monster does not mean that the reader should not do so himself, for "[v]ult enim deus interdum ventura significare" ("God sometimes wishes to indicate what is to come") (11.3.4; trans. Brehaut). These warnings do differ in kind from the meanings communicated in the *Physiologus,* for the latter relate scripturally-based spiritual truths whereas the former often function as a kind of prophecy:

> Quaedam autem portentorum creationes in significationibus futuris constituta videntur. Vult enim deus interdum ventura significare per aliqua nascentium noxia, sicut et per somnos et per oracula, qua praemoneat et significet quibusdam vel gentibus vel hominibus futuram cladem; quod plurimis etiam experimentis probatum est. (Isidore, *Etymologies* 11.3.4)
>
> Certain creations of portents seem to have been made with future meanings. For God sometimes wishes to indicate what is to come by disgusting

> features at birth, as also by dreams and oracles, that he may give forewarning by these, and indicate to certain nations or certain men coming destruction. This has been proved by many trials. (trans. Brehaut)

Yet, though the thing being made known varies in kind from the *Physiologus* to the *Etymologies,* the authority for the knowledge and His centrality in the entire scheme of knowing, whether the frame is spiritual or physical/etymological, remains the same. God is in the foreground of both kinds of knowledge, in contrast to Latin encyclopedias such as Pliny's *Natural History* from which God and spiritual significance have been banished.

Thirdly, although Isidore himself may not give a "higher meaning," he makes it very clear in what direction the reader should be looking for interpretation. In the first section of Book 11, "De homine et partibus eius," Isidore explains exactly how one should look up from the earth to God, from the material to the ethereal:

> Graeci autem hominem ανθρώπον appellaverunt, eo quod sursum spectet sublevatus ab humo ad contemplationem artificis sui. Quod Ovidius poeta designat, cum dicit (Metam. I, 84):
>
> > Pronaque cum spectant animalia cetera terram,
> > os homini sublime dedit caelumque videre
> > iussit, et erectos ad sidera tollere vultus.
>
> Qui ideo erectus caelum aspicit, ut Deum quaerat, non ut terram intendat veluti pecora, quae natura prona et ventri oboedientia finxit. (11.1.5)
>
> The Greeks called man ανθρώπον, because he observes upwards, having been raised from the earth to contemplation of his maker. Thus meant the poet Ovid, when he said [Metam. I, 84]:
>
> > And when they saw the other animals on the earth stooped over,
> > He gave to man an elevated face and ordered him to see the heavens,
> > And to raise his ennobled features to the divine.
>
> By which, therefore, man, standing upright, saw the heavens, so that he should search for God, and not be inclined toward the earth, as it were, to sin, which a bent nature and obedience to the belly forms. (my translation)

In Ovid, the vision of the animals themselves prompts the elevation of mankind's contemplation to the proper sphere, the heavens. Yet one might argue that this indicates not that man should look towards the heavens for some indication as to how to regard physical reality, but that man should ignore earthly matters entirely and spend his time contemplating the heavens, i.e., God, as such. Certainly if taken out of context, one could read the passage in this way; however, one must also consider the nature of the work in which these instructions are found. The *Etymologies* is comprised of twenty books that explore the material world in exhausting, occasionally mind-numbing detail; the chapter on man, from which the above excerpt is taken, discusses physical detail at the most minute level, devoting endless pages to the "meanings" of such things as the senses, body parts, and even hair and veins. To take the instructions to look towards the heavens as meaning that one should ignore the physical world entirely would be to negate the entire structure and function of the work in which those instructions appear; it would render the *Etymologies,* as well as Isidore's other work explaining the physical world, *De Natura Rerum,* moot. It seems unlikely that Isidore would have wanted to disown his work in this way and far more likely, given the context, that he was indicating the direction in which etymological interpretation of material reality ought to guide his reader. It follows, then, that even when Isidore himself does not interpret a monster, the reader still knows that it can be "read" and in what direction that "reading" should go.

Looking at an interpreted monster will show by example how to interpret and will also demonstrate what a Christian reader can do with a pagan source. Isidore spends around two-thirds of "De portenta" describing the different types of deformities and monstrosities whose physical existence he does not seriously question (11.3.6–27). Isidore then proclaims that Dicuntur autem et alia hominum fabulosa portenta, quae non sunt, sed ficta in causis rerum interpretantur" ("Other fabulous monstrosities of the human race are said to exist, but they do not; they are imaginary. And their meaning is found in the causes of things. . . .") (11.3.28; trans. Brehaut). In spite of the fact that he thinks some monsters are fictional, Isidore still devotes a significant amount of space to their description in order to get at, as he says, "their meaning," a further indication of the *Etymologies*' true and higher purpose. In some ways, this may seem similar to Pliny's strategy concerning the phoenix, for example, but it is not. Whereas Pliny catalogued what was known, including widely reported fabrications, Isidore aimed to record important spiritual truths which remain valid spiritually even if untrue in a physical sense. The sense in which fictional monsters are "true" or relate a truth is literary. Thus, Isidore willingly interprets monsters that exist only in fiction, such as the sirens:

> Sirenas tres fingunt fuisse ex parte virgines, ex parte volucres, habentes alas et ungulas: quarum una voce, altera tibiis, tertia lyra canebant. Quae inlectos navigantes sub cantu in naufragium trahebant.

> Secundum veritatem autem meretrices fuerunt, quae transeuntes quoniam deducebant ad egestatem, his fictae sunt inferre naufragia. Alas autem habuisse et ungulas, quia amor et volat et vulnerat. Quae inde in fluctibus conmorasse dicuntur, quia fluctus Venerem creaverunt. (11.3.30–1)
>
> The three sirens are shaped partly as young women and partly as birds, having talons and wings: they sing, the first with her voice, the second with her flute, and the third with her lyre. Through this allure they lead sailors to shipwreck with their song.
>
> In truth, however, they were whores, because they draw those who see them into desire, who by their falsehoods are brought to shipwreck. Also, they have wings and talons because lust flies and wounds. From this source it is said they linger in the ocean waves, because Venus was created in the waters. (my translation)

In spite of their merely fictional existence, Isidore can extract not just a moral, but a truth ("veritatem") from the legend of the monstrous sirens. He goes on to discover similar moralistic truths in the monsters of classical fiction, such as the Gorgons, Scylla, and Cerebus (11.3.29, 32, 33). Truth in the case of fictional monsters is metaphorical and literary, but nonetheless important and real, as one might expect in a treatise on the meanings behind words; the *Etymologies* is, after all, a literary venture.

Isidore demonstrates how a Christian might make use of the truth behind a fictional monster when he quotes St. Ambrose on the serpent Hydra:

> Huius mentionem facit Ambrosius in similitudinem haeresium, dicens (de Fid. I, 4): "Haeresis enim velut quaedam hydra fabularum vulneribus suis crevit; et dum saepe reciditur, pullulavit. . ." (11.3.35)
>
> Ambrose makes mention of this [i.e., the Hydra] in an analogy with heresy, saying [de Fid. I, 4]: "Heresy grew, as it were, like a certain hydra of legend grew through its wounds; and as often as it is cut away, it sprouts back . . ." (my translation)

This use would seem to differ from the use made of the portents Isidore describes earlier in the chapter which are designed by divine will to foretell a specific event:

> Alexandro ex muliere monstrum creatum, quod superiores corporis partes hominis, sed mortuas habuerit, inferiores diversarum bestiarum, sed viventes, significasse repentinam regis interfectionem: supervixerant enim deteriora melioribus. (11.3.5)

> Alexander saw signified the sudden death of the king from a female monster, because the upper part of the body [was] human, but had withered, and the lower [part was composed] of diverse beasts, but living: to wit, the worse overtakes the better. (my translation)

But however different portentous births may be from metaphorical fictional monsters, one aspect remains common to both scenarios: both are meant to be read, after which both will reveal, show, make known something true, a message from God.

One might now wonder what to do with Isidore's uninterpreted monsters, like the Blemmyae:

> Blemmyas in Libya credunt truncos sine capite nasci, et os et oculos habere in pectore. Alios sine cervicibus gigni, oculos habentes in humeris. (11.3.17)
>
> The Blemmyaes, born in Libya, are believed to be headless trunks, having mouth and eyes in the breast; others are born without necks, with eyes on their shoulders. (trans. Brehaut)

Granted, Blemmyaes comprise an entire race, not a single monstrosity, but Isidore makes very little distinction between monstrous individuals and monstrous races: "Sicut autem in singulis gentibus quaedam monstra sunt hominum, ita in universo genere humano quaedam monstra sunt gentium, ut Gigantes, Cynocephali, Cyclopes, et cetera" ("And just as there are monstrous individuals in separate races of men, so in the whole humankind there are certain monstrous races, as the Gigantes, Cynocephali, Cyclopes, and the rest") (11.3.12; trans. Brehaut). When discussing the various deformities that constitute true portents and the merely portentous, Isidore groups together individuals and entire races:

> Portenta igitur vel portentuosa existunt alia magnitudine totius corporis ultra communem hominum modum, quantus fuit Tityon in novem iugeribus iacens, Homero testante; alia parvitate totius corporis, ut nani, vel quos Graeci Pygmaeos vocant, eo quod sint statura cubitales. . . . Alia, quae in parte transfigurantur, sicut qui leonis habent vultum vel canis, vel taurinum caput aut corpus, ut ex Pasiphae memorant genitum Minotaurum. (11.3.7,9)
>
> Therefore portents or the portentous appear sometimes as great size in the entire body in an otherwise generally human manner, as large as was Tityon lying through nine acres, as Homer testified; sometimes as smallness of the whole body, as with dwarves, or what the Greeks call Pygmies,

> who are one cubit tall. . . . Sometimes one is transformed in part, as when they have the face of a lion or a dog, or a bull's head or body, as the race generated by Pasiphae called minotaurs. (my translation)

If individual monsters are meant to be "read" and little or no distinction is made between an individual monster and a monstrous race, it follows that monstrous races are to be "read" in the same way as individuals are. In addition, Pliny states quite clearly that Pygmies and Minotaurs are portentous, but then he does not interpret them. What, then, is the reader to do?

While one may be tempted to look ahead to the moralized monsters of the later Middle Ages for an obvious answer (Friedman, *Monstrous Races* 108–30), I believe a better answer lies in Isidore's own words and their implicit connection to St. Augustine's *City of God*. After explaining how individual portents work, Isidore writes, "[s]icut autem in singulis gentibus quaedam monstra sunt hominum, ita in universo genere humano quaedam monstra sunt gentium, ut Gigantes, Cynocephali, Cyclopes, et cetera" ("and just as there are monstrous individuals in separate races of men, so in the whole human kind there are certain monstrous races, as the Gigantes, Cynocephali, Cyclopes, and the rest") (11.3.12; trans. Brehaut). He includes Blemmyaes and Pygmies in this list as well. Augustine, with whose work Isidore was undoubtedly familiar, says something suspiciously similar: "Qualis autem ratio redditur de monstrosis apud nos hominum partubus, talis de monstrosis quibusdam gentibus reddi potest" ("Furthermore, the same explanation that is used to account for monstrous human births among our race can be applied to certain monstrous races also") (16.8; trans. Sanford and Green). Isidore follows Augustine's jump from individual monsters to monstrous races but leaves out Augustine's explanation for having made such a move:

> Deus enim creator est omnium, qui ubi et quando creari quid oporteat vel oportuerit, ipse novit, sciens universitatis pulchritudinem quarum partium vel similitudine vel diversitate contexat. (16.8)
>
> For God is the creator of all things, and he himself knows at what place and time a given creature should be created, or have been created, selecting in his wisdom the various elements from whose likenesses and diversities he contrives the beautiful fabric of the universe. (trans. Sanford and Green)

Thus the purpose or "higher meaning" of the monstrous races of mankind is the contemplation of the glorious superabundance of God's creation, in a word, wonder. Blemmyaes and Pygmies and all the other monstrous races signify His power, wisdom and presence in all of creation. Just as one may interpret a single monster, whether real or imaginary, as a manifestation of a single spiritual reality, one may also interpret the presence of a myriad of monstrous races on the earth as the manifestation of God's infinite power and knowledge. In the presence of such diversity, one can only look up to the heavens as Isidore instructed man to do, for to look down to the earth for any explanation can only result in confusion, not edification.

Augustine offers another potential explanation for monstrous races, and this explanation also links the concepts of the individual monster and the monstrous race in a way the reader may find illuminating for developing an understanding of Isidore's insistence on coupling the two apparently divergent concepts of the monstrous:

> [Q]uid si propterea Deus voluit etiam nonnullas gentes ita creare, ne in his monstris, quae apud nos oportet ex hominibus nasci, eius sapientiam qua naturam fingit humanam velut artem cuiuspiam minus perfecti opificis putaremus errasse? Non itaque nobis videri debet absurdum ut quem ad modum in singulis quibusque gentibus quaedam monstra sunt hominum ita in universo genere humano quaedam monstra sint gentium. (16.8)
>
> [W]hat if God willed to create some races of this sort expressly to prevent us from thinking that the wisdom by which he moulds the forms of men was at fault in the case of such monsters as are duly born among us of human parents, as if it had been the craft of an unskilled artisan? It should not then seem to us unnatural that, even as there are certain monsters among individual races of men, so also within the human race as a whole there may be certain monstrous tribes. (trans. Sanford and Green)

Once again, the individual monster and the monstrous race are joined. Each depends upon the other for the proper conveyance of its meaning or purpose, and inevitably the final determinant and referent of any meaning is, of course, God.

Two objections may be made to this explanation. First, it may appear that individual monsters are portents in the strict sense of the word—warnings about the future—whereas monstrous races are metaphoric illustrations of God's inscrutable yet wondrous plan and that these are two very different functions. The inclusion of the fictional monster as a form of literary truth adds a third possible function to the term "monster," which complicates the issue even further. I do not believe, however, that Isidore would have sensed any contradiction between or conflict of interest among the three possible functions of the monstrous. I base this assertion on Isidore's initial etymological explanation of the terms he uses, "[p]ortenta autem et ostenta, monstra atque prodigia" ("portents and wonders, monsters and prodigies") (11.3.2; my translation):

> Nam portenta dicta perhibent a portendendo, id est praeostendendo. Ostenta autem, quod ostendere quidquam futurum videantur. Prodigia, quod porro dicant, id est futura praedicant. Monstra vero a monitu dicta, quod aliquid significando demonstrent, sive quod statim monstrent quid appareat. (11.3.3)
>
> For portents are asserted to be named from portending, that is, from displaying before. And wonders because they are seen to display something in the future. Prodigies because they say in future, that is they predict future things. Monsters, in truth, are named from "omen," because in signifying something they point it out, or because they immediately show what may appear. (trans. Wigginton and Stephens)

Portents, it seems, reveal or make the future known; monsters, on the other hand, simply make meaning known. Thus the various categories of the monstrous may serve slightly different purposes, but the ultimate end of each sort is to make known, whether the fact to be revealed is a future event, a literary meaning, or an eternal truth; but all such facts derive from the same divine origin and ultimately refer back to and reflect Him. That Isidore groups all permutations of the monstrous together and talks about them as if they were very similar, if not the same, indicates how little import he places on the difference between "making known" and "making known the future."

Secondly, one might argue that if individual monsters and monstrous races are not, in fact, mistakes of nature, then the very existence of a "monster" in any common sense of the word is precluded; there can be no monsters. Once again, Isidore can reply to such an objection far more lucidly than I could:

> Portenta esse Varro ait quae contra naturam nata videntur; sed non sunt contra naturam, quia divina voluntate fiunt, cum voluntas Creatoris cuiusque conditae rei natura sit. Vnde et ipsi gentiles Deum modo Naturam, modo Deum appellant. Portentum ergo fit non contra naturam, sed contra quam est nota natura. (11.3.1–2)
>
> Portents, Varro says, are those births which seem to have taken place contrary to nature. But they are not contrary to nature, because they come by the divine will, since the will of the creator is the nature of each thing that is created. When, too, the heathen themselves call God now nature, now God. A portent, therefore, happens not contrary to nature, but contrary to known nature. (trans. Brehaut)

Although he may be begging the question, Isidore illustrates how his world view precludes not monsters but natural, i.e., divine, mistakes. The common perception of a monster as a being formed against nature merely needs minor modification to maintain its validity; that is, a monster is not deformed against nature itself, but rather against known nature, what humankind assumes to be the ordinary and natural type of a creature. Since the nature of a creature is "the will of the creator," and since the creator does not make mistakes, a monster cannot be formed against nature, i.e., mistakenly. Monsters thus proceed from God and, in their apparent violation of what looks natural, attempt to tell humankind something meaningful. Such splitting of semantic hairs would in no way violate the common identification of a monster; one would still clearly recognize a monster when confronted by one but would also have to acknowledge it as formed within God's plan and not against it.

Isidore's project, then, was to wed Pliny's obsession with physical knowledge to the idea of divine meaning epitomized in the *Physiologus.* He "frame[d] pagan and mundane knowledge within a new scene of Christian reading" (Amsler 133). In a literary sense, Pliny had catalogued signifiers and the *Physiologus* had explained the signified, which was in all cases God Himself. Isidore's *Etymologies* united signifier and signified and through the explanations of word origins attempted to eliminate the slippage that must inevitably occur between the two. In doing so, Isidore must manufacture a "verbal ontology" in which things and words are essentially the same entity, a system in which one might, therefore, reasonably be able to access divinity, or at least divine intention, through words. "Even as Isidore continues the older encyclopedic discourse of Pliny's *Historia naturalis,*" writes Amsler, "he formalizes pagan learning in order to present it systematically to Christian monastic readers as aids to their proper reading of the sacred texts" (134). Such "formalization" is, I would argue, closely related to the project of the *Physiologus* in which, though the meaning of a monster is not divined through analysis of its name, signification is determined by reference to God's intent as revealed through the verses of the Bible. Thus Isidore's strategy in the *Etymologies* appears to be almost as closely related to that of the *Physiologus* as it is to that of Pliny's *Natural History* whose influence has long been acknowledged.

Isidore does clearly replicate the completeness of Pliny's *Natural History,* if not its concentric organization of the material universe. The *Etymologies,* however, goes beyond the *Natural History* in this regard in a very interesting and revealing way. Isidore's "verbal ontology" not only reconciles pagan heritage with Christian significance but also gives the reader an avenue of access to divine knowledge which is, by its very definition, complete:

> [T]he divine world subsists implicitly in Isidore's text, in the grammarian's authority to account for the origins of words and things. Isidore' encyclopedic grammatical discourse writes the knowledge of things into the

> knowledge of words and thus shrinks the universe into a one-volume library, conveniently located on a monastic shelf. (Amsler 135)

The completeness of Isidore's "one-volume library" derives from the fact that though it "is not exhaustive, yet [it] is the pretext for knowledge" (Amsler 137). Isidore thus surpasses Pliny, who has actually done a much better job of collecting empirical facts, in that the subtext of his entire work is not the world, but the Word, and, as everyone knows, "In the beginning was the Word, and the Word was with God, and the Word was God" (John 1.1). For Isidore, words are inseparable from divine intention, and this is the *Etymologies*' ubiquitous and most important message.

Now it is time to ask what the *Etymologies* communicates about the ancient literary heritage of the medieval monster. The monster serves as an ideal case study of the method by which early Christianity assimilated and adjusted pagan knowledge; the power possessed by the figure of the monster made it a particularly useful tool of Christian hegemony. Williams explains that power:

> Thus the monstrosity of a human figure with three heads or a tree with the power of speech functions to upset the mental expectations about the relation of the sign to what it is supposed to signify and to underscore the element of the arbitrary in the relation of the two. (5)

Christianity took full advantage of the anxiety, or wonder, caused by the revelation of arbitrariness. The *Physiologus* converted this wonder to spiritual contemplation through biblical references and eased anxiety through the reassurance that the apparent disjunction of the monster in fact communicated a divine message. The *Etymologies* filled up the arbitrary space created by the monster between signifier and signified with God, through whose divine intention signifier and signified are reunited via "verbal ontology." Christian cosmology thus recruits the monstrous to further its own theological ends; it domesticates monsters and brings them back within the religious metanarrative.

Yet the monster is clearly not comfortable in this role, which is why interpretations of monsters, such as the sirens in the *Etymologies,* often ring hollow. Having awed the reader with the description of half-fish/half-woman monsters, beings that defy categorization, Isidore disappoints when he reduces them to mere "whores"; for what makes the monster so intriguing as a subject is its ability to resist domestication and categorization. Williams has explained that "the monstrous has frequently been defined as enigma" (85), and such enigmatic status, and not a clear and categorical interpretation, gives the monster its true theological power:

> In the Middle Ages and other periods and cultures in which the monster flourished, the existence of a transcendent, ineffable reality superior to and paradigmatic of mundane reality was undoubted. The representation of this essentially unrepresentable reality was the goal of both philosophy and art. The limitations of discursive language seem to have been recognized almost from the beginning of philosophical thought, and the general nature of those limitations identified as language's need for a sign to represent a truth, which sign, by its nature, remains different and distinct from what it signifies. (Williams 85).

Such ineffability, Williams continues, could best be expressed by the monstrous enigma:

> Throughout the Middle Ages enigma was revered as the most suitable expression of divine mysteries precisely because its obscurity suited the extradiscursive nature of its subject. . . . The monstrous enigma deforms the fundamental of signification to communicate what otherwise could not be communicated. (85)

Thus the awesome, mute power of the monster as a vehicle for the ineffable, i.e., the divine, serves the needs of religion better than an explicit theological interpretation that eliminates all forms of arbitrariness; and it is, as Williams has pointed out, the sudden realization of arbitrariness or "disorder"—"the jarring and unsettling inaccuracy and impropriety on which enigmatic understanding is based" (Williams 85)—that one might term "wonder" (Bynum 7).

In a sense, according to Williams' reasoning, the *Physiologus*, the *Etymologies,* and later the *Liber Monstrorum* fail as theological treatises on the monstrous because the monster, enigmatic, chaotic and awesome, resists the kind of Christianized ordering of the world these works take as their unquestioned subtext. Yet the way I have characterized the monstrous makes it the ideal vehicle for the ineffable and the divine, and in this way, too, the monster is re-integrated yet again into the Christian symbolic. This form of domestication, however, is more suited to its nature, for it remains an expression of awe, contradiction, wonder and transcendence instead of a mere tool subdued and enlisted in the Christian paradigm.

Because of the monster's peculiar theological suitability to the ineffable rather than interpretation, the reader encounters a great irony in Isidore's passage on monsters. While the interpreted monsters clearly are intended to serve Christian ends, through both metaphorical explanation of individual monsters and the larger etymological project, such explicit domestication does not serve such ends as effectively as the simple enigmatic presence of the uninterpreted variety. The Blemmeyae just sitting there with no apparent meaning or function are actually more powerful representations of pure wonder—the ineffable—than any etymological explanation of their name could make them. Such mute power also renders Augustine's speculations as to divine motivation almost counterproductive, as would be any human explanation that attempted to account for their monstrous presence. So when Augustine asks, "Quid dicam de Cynocephalis?" ("What am I to say of the Cynocephali?") (16.8; trans. Sanford), he would perhaps do a better job communicating the power of the divine if he did not attempt to answer. "Nondifferentiation and disorder, since they are proper to the divine, have precedence over order and differentiation," and the cynocephalus "disperses elements of human anatomy and those of animal, to recombine them in the figure that confounds the very principle of differentiation and of order" (Williams 84). The human-canine hybrid in its "simplicity, unity, nondifferentiation, stillness and silence" (Williams 84) represents Divine Chaos and resists being pinned down and domesticated by a static and orderly interpretation.

Christianized monsters become less interesting and less effective precisely due to the Christian imperative to organize, catalogue, and interpret them, but this imperative is itself the characteristic that defines the medieval episteme, as the *Etymologies*' popularity in part proves. Concerning the "mental Model of the Universe" adopted by medieval humankind, Lewis remarked, "Of all our modern inventions I suspect that they would most have admired the card index" (10). All knowledge thus can and should be categorized and filed, including the monster, which resists categorization by its very being. Yet one simply cannot leave the monster unexamined or unexplained entirely: Isidore may have allowed the Blemmyaes, Panotii, and Sciopods to sit on the page unmolested, but he insisted on explaining Satyrs, Gorgons, and Sirens; and the *Beowulf* poet, in spite of his great theological subtly, must explain that Grendel is "in Caines cynne—Þone cwealm gewræc / ece Drihten, Þæs Þe he Abel slog" ("the kin of Cain—the eternal Lord avenged the murder in which he killed Abel") (*Beowulf* 107–8; my translation). One wonders whether these two impulses, wonder and explication, can be reconciled.

Part of the conflict between wonder and explication may have to do with the fact that two different kinds of activity are being confused. Pliny, for example, dealt with observations and empirical facts, even incorrect empirical facts, which involve organization on the physical plane. In contrast, early Christians were categorizing not facts but literary references, and literature begs for explication and interpretation in a way that simple physical presence, and perhaps the wonder it produces, does not. The contrast can be made concrete by considering the circumstances under which Pliny died. The eruption of Mt. Vesuvius prompted Pliny to scientific and physical observation of the phenomenon, whereas a similar event in the seventh century would have sent Isidore running for his Bible in an effort to interpret the volcanic eruption in a religious and literary fashion. Thus the change that takes place from the pagan to the early Christian world involves not just the replacement of human with divine *auctoritas* and the imposition of meaning and interpretation, but also a kind of epistemic shift from the scientific to the literary, perhaps not surprising in a culture that believed the Word was God.

Even so, it seems that the monster itself presents the reader, appropriately, with a conundrum: the monster is, in its category-defying aspect, the most suitable expression of mystical enigmas, of the ineffable, as Williams has pointed out; yet its presence in such encyclopedic works as the Etymologies as a separate category of signifier, and likely an interpreted signifier at that, testifies to the monster's presence on the organized, classified, and explicable medieval landscape that Lewis documented. But what looks like a dilemma here may in fact be two separate steps in the same (Christian) process, according to Bynum, who writes that "wonder as a response was not devalued or dismissed [in the Middle Ages], even in a philosophical and theological tradition that (as Katharine Park has aptly put it) 'de-wondered' anomalies by insisting on an increasingly ordered world, whose laws were decipherable by the wise" (Bynum 10). Indeed, wonder, the response to the ineffable, may act as the catalyst for cataloguing and interpreting: "admirari (to wonder at) is sometimes contrasted to rimari (to pry into), although it is sometimes seen as an inducement to such prying" (Bynum 7). In fact, by prying into a wonder, in this case a monster, as Isidore, the Physiologus, and others do, one arrives eventually at the cause or meaning of the wonder, which is always God, the greatest of all inducements to wonder. Not prying at all—as, for example, Pliny does, in spite of his great efforts at collecting—characterizes the pagan perspective which must be corrected by prying, much as the Physiologus does with material handed down from Pliny. Lack of prying and its association with the pagan world view, along with a belief in God's centrality to all forms of knowledge, continued to characterize the early medieval episteme through the Anglo-Saxon Age, as the following chapter will attest.

Chapter Two
The Anglo-Saxons

The inquiry into early medieval monsters begins in a perhaps unlikely place: the *Enigmata* of Aldhelm, Bishop of Wessex (d. 709/710) (Lapidge and Rosier, Introduction 6). Aldhelm serves as a useful introduction not only because "in Anglo-Saxon times Aldhelm's writings were perhaps the best known of any Anglo-Saxon author" (Lapidge and Rosier, Introduction 5), but also because Pliny, the *Physiologus*, and Isidore were all sources for the subject matter of the *Enigmata* (Lapidge and Rosier, Notes 247). Perhaps even more importantly, Aldhelm provides a bridge between two periods by virtue of Isidore's demonstrable influence upon him: "In the final analysis, the linguistic practice of the *Enigmata* reveals the decisive influence of Isidore on Aldhelm's habits of thinking and composing" (Howe, *Aldhelm's "Enigmata"* 58). Howe goes even further in his study of catalogue poetry, suggesting an Isidorian influence on Aldhelm not just in the realm of literary composition, but in the very pattern of his thought processes:

> Within a generation or so after Isidore's death in 636, Aldhelm (640?–709?) had mastered the *Etymologies* so thoroughly that he was able to borrow not only information but also patterns of thought and organization. His immersion in the *Etymologies* shaped his style and to some extent as well his choice of subjects. . . . For Aldhelm, and by extension, other Anglo-Saxon writers, the encyclopedias served from the start as examples of intellectual practice which demarcated and defined the essential subjects and methods of the culture. (Howe, *Catalogue Poems* 67)

The *enigmata* themselves are "'Riddles,' or better perhaps, 'Mysteries'" (Lapidge and Rosier, Introduction 61). The *Enigmata* presents one hundred riddles whose answers vary from the most mundane (cauldron, pillow) to the most magnificent (Pleiades, the Colossus) and include various monsters and marvels (Minotaur, unicorn, Scylla). An enigma aims "to evoke recognition of the metaphor" in the riddle "and hence appreciation of the congruence between elements which may be in opposition . . . and may even be antithetical" (Lapidge and Rosier, Introduction 61). In constructing and then breaking down unlikely metaphors, riddles implicitly comment on organizational categories:

> The human learning process involves classification and the intelligible ordering of experience; but it also involves the ability to transcend conceptual categories. The transcendence of the normal conceptual categories draws attention to the riddle-subject and leads to fresh perception of its properties. (Lapidge and Rosier, Introduction 61–2)

In his collection of one hundred seemingly random riddles, Aldhelm demonstrates an even greater ambition: "(H)is theme will be the entirety of creation, visible and invisible, and his intention will be 'to reveal the hidden mysteries of things' (prol. 7–8: pandere rerum enigmata clandistina)" (Lapidge and Rosier, Introduction 63). Thus Aldhelm aims not just to question certain conceptual categories, but also to show the transcendence of the visible creation by the invisible creator. In this endeavor, Aldhelm rejects Pliny's strategy of organization for its own sake and substitutes the idea of divine transcendence as his central organizing principle.

The specific form the riddles take points to this higher purpose. Unlike the *Exeter Book* riddles, which are difficult, the *Enigmata* actually has the "answer" to each riddle prominently displayed at its beginning. Thus, as Howe has pointed out, the purpose of such riddles cannot be the discovery of the answer, but is rather a didactic linguistic exercise: "Such riddles ask 'What does my name mean?' rather more than 'What am I?'" (*Aldhelm's "Enigmata"* 37). Answering the more pertinent question becomes "a recreation of this act of naming: to solve it means to participate in the initial act of identification and thus of naming. It means, in short, to remember the first act of riddling in Christian history, Adam's naming of the animals in Eden" (Howe, *Aldhelm's "Enigmata"* 57). Contemplation of an enigma does not aim only to sharpen one's wits, but also to instruct one in Christian doctrine and its manifestations in the world.

Aldhelm's preface to the *Enigmata* begins a simultaneous use and rejection of ancient sources in favor of a higher spiritual authority. Aldhelm writes:

> Castalida nimphas non clamo cantibus istuc
> Examen neque spargebat mihi nectar in ore;
> Cynthi sic numquam perlustro cacumina, sed nec

> In Parnasso procubui nec somnia vidi.
> Nam mihi versificum poterit Deus addere carmen
> Inspirans stolidae pia gratis munera menti. (*Riddles*)
>
> I do not declaim my verses in the direction of the Castalian nymphs, nor has any swarm [of bees] spread nectar in my mouth; by the same token I do not traverse the summits of Apollo, nor do I prostrate myself on Parnassus, nor am I entranced by any poetic vision. For God shall be able to augment the poetic undertaking for me, freely breathing His holy gifts into my obtuse mind. (trans. Lapidge)

Here Aldhelm rejects not just authority but also pagan lyric and epic structures. His rejection of ancient pagan authority turns into outright hostility and correction in several of the *Enigmata,* including the riddles whose answers are "Pleiades" ("Nos Athlante satas stolidi dixere priores" ["The stupid ancients said that we were the offspring of Atlas"] (*Riddles* 8; trans. Lapidge)) and "eagle" ("'Armiger infausti Iovis et raptor Ganimidis' / Quamquam pellaces cantarent carmine vates, / Non fueram praepes, quo fertur Dardana proles" ["Although deceitful poets might sing in their verses {that I am} the weapon-bearer of unlucky Jove and the abductor of Ganymede, I was not that bird by whom the Trojan youth was carried off"] (*Riddles* 57; trans. Lapidge)). But even as Aldhelm rejects and corrects the ancients, principally Vergil, he also uses them to fashion clues to the answers of his riddles. Aldhelm feels free to use pagan sources, much as Isidore did, to construct his treatise on "the hidden mysteries of things" (*Enigmata* pref.; trans. Lapidge), but the use he makes of them does not oblige him to treat the ancients with respect or admiration, which are reserved solely for God, the real and ultimate source and the corrector of the ancients. In this way, he conforms to the practice of his culture, as did his predecessor Augustine and, as will be seen shortly, his contemporary, the author of the *Liber Monstrorum.* In contrast, Aldhelm does not comment on his Christian sources, such as Isidore, *Physiologus,* and St. Augustine; perhaps it goes without saying that they are neither stupid nor deceitful and therefore not in need of correction.

In terms of organization, the *Enigmata* resembles the *Physiologus* in at least two ways. First, the *Enigmata,* like the *Physiologus,* appears to have no organizing principle. The one hundred riddles include a vast array of subject matter which appear to be in no particular order. "Pleiades" (no. 8) is followed by "Diamond," "Dog," and "Bellows" (nos. 9, 10, 11, respectively). The ordinary sits beside the marvelous, the animate beside the inanimate, the tangible beside the intangible. However, also much like the *Physiologus,* organization is both subtle and cyclical. Lapidge and Rosier observe some ingenious Biblical pairings in the *Enigmata:*

> Aldhelm's *Enigmata* explore hidden and subtle relationships between objects of the visible world. Sometimes the relationship is immediately clear from Aldhelm's juxtaposition of two *enigmata:* thus Raven (lxiii), the first animal dispatched from the Ark, alongside Dove (lxiv); or Apple-tree (lxxvi), the source of man's downfall, alongside Fig-tree (lxxvii), which supplied the covering for his shame. (Introduction 63–4)

Lapidge and Rosier also detect organization around the four cosmic elements of earth, air, fire and water (Introduction 64). While *Physiologus* may not have been organized around any such complex ideas, the opening section on the lion did point to the circular nature of the work itself and to the authority of scripture as revealed by the work.

I likewise detect a similar circularity in the *Enigmata.* Aldhelm made his first enigma "Earth," who tells us, "Altrix cunctorum, quos mundus gestat, in orbe / Nuncupor" ("I am called the nurse of all things in my sphere, which the universe sustains") (*Riddles* 1; trans. Lapidge). Aldhelm's final enigma, "Creation," informs the reader similarly that "Nam Deus ut propria mundum dicione gubernat, / Sic ego complector sub caeli cardine cuncta" ("For as God governs the universe with His own edict, so do I encompass all things beneath the pole of heaven") (*Riddles* 100; trans. Lapidge). In addition to the repetition of "mundus/m," one notes the similar phrasing of "cunctorum . . . in orbe" and "sub caeli cardine cuncta"; such phrases emphasize completeness and the enclosure of the material world between earth and sky. Both enigmas also emphasize extremes of heat and cold: "Prole vireas aestate, tabescens tempore brumae" ("In summer I am verdant with offspring; in winter-time I languish") (*Riddles* 1; trans. Lapidge), and "Frigidior brumis necnon candente pruina, / Cum sim Vulcani flammis torrentibus ardens" ("I am colder than winter and glistening hoar-frost, although I burn hot in the searing flames of Vulcan") (*Riddles* 100; trans. Lapidge). By emphasizing completeness and contradiction, and by repeating key words and concepts, both enigmas stress the inclusiveness of their subjects, terra and creatura, which are ultimately commentaries on God's own inclusiveness, interconnectedness, and ability to contain and transcend, if not reconcile, apparent contradictions. The *Enigmata* creates a perpetual circularity from the material world to God, to the material world to God, ad infinitum.

Even if one ignores the circular implication of ending the *Enigmata* with the creation, one can still see the cycle completed by the *Enigmata.* Aldhelm begins with the earth, which holds and sustains all things, and ends with creation, which encompasses all things. Between the two fall all the *enigmata* Aldhelm has constructed, which are also all the things God has created. This inclusiveness is literal and figurative, linear (in Aldhelm's written work) and three-dimensional (in God's work). Just as all the *visibilia* and *invisibilia* of the *Physiologus* are contained in the lion, so all the *enigmas* of the *Enigmata* are contained between the inner sphere of the earth and the outer sphere of creation.

This sort of interconnectedness and Aldhelm's simultaneous rejection and use of ancient authority are clearly visible in a monstrous enigma, the unicorn, worth quoting here in full:

> Collibus in celsis saevi discrimina Martis,
> Quamvis venator frustra latrante moloso
> Garriat arcister contorquens spicula ferri,
> Nil vereor, magnis sed fretus viribus altos
> Belliger impugnans, elefantes vulnere sterno.
> Heu! fortuna ferox, quae me sic arte fefellit,
> Dum trucido grandes et virgine vincor inermi!
> Nam gremium pandens mox pulchra puerpera prendit
> Et voti compos celsam deducit ad urbem.
> Indidit ex cornu nomen mihi lingua Pelasga;
> Sic itidem propria dixerunt voce Latini. (*Riddles* 60)

> In no way do I fear the attacks of cruel Mars, even though the hunter with his vainly baying hound should be babbling, a bowman shooting iron-tipped arrows; rather, sustained by my immense strength, I behave as an aggressive warrior (and) bring down mighty elephants. Alas, cruel Fortune, which thus tricked me by craft, since I slaughter mighty beasts but am overcome by a harmless virgin! For, laying bare her breast, the beautiful young woman straightway captures me and, having thus fulfilled her wish, she leads me back to a lofty city. The Greek language gave me my name because of my horn; the Latins call me likewise in their language. (trans. Lapidge)

Obviously, the first level of "hidden mystery" here explores the irony of the unarmed gentleness of the virgin overcoming the great strength and courage of the warlike beast, and the moral of the story is quite clear. However, the inclusion of the lament to Fortune complicates, or rather extends, this simple reading and suggests that the reader look at what Aldhelm had to say about Fortune:

> Facundum constat quondam cecinisse poetam:
> 'Quo Deus et quo dura vocat Fortuna; sequamur!'
> Me veteres falso dominam vocitare solebant,
> Sceptra regens mundi dum Christi gratia regnet. (*Riddles* 7)

> It is well known that an eloquent poet once sang: "where God and where hard Fortune calls, let us follow!" (Vergil, *Aen.* XII. 677). The ancients were accustomed—wrongly!—to call me mistress, as being the one who ruled the sceptres of the world—until (the advent of) Christ's grace which shall rule forever. (trans. Lapidge)

The unicorn speaks in the first person and laments Fortune's capricious trickery in determining his fate. This implies that he believes "fortuna ferox" to be the master, or mistress, of his destiny, much as one who, suffering under an unbearable situation, by vainly asking God, "what have I done to deserve this?" implies that s/he believes God controls the situation and can ameliorate it. By extension, this suggests that the unicorn himself is one of the mistaken ancients who was accustomed to call "fortuna" "dominam."

This may seem a capricious interpretation, but closer inspection of unicorn iconography and metaphor may bolster its probability. The image of the unicorn with which the reader is most likely familiar is that of the subdued creature with its head resting in a young virgin's lap, a ubiquitous image made famous by the Unicorn Tapestries at the Cloisters and the *Lady with the Unicorn* at the Musee de Cluny. In these, the iconography of religion has merged with that of romance. In the former, the virgin represents the Virgin, the unicorn represents Christ, and the capture of the unicorn by the virgin depicts an allegory of the Annunciation and the Incarnation. In the latter, the virgin becomes the coy lady of medieval romance and the unicorn is her hapless lover. Both elements were often simultaneously meant and presented no difficulties to their audience (Freeman 33–66).

However, both tapestries are late fifteenth-century creations and epitomize the zenith of iconographic development. In his historical study of the unicorn, Beer has indicated that the fixed symbolism of the unicorn as Christ "captured" by the Virgin Mary was a relatively late occurrence, coming about sometime in the twelfth century (R. Beer 78–97). This is not to say that the unicorn and virgin were not used in this symbolic fashion before the twelfth century, for they certainly were; however, the unicorn as a symbol had many more potential meanings, both positive and negative, prior to the twelfth century, and these meanings would have been at Aldhelm's disposal.

To begin to unravel the enigma of the unicorn, the reader must consult what Aldhelm's sources and contemporaries had to say about the creature. The *Physiologus* puts in place the principle Christian metaphors to be derived from the unicorn and its behavior. After recounting its appearance and the method of its capture, the *Physiologus* says:

Sic et dominus noster Iesus Christus, spiritalis unicornis, descendens in uterum uirginis, per carnem ex ea sumptam, captus a Iudaeis, morte crucis damnatus est; de quo Dauid dicit: Et dilectus sicut filius unicornium [Ps. 28.6]; et rursum in alio psalmo ipse de se dicit: Et exaltabitur sicut unicornis cornu meum [Ps. 91.11]. Et Zacharias dicit: Suscitauit eum cornu salutis in domo Dauid pueri sui [Luc. 1.69]. Et in Deuteronomio Moyses benedicens tribum Ioseph: Primitiuos tauri species eius, cornua eius tamquam cornua unicornis [Deut. 33.17].

Quod autem unum cornu habet in capite significat hoc quod dicit saluator: Ego et pater unum sumus [Ioh. 10.30]. Caput enim Christi, deus [I Cor. 11.3], secundum apostolum. Acerrimum uero quod dicit eum, id est quod neque principatus, neque potestates, non throni neque dominationes intelligere potuerunt, nec infernus tenere ualuit. Quod autem dicitur pusillum animal: propter incarnationis eius humilitatem; dicente ipso: Discite a me, quia mitis sum humilis corde [Matt. 11.29]. In tantum autem acerrimus, ut nec ille subtilissimus diabolus intelligere aut inuestigare potuit, sed sola uoluntate patris descendit in uterum uirginis Mariae pro nostram salutem: Et uerbum caro factum est, et habitauit in nobis [Ioh. 1.14]. Quod autem est similis haedo unicornis—et saluator noster secundum apostolum: Factus est in similitudinem carnis peccati, et de peccato damnauit peccatum in carne [Rom. 8.3]. Bene ergo dictum est de unicorne. (*Physiologus* 31–2 [versio B])

In this way our lord Jesus Christ, the spiritual unicorn, descended into the womb of the virgin, assumed human flesh, was captured by the Jews, and was sentenced to death on the cross; concerning this David said: and as the beloved son of the unicorn [Ps. 28.6]; and yet again in another psalm it is said of him: And my horn shall be exalted like that of the unicorn [Ps. 91.11]. And Zachariah said: he has raised up a horn of salvation to us, in the house of David his servant [Luc. 1.69]. And in Deuteronomy Moses blesses the tribe of Joseph: His beauty as of the firstling of a bullock, his horn as the horn of the unicorn [Deut. 33.17].

That he has one horn on his head signifies what the savior said: I and the father are one [John 10.30]. He is said to be shrewd since neither principalities, powers, thrones, nor dominations can comprehend him, nor can hell hold him. He is small because of the humility of his incarnation. He said "Learn from me; for I am gentle and lowly in heart" [Matt. 11.29]. He is so shrewd that that most clever devil cannot comprehend him or find him out, but through the will of the Father alone he came down into the womb of the Virgin Mary for our salvation. "And the Word became flesh and dwelt among us" [John 1.14]. The unicorn is like the kid, as is our Savior according to the Apostle: "He was made in the likeness of sin-

> ful flesh and for sin he condemned sin in the flesh" [Rom. 8.3]. This was spoken well of the unicorn. (*my translation;* trans. Carmody)

The *Physiologus* provides a variety of positive interpretations of the unicorn, many of which do not depend on its interaction with the virgin. Importantly, however, it also sets up the correspondence of the virgin/Virgin, a correspondence that will influence every interpretation of the unicorn story that attempts to account for the young woman's presence in the unicorn's description.

But not all interpretations of the unicorn and its behavior even mention the virgin, and not all interpretations are spiritually positive.

> In the thirty-fourth chapter of Isaiah unicorns appear as one symbol for the heathens which the prophet is threatening in so formidable a manner. The unicorn was identified by the Church Fathers with everything resisting the domination of Christ and contrary to the Church. In Psalm 37, Jerome speaks of enemies of the Lord who are as overweening as unicorns, although this interpolation does not appear in the original text. (R. Beer 24)

Early interpreters felt free, or freer than their late medieval counterparts, to use the unicorn-as-symbol in negative as well as positive ways. I believe Aldhelm is using it in a negative but unique way in his enigma to represent the pagan past. Not only does the unicorn call out to Fortune—"Heu! fortuna ferox"—as though she is his "mistress," as pagans did, but it also rather pointedly refers to the pagan god "discrimina Martis," thereby orienting its belief system in a mistaken pagan past. This phrase could also function simply as a poetic reference to human hunters, but such use does not negate the antique effect of the word "Martis."

In addition, the use of the word "moloso" helps orient the enigma's speaker in a classical past. The translator's rendering, "vainly baying hound," is somewhat misleading, bringing to mind, as it does, the elaborately staged medieval hunt with mid-sized, flop-eared foxhounds in full song. A "moloso," or Molossian, was a very specific and famous kind of Roman war dog. Extinct by Aldhelm's time, this ancestor of today's mastiff was of "sufficient strength to knock or drag an armed man off his horse, disembowel and dismember him" (Thurston 49), and was often set upon gladiators in the Circus. That Aldhelm referred to this specific Roman breed, which was "frustra latrante"—snarling, not just baying—provides an even starker contrast between the violent ancients and the gentle, "inermi" virgin/Virgin.

Gregory the Great's interpretive use of the unicorn in some sense resembles the one put forth here and bolsters my conviction that the unicorn represents a negative pagan past put to good use within a Christian framework:

> Gregory rediscovered the contradiction of the unicorn's power for good and for evil in a historical character. In a lengthy theological treatise, he compared Saul of Tarsus to a unicorn when he frenziedly persecuted Christians. But God succeeded in tethering this unicorn to the manger, fed it the fodder of the holy script, and harnessed it to his plough. Thus Saul became converted into Paul—God placed his trust in that unicorn. (R. Beer 24)

Like Paul, a potentially dangerous pagan past, whose literature and philosophy were nonetheless intellectually appealing, could be harnessed and integrated into the community of believers and transformed into a useful tool of the Almighty.

Some interpretive difficulties arise when trying to establish that the unicorn is, in fact, being captured in order to be put to the service of the Church, for although the "harmless virgin" tames him, the enigma, being enigmatic, fails to clarify to what use the beast will be put. Aldhelm's use of the term "lofty city" ["celsam . . . ad urbem"] may offer a clue. Although Lapidge and Rosier tell us that "[i]t is not clear what is meant by the 'lofty city' to which the unicorn is led" (Notes 252), Aldhelm could certainly have the *City of God* in mind here. This possibility is bolstered by the fact that Aldhelm's choice of a city is unusual if not unique in the medieval depiction of the unicorn. The *Physiologus,* the source for the notion that the captured unicorn is led anywhere, says that it "exhibetur in palatio regis" ("is displayed in the palace of kings") (*Physiologus* 31 [versio B]; my translation). Alternately, the unicorn and maiden are often portrayed in an enclosed garden, "the *hortus conclusus,* an attribute of the Virgin Mary, inspired by a verse in the Song of Songs" (Freeman 136). Aldhelm rejected both these well-known possibilities as his unicorn's ultimate destination, and such blatant rejections indicate that his choice, a lofty city, must serve some symbolic purpose. Augustine's *City of God* functioned as the source for the enigma on the peacock (Lapidge and Rosier, Notes 249), and Aldhelm was also apparently familiar with a wide range of Augustine's works, as indicated in his tenth *De Metris* (*Aldhelm: The Poetic Works*).

The words Alhelm chooses may bolster this point. "Celsam urbem" literally translated means "lofty city," and "celsam" may mean lofty in the secular sense—"high in rank or dignity"—or in the religious sense—"spiritually exalted," according to the *Dictionary of Medieval Latin from British Sources.* That Aldhelm may have meant lofty in the religious sense is supported by the fact that he clearly used the word in this way in his *Carmina Ecclesiastica,* 3.28 and 4.12, to describe the Virgin and the apostles' vocation (*Aldhelm: The Poetic Works*). The word "urbem" possesses less clear connotations and may, admittedly, not refer specifically to Augustine's great work. However, the *Oxford Latin Dictionary* notes that in many cases "urbs" refers to the city of Rome itself, the seat of Christianity to which all roads, including the pagan unicorn's, apparently lead. So the "lofty city" could simply refer to Rome, or even heaven, but either will work equally well for this interpretation, which can be summed up as follows: the ancients (the unicorn) mistakenly followed a false god (Fortune) until Christ was born from Mary (the beautiful virgin) who led them to the one true God in heaven or to the community of believers (the lofty city) which makes use of them (the ancients) for Christian edification, as in this very treatise. As Howe notes of another enigma, "the chaos of paganism was replaced by the order of Christianity. . . . the didacticism of the name riddle is turned to a doctrinal end" (Howe, *Aldhelm's "Enigmata"* 56).

In this interpretation the enigmas of the unicorn and Fortune demonstrate between them the theological interconnectedness of Aldhelm's *Enigmata* which is, I have argued, one organizational principle of this work. These two riddles also show how Aldhelm used ancient authority while simultaneously subverting it, for the source for the enigma on Fortune, Vergil's *Aeneid* (Lapidge and Rosier, Notes 248), is very specifically rejected in favor of the Christian (and Christianizing) source for the enigma of the unicorn, Isidore's *Etymologies* (Lapidge and Rosier, Notes 252) augmented by Aldhelm's own very Christian touches. Thus the "hidden mystery" Aldhelm has revealed about the unicorn involves the monster's didactic connection both to pagan antiquity and Christianity; it can even act as a connecting bridge between the two worlds by showing how the latter can make use of the former for its own ends. Pagan antiquity is a monster that can nevertheless be tamed and assimilated by Christianity, and along the way the monster itself becomes a metaphor. In addition, the organization of discrete categories as found in Pliny is replaced by a series of interconnections whose ultimate direction always remains divine *invisibilia.* Such a strategy confounds the categories of monster and not-monster, as well as of mundane and extraordinary, since all participate in a single transcendent truth in much the same way that pagan antiquity, despite its religious allegiance, participates in Christian instruction.

Orchard has established a link between Aldhelm's *Enigmata* and the *Liber Monstrorum* via their shared attitude toward a pagan past that has been usurped by a Christian present (94–104). Lapidge has argued in addition that Aldhelm and the anonymous author of the *Liber Monstrorum* "appear to have drawn on the same monastic library" and that the author of the *Liber Monstrorum* may have known Aldhelm's work (Lapidge 176). The *Liber*

Monstrorum exists in at least five manuscripts dating from the ninth and tenth centuries (Orchard 86), although Lapidge has argued that its date of composition falls within the century 650–750 A.D. (164–5). Its insular origin has long been recognized, as has its link to *Beowulf* through the reference to Hygelac (Orchard 86; Ogilvy 206). More important for the present purposes are the links the work itself establishes between an erroneous and ominous pagan past inhabited by hostile monsters and a progressive and harmonious present governed by Christianity. As its title indicates, this is a book of monsters, but the anonymous author has further divided this category into three subcategories: "de monstruosis hominum partibus . . . et de ferarum horribilibus innumerosisque bestiarum formis et draconum dirissimis serpentiumque ac uiperarum generibus" ("the monstrous parts [or 'births'] of men . . . and the horrible and innumerable forms of wild beasts, and the most dreadful kinds of dragons, and serpents, and vipers") (*Liber Monstrorum* prologue; trans. Orchard). These are further divided into very small sections, each concerned with one specific monster. Book one, on human monsters, contains fifty-six monsters; book two, on beasts, has thirty-six; and book three, on serpents, consists of only twenty-four monsters.

The author does not appear to have had a reason like Pliny's for such minute divisions; he does not provide a table of contents so the reader can look up the entry s/he wants. Indeed, the author's detailed list of monsters actually seems to have intended quite the opposite:

> De occulto orbis terrarum situ interrogasti et si tanta monstrorum essent genera credenda quanta in abditis mundi partibus per deserta et Oceani insulas et in ultimorum montium latebris nutrita monstrantur . . . (*Liber Monstrorum* prologue)
>
> You have asked about the secret arrangement [or 'filthiness'] of the lands of the earth, and if as many kinds of monsters are to be credited as are demonstrated in the hidden parts [or 'births'] of the world, raised throughout the deserts and the islands of the Ocean and in the recesses of the farthest mountains . . . (trans. Orchard)

The author of the *Liber Monstrorum* does not merely wish to catalogue a list of interesting monstrosities; he aims to make known "secret arrangement(s)" and "hidden parts of the world." His work will reveal the truth of those things and places that are secret and hidden and will likewise expose the lies popularly reported about monsters and their habitats. This intent implies that the entire work, not just selective parts of it as in Pliny or even Isidore, must be read in order to be completely understood and in order for the truth to be made completely known, thereby demonstrating, like the *Enigmata,* the interconnectedness of its organizational strategy.

In spite of the author's rather dismissive attitude, he himself recognizes the genuine difficulty of distinguishing fact from fiction and the allure that monstrous fantasies exercise over the human psyche. He admits that:

> Quaedam tantum in ipsis mirabilibus uera esse creduntur, et sunt innumerabilia quae si quis ad exploranda pennis uolare potuisset et ita rumoroso sermone tamen ficta probaret, ubi nunc urbs aurea et gemmis aspersa litora dicuntur, ibi lapideam aut nullam urbem et scopulosa cerneret. (*Liber Monstrorum* prologue)
>
> Only some things in the marvels themselves are believed to be true, and there are countless things which if anyone could take winged flight to explore, they would prove that, although they should be concocted in speech and rumour, where now there is said to lie a golden city and gem-strewn shores, one would see there rocks and a stony city, if at all. (trans. Orchard)

Orchard describes this contrast as that "between the glittering of fiction and the harshness of fact" and sees it as foreshadowing a tension that runs throughout the *Liber Monstrorum,* "namely that between Christian and pagan lore" (90). The author's purpose, then, is to lead the reader to see the reality of the "rocks and a stony city." Importantly, however, the author does not dismiss all monsters as entirely fictitious; he leaves open the possibility of the existence of the "stony city" which may very well be real, but not as glamorous as rumor would have it, a veritable ruin, in fact. His description of the work he is composing is instructive in this light:

> . . . per haec antra monstrorum marinae puellae quandam formulam sirenae depingam, ut sit capite rationis quod tamen diuersorum generum hispidae squamosaeque sequuntur fabulae. (*Liber Monstrorum* prologue)
>
> . . . throughout these monster-filled caverns I shall paint a little picture of a sea-girl or siren, which if it has a head of reason is followed by all kinds of shaggy and scaly tales. (trans. Orchard)

The author sees his job, then, as discovering the "head of reason" amidst the "shaggy and scaly tales" and thereby making known the truth of hidden places and the secrets they contain. That monsters can serve some function in revealing truth is demonstrated by his use of the mermaid here as a metaphor for the truth he aims to make known.

The author of the *Liber Monstrorum* takes a highly hostile attitude toward some of the monsters he describes, an attitude which "represents a considerable departure from the less antagonistic approaches of such predecessors as Augustine, Isidore, or Pliny" (Orchard 89–90). But for Pliny, a pagan, monsters were merely part of the world, ubiquitous but not even warranting their own category; and for Isidore and Augustine, monstrosity only had importance in a spiritual or symbolic sense, since the "naturalistic interpretations of St. Augustine and Isidore of Seville" reflected "merely special, extreme cases of natural phenomena and [were] hence a part of the natural and divine order" (Le Goff, *Time, Work, and Culture* 194). Friedman describes Augustine's attitude best when he notes that it "combined missionary zeal with the Roman cosmopolitan tolerance of ethnic diversity" (*Monstrous Races* 90). In this light, it becomes clear that the *Liber Monstrorum* took an unusual approach to its subject, and one might reasonably ask if the author had a particular purpose beyond simple disgust for doing so.

Augustinian inclusiveness did not carry over into the *Liber Monstrorum,* but although one does sense a great deal of hostility in the *Liber Monstrorum*'s author towards his subjects, he rarely directly states his antagonism. More often, he simply distances himself from the story he is reporting and thereby implicitly refuses to take responsibility for its veracity or its falseness. Almost every entry on every monster begins with some variation of "it is said" or "they say that." Typical entries look much like these:

> Mulieres, ut ferunt, iuxta montem Armeniae nascuntur pellibus indutae, barbam usque ad mammas prolixam habentes, quae sibi, dum uenatrices sunt, tigres et leopardos et rapida ferarum genera pro canibus nutriunt. (1.22)
>
> Women, so they say, are born near the mountain of Armenia covered with hair, having long beards down to their breasts, who, since they are huntresses, rear tigers and leopards and swift kinds of wild animals instead of dogs. (trans. Orchard)
>
> Hippotami beluae in India esse perhibentur maiores elefantorum corporibus, quos dicunt in quodam fluuio aquae impotabilis demorari. (2.9)
>
> Hippopotami are said to be beasts in India greater in body than elephants, and they say that they live in a certain river with undrinkable water. (trans. Orchard)

These phrases of which the *Liber Monstrorum*'s author is so fond serve at least two functions. First, as previously mentioned, they allow him to distance himself from material that, as he made clear in the prologue, he finds of at least questionable merit and truthfulness. Secondly, this method also refers to authority in a typically medieval fashion. Although he may not give the authority's name, he makes certain that the reader understands that the information he reports comes from somewhere besides his own imagination, even if it comes from someone's else's imagination.

But how can the reader tell what to believe and what not to believe? The author of the *Liber Monstrorum* admits that he mixes truth and falsehood in his descriptions:

> . . . de his tibi sermo pauca depromet beluis et horribilibus ignotarum formis bestiarum quae in fluminibus uel stagnis paludibusque, siue in desertis orbis terrarum latebris fuisse quondam, poetae ac philosophi aurato sermone in suis litteraturis inaniter depingunt. (2. prologue)
>
> . . . a discussion will provide you with a few things concerning these [real] beasts and the horrible forms of unknown beasts which the poets and philosophers emptily depict in the gilded discourse of their writings to have once existed in rivers or lakes and swamps, or in the deserted recesses of the globe. (trans. Orchard)
>
> In his namque serpentibus quos superius descripsimus, quaedam uera, quaedam namque omni ueritate carentia reperiuntur. (3. epilogue)
>
> Now, amongst these serpents which we have described above, some true things are found, and some lacking all truth. (trans. Orchard)

In order to gauge the degree of veracity in these monstrous accounts, one must look to the author's specific sources because not all authorities are created equal. The reader must look to written sources in his/her evaluation of the truth precisely because it is the truth as expressed in words that is the author's subject; truth as revealed by nature—the fact that one can or cannot, for example, go out and capture a hydra to confirm or deny its material existence—does not come under discussion. Such truth as found in words can trace its ancestry back not only to Isidore, who after all was contemplating exactly this relationship, but also to the *Physiologus,* the supposed sayings of the "naturalist." In his preoccupation with truth-in-words, the author of the *Liber Monstrorum* shows no change from the attitude of his late antique and patristic sources.

Whereas most of the *Liber Monstrorum*'s sources are designated by the non-judgmental "they say" construction, a very few are openly hostile or openly approving, and these judgmental entries can help the reader find his/her way. Orchard provides what he terms "a fairly cautious list" (318) of sources for each section of the *Liber Monstrorum,* and what one first notices about this catalogue of sources is that pagan and Christian, sacred and secular, are freely mixed together as haphazardly, apparently, as Aldhelm mixed the ordinary and the extraordinary. So, for example, book one's eighth through eleventh entries have as their sources Augustine, *The Wonders of the East,* Isidore, and Vergil,[1] respectively (Orchard 318). A cursory glance at this list of source materials tells the reader very little, except that the author apparently knew his Vergil as well as he knew his Augustine; one must look at the texts of the monsters instead.

The author of the *Liber Monstrorum* usually does not comment on the quality of his source, even when uncovering commonly accepted truths as lies, e.g., "in Perside fingunt esse bestias quas conopenos appellant, quibus sub caninis capitibus equina dependet per ceruices iuba et ore naribusque ignem flammamque expirant" ("in Persis they imagine that there are beasts which they call Conopeni, beneath the dog-shaped heads of which a horse-like mane hangs from their neck, and they breath fire and flame from their mouth and nostrils") (2.13; trans. Orchard). However, in a few instances, the author pronounces a scathing judgment on the falsehood he has uncovered and its lying source:

> Et scribunt Romani cum Graecis per ipsas poeticas incredibilium rerum fabulas, bipedes equos in mari esse Tyrrheno, qui parte corporis priore equorum figuras et posteriore piscium habeant. (2.28)
>
> And along with the Greeks the Romans write in their poetic fantasies of incredible things, that there are two-footed horses in the Mediterranean, which have most of the front part of their body in the shape of horses, and the rear of fish. (trans. Orchard)
>
> In his enim poetarum fictionibus describitur quod angues gemini cum monstris et nubes ex aere latrantes Cleopatram ad Nilum fugassent exterritam, que cum Antonio contra Cesarem nauale proelium gessit. Et sicut huic mendacium a tergo reginae monstra et angues finxit aethereos, ita et fallaces poetarum fabulae sibi plurima quae non fiunt uoluntarie fingunt. (3.23)
>
> For it is described in these fictions of poets that twin snakes with monsters and clouds barking from the sky chased off to the Nile the terrified Cleopatra, who along with Anthony waged a naval battle against Caesar. And just as a lie has created monsters and etherial snakes on this queen's back, so too do the lying fables of poets willfully fake very many things for themselves which do not occur. (trans. Orchard)

The source for the first excerpt is Servius' *In Georgica* while the source for the second is Vergil's *Aeneid* (Orchard 318–20). Although the author does not say exactly who his sources are, the reader can tell that they are classical pagans, that they are poets, and that he considers their writings and their monsters to be "lying fables." Indeed, all the material which the author of the *Liber Monstrorum* considers spurious has either a pagan or a secular source; none of the material whose veracity is questionable derives from a patristic or explicitly Christian source. While such a conclusion may not be particularly surprising, it does point to the central organizing principle of the work in question as well as to the alien, premodern method for determining truth.

Plenty of the *Liber Monstrorum*'s sources are patristic and Christian, but they receive the kind of vague, non-judgmental treatment mentioned above ("it is said," "I have read," etc.), except for one:

> Et quendam hominem fideli historia lunatas habuisse plantas duorum non amplius digitorum conperimus; cuius quoque manus in huius normae mensuram editae describuntur. (1.25)
>
> And in a reliable (or 'faithful') narrative we find that a certain person had crescent-shaped feet with no more than two toes, and that their hands also are described as being formed after the measure of this pattern. (trans. Orchard)

The source for this account is Augustine's *City of God* 16.8 (Orchard 319), and "Augustine's tale is faithful precisely because it is full of faith (*fides*)" (Orchard 90). The author of the *Liber Monstrorum* would agree, adding that "reliable" is implicit in and inseparable from the word "faith(ful)." Although the author only approves of his source this once, he also never designates as imaginary or deceitful any entry whose only known source is Christian. He may reserve judgment ("they say"), but he never dismisses Christian sources as he does pagan sources. By extension, since Augustine makes this monster credible, all monsters derived from the *City of God,* 1.1; 1.4; 1.8; 1.16; 1.17; 1.19; 1.21; 1.23–25; 1.27; 1.29; 1.49; 1.53 (Orchard 318–20), must also be credible. Such extensive use of the *City of God* indicates familiarity with the work, making it quite surprising that the author did not borrow, along with the descriptions of monsters, Augustine's "Roman cosmopolitan tolerance of ethnic diversity."

When discussing the organization of the *Liber Monstrorum,* Orchard describes the book as "[a] catalogue of almost 120 monstrosities . . . divided up into three books of diminishing length (and, one suspects, dwindling authorial interest) . . ." (87). The parenthetical comment could be adjusted to read "dwindling use of Christian sources," for while book one contains fourteen monsters with their roots in *City of God* alone and an additional five with other Christian writers as their sources, book two lists only five monsters from explicitly Christian sources (2.2; 2.4; 2.18; 2.24; 2.25), and book three lists only five as well (3.6; 3.9; 3.14; 3.15; 3.18) (Orchard 319–20). Even considering the decreasing length of the three books, one cannot help but notice a significant decrease in the percentage of entries taken from Christian sources from book one to book three. I count nineteen entries from Christian sources, approximately one-third of the total, in book one. In contrast, book three's five entries from Christian sources account for about one-fifth of that book's total (Orchard 318–20). One can observe this phenomenon in reverse in the *Liber Monstrorum*'s use of the pagan poet Vergil. Book one contains eighteen entries whose source is either Vergil's *Aeneid* or *Georgics,* also approximately one-third of the total entries for book one. Book three, however, has eleven entries from Vergil, almost half of the total of that book (Orchard 318–20). So while the author decreases his use of explicitly Christian sources as he composes the *Liber Monstrorum,* he also increases his use of pagan lore.

This pattern does not appear to have much to do with the kinds of creatures he happens to be describing in each book, for whereas book one on human monsters and human hybrids would logically take much of its material from classical sources where such hybridization occurs frequently, in fact book one contains more and a larger percentage of Christian sources than the remaining two books. Interestingly, the second book takes as its major sources the problematic *Alexander's Letter to Aristotle* and *Wonders of the East,* which are neither explicitly Christian nor pagan, even if they are about pagans. Seventeen of the thirty-six entries of book two use one of these as a source, compared to five that use Vergil and five that use Christian sources. Nine of the remaining entries have no known source (Orchard 318–20).

One must also consider the entries that the poet has clearly censured for dishonesty and impiety. They number twelve: three from book one (37, 42, 45); seven from book two (8, 10, 14, 15, 28, 33, 34); and two from book three (13, 23). All censured entries have as their source a pagan author except for book two, 10 and 15, whose source is the problematic *Wonders of the East,* and by far the most popular pagan authority to be censured is Vergil, whose six reprimands are distributed equally throughout the three books, with two censured entries in each section (1.42, 46; 2.8, 14; 3.13, 23) (Orchard 318–20). However, if one considers the decreasing number of entries in each book as the work progresses, one will see that Vergil becomes increasingly responsible for the number of monstrous "lies" in the *Liber Monstrorum.* That is, while he is the source for half the censured entries that appear in the work, the two "lies" for which he is responsible in book one constitute slightly less than 1/25 of the complete number of entries. This ratio increases to 1/18 in book two and to 1/12 in book three. These percentages are small, to be sure, but their significance lies in the way they conform to general scheme of the *Liber Monstrorum* in which the reader progresses (regresses?) from faithful to faithless, from true to false, from good to bad.

What sort of pattern might be extracted from this amalgam of disparagement, percentages, increases and decreases? First, the percentage of Christian sources decreases while the percentage of pagan sources increases. The number of censured entries, if plotted on a graph, would describe a sort of parabola (3–7-2), but a single pagan author, Vergil, remains responsible for fully half those censured. The ratios of censured Vergillian material to the number of entries per book rises steadily, and this rise resembles the aforementioned increase in pagan sources generally. Augustine remains the only praiseworthy, clearly reliable source. Orchard's interpretation of these trends can help:

> The first few chapters of Book I, for example, rely heavily on material derived from Christian prose sources, particularly Augustine, whilst the Book ends with a string of sections adapted from Vergil. During the middle portion of Book I the author is implicitly following his own model, outlined in the Prologue, namely that of the siren . . . This model of the siren applies not simply to Book I, of course, but to the whole work, which commences by discussing monsters who share human shape and reason (Book I), and finishes by considering in turn tales (and tails!) both shaggy (Book II) and scaly (Book III). (94)

Such an interpretation is instructive, but needs augmenting. I would argue that it is not so much the resemblance of the monsters themselves to "human shape and reason" in book one that calls forth the model of the siren with a head of reason but rather the nature of the source materials. As noted, book one relies quite heavily on Christian sources, Augustine in particular, and these sources, in addition to the monsters' resemblance to humankind, constitute the "head of reason." At the "head" of book one, and thus of the entire work, seven of the first ten entries derive from explicitly Christian sources (1, 3, 4, 5, 7, 8, 10), three of which are Augustine (1, 4, 8) (Orchard 318). So the *Liber Monstrorum* begins with reference to Augustine's *City of God,* that "fideli historia" (1.25) full of rationality ("rationis") (1. prologue); Augustine, Isidore (5, 10), and Jerome (3, 7) (Orchard 318) comprise the "head of reason."

Likewise, I do not believe necessarily that the decreasing resemblance to humankind through books two and three reflects the model of the siren; instead, the increasing use of pagan sources, particularly the "lying poet" Vergil, recalls the monstrous form of the sea-girl. Despite Orchard's pun on tale/tail quoted above, the text itself does not say "caudae" but rather "hispidae squamosaeque . . . fabulae" (*Liber Monstrorum* prologue). The text refers not to physical monstrosity in this part of the sea-girl metaphor but to "fabulae," stories, gossip or myths. The siren's head of reason is followed not only by a physically monstrous tail, but by a series of monstrous lies whose lack of veracity derives ultimately from their pagan sources. Just as the *Liber Monstrorum* begins with the "reasonable" Augustine, it ends with an increasing reliance on Vergil. Of the final ten entries in book three, five (16, 17, 20, 23, 24) have Vergil as their source, one of which (23) is censured. One entry (22) derives from Servius, and another (21) from *Alexander's Letter to Aristotle* (Orchard 320). Having begun with a patristic head of faith and reason, the *Liber Monstrorum* ends with "scaly and shaggy tales"—*not* tails—primarily from Vergil's "lying fables" (3.23).

The *Liber Monstrorum*'s ideas about authority seem relatively clear: Christian authors are reliable and pagan authors—especially poets, although orators and scientists are also censured (2.1), as is the letter-writing Alexander the Great—are liars. Theological allegiance alone is enough to determine truth or falsehood about monsters. The degree to which a particular monster is fantastic or grotesque has little to do with veracity, for many of the monsters whose existence remains at least unquestioned and who derive from a Christian source are no less marvelous than some of Vergil's censured monsters, such as the "monstrum quoddam nocturnum" ("certain monster of the night") (1.42; trans. Orchard) that habitually flew screaming through the night sky. Although it is not described in exceptionally unbelievable terms, the report of it is nevertheless "dici nefandum est" ("impious to be said") (1.42; trans. Orchard) simply because the description comes from Vergil and not Augustine or Isidore. My point in dwelling on this method for determining truthfulness is to show that the monsters themselves as potential physical realities have lost any relevance. Instead, the author focuses the reader's attention on distinguishing between "quaedam uera, quaedam namque omni ueritate carentia" ("some true things, and some lacking all truth") (3. epilogue; trans. Orchard) as an exercise in theological instruction and secular pagan denigration. That the screaming flying monster is "impious" ("nefandum") instead of "falsus" or an "erratum" indicates that physical reality is not just secondary to orthodoxy, but is simply not under discussion.

Following Orchard, I have dwelt at length on the organizational structure of the *Liber Monstrorum* but have only briefly addressed the issue of its didactic completeness. This completeness does not greatly resemble, for example, Isidore's or Pliny's because the author makes no effort to include everything:

> Haec sunt inmania monstra de quibus me fluctus tuae postulationis tundebat et ea quae de spumosis fabularum gurgitibus ad haec litora congessi. Adhuc tamen innumberabilia sunt quae et in terris et in mari fuisse dixerunt. De quibus tediosum est plus scribere uelle . . . (1. epilogue)
>
> These are the huge monsters concerning which the wave of your request buffeted me, and those are the ones which I have gathered to these shores from the foaming torrents of fable. But there are still innumerable things which they have said have existed both on land and in the sea, concerning which it is tedious to wish to write more . . . (trans. Orchard)

The author's mention of incompleteness would seem to violate the principle of doctrinal completeness for which I believe the *Liber Monstrorum* strives, but this apparent violation stems from a misunderstanding of the author's purpose. That is, in spite of the author's stated intention to make known "[d]e occulto orbis terrarum situ" ("about the secret arrangement [or 'filthiness'] of the lands of the earth") (1. prologue; trans. Orchard), he does not aim to make every detail or every monster known; for that sort of information one must look to Pliny. But I do believe the *Liber Monstrorum* does achieve a certain kind of completeness through its encyclopedic nature.

Howe writes of the encyclopedic form of Old English catalogue poems, and while the *Liber Monstrorum* is certainly not a poem or even poetic, it is very much a catalogue, a list. To speak of an "encyclopedic catalogue" (Howe, *Catalogue Poems* 16) seems contradictory, for "encyclopedic" implies completeness while a catalogue "does not indicate to the reader that a subject has been brought to a final, immutable state. Rather it suggests that the work remains in progress" (Howe, *Catalogue Poems* 44). The completeness of a catalogue refers both to its capacity to incorporate new and relevant information as it becomes available and to its ability to supply the information needed for the reader to get the "big picture." The *Liber Monstrorum* conforms to both these criteria, for one could easily imagine the form additional entries could take were any future compiler to become convinced of the need for them, and the source exercise I have outlined here reveals the "big picture" of Christian authority and truth. In this way the *Liber Monstrorum* resembles Isidore's *Etymologies,* a catalogue that "offers the necessary education for biblical exegesis" (Howe, *Catalogue Poems* 58). The *Liber Monstrorum* offers the necessary education for determining authorial reliability within the Christian metanarrative. While such a pointed message may seem unencyclopedic to those of us imbued with post-Romantic ideas of scholarly truth, the *Liber Monstrorum* actually conforms to the encyclopedic schemes of its predecessors and contemporaries: "Like the later encyclopedists, Pliny understood that no work, not even a compilation of facts, could or should be free of ideological intent . . ." (Howe, *Catalogue Poems* 31).

The author of the *Liber Monstrorum*'s ideological intent is unpoetically obvious: he proposes to reveal through praise, disparagement, and the carefully arranged pattern of his sources the only truth that matters at all: the inherent and eternal superiority of the Christian to the pagan. This truth is, in a sense, complete in that beyond this, the reader really does not need to go; all relevant information is contained within the doctrine of Christianity which transcends, encompasses and uses pagan literary "lies." The monsters themselves function only in service to demonstrate this truth, and the author even seems to find discussion of particular monsters tiresome. In the epilogue he confides, "[s]unt quoque plurimi adhuc serpentini generis angues . . . de quibus iam nihil singulare et admiratione dignum reperri" ("[t]here are also still very many snakes of serpentine kind . . . concerning which I have now found nothing remarkable or worthy of notice") (3. epilogue; trans. Orchard). Obviously the monsters themselves do not concern the author overmuch, and he feels no need to include all those of which he is aware in his book. Instead, the "occulto . . . situ" refers to the hidden, but recoverable, pattern of authority so deftly woven into a rather tedious list of monsters. The view this arrangement makes known is that with which no good Christian would disagree: Christianity represents the "head of reason" that supersedes a monstrous pagan past, however poetically seductive that past may be.

The *Liber Monstrorum*'s strategy might best be described as rejection and re-incorporation of pagan (mis)information into a literary endeavor for Christian truth. Like Isidore, the author must reject the classical monster on whatever plane it appears: historical, literal, fictional; but then, because his organizing principle is the transcendence and all-inclusiveness of the Christian faith, he must re-incorporate monstrous information into a Christian literary project. In a kind of literary hostile takeover, the *Liber Monstrorum*'s author integrates pagan sources into the Christian symbolic, thereby assimilating the competition instead of obliterating it.

The author of the *Liber Monstrorum* uses two quite problematic but popular works as sources, especially in book two, that deserve further comment: the *Wonders of the East* and *Alexander the Great's Letter to Aristotle*. These sources present to the reader a view that is by no means encyclopedic or complete, but rather geographically linear. Instead of depicting a God's eye view of the physical world, these works describe an entirely earth-bound, horizontal perspective that never becomes omniscient even though it may provide the reader with complete, even painstaking, detail of the physical world. The worldly limitations of these works, I will argue, derive from the definitively pagan point of view they pretend to represent. By adopting their epistolary form and using them as sources, the *Liber Monstrorum* functions as a commentary on and correction of their paganism.

The *Wonders of the East,* also commonly known as the *Marvels of the East* and occasionally as *De Mirabilibus Orientis,* survives in three manuscripts: an Anglo-Saxon version in the *Beowulf* ms. (BM Cotton Vit. A.15, c. 1000); an Anglo-Saxon version alongside a Latin version in Cotton Tib. B.5 (c. 1050); and a Latin version in Bodley 614 (early twelfth century) (James 2–6). Concerning the question of the *Wonders*' provenance, Sisam concluded that the *Wonders* "was compiled by an Anglo-Saxon whose simple Latin was influenced by his native idiom" (Sisam 76). In addition to his syntactical argument, Sisam reasons that "the only extant Latin manuscripts T and B are English, and the only known vernacular rendering is the Anglo-Saxon" (76). Cotton Vitellius is the shortest and least attractive text, with thirty-two wonders. Cotton Tiberius contains an additional five (33–37/8), and Bodley 614 adds another twelve (38–49/50) (Orchard 20–22).[2] These alternative endings will have profound implications later in my argument.

M.R. James identified as one of the primary sources for the *Wonders* the pseudo-epistolary *Fermes' Letter to Emperor Hadrian.* Fermes supposedly traveled to the remote East to capture and bring back to Hadrian marvelous animal and human specimens. James notes that "the epistolary pretense is flimsy; the document is but a collection of marvels rather ill put together" (9), but this evaluation is beside the point. Whoever forged the "letter" went out of his way to make is clear to his audience the perspective from which he meant this composition to be read: that of a pagan in the east communicating with his emperor, also a pagan. Orchard lists five extant copies of this letter and notes their connection to the *Wonders:* "The Anglo-Saxon versions of the *Wonders* derive ultimately from a text represented in mainly continental manuscripts in many different forms, almost all of which share a basic epistolary framework . . ." (22–3).

In addition to identifying an epistolary source for the *Wonders,* James has also noted an analogue for this text in the *Epistola Premonis regis ad Traianum imperatorem.* The chaotic history of this work demands lengthy quotation:

> In a Strasburg MS. (marked C. iv. 15) of the eighth or ninth century, which perished in the fire of 1870, was a tract called *Epistola Premonis regis ad Traianum imperatorem.* It was fortunately printed by Graff in *Diutiska,* ii. 292 (1829) . . . but in fact it is much nearer to *M[arvels]* than

> to *F*[*ermes*], of which it practically presents a shortened text. . . . [I]t everywhere omits the particulars of distances which are common to *F*[*ermes*] and *M*[*arvels*]. When it rejoins the text of *F*[*ermes*] and *M*[*arvels*] it agrees with the latter. . . . Thus *P*[*remonis*] and *M*[*arvels*] have closely followed an ancestor now lost, but *M*[*arvels*] represents it far better than *P*[*remonis*], having retained part at least of the framework of an itinerary which *P*[*remonis*] has wholly dropped. (James 33–5)

Orchard has identified three MSS of the *Premonis,* two of which are now lost (23). Both James and Orchard chart in exhausting detail the correspondences between the *Wonders, Fermes,* and *Premonis* (James 37–40; Orchard 24–5). The *Premonis,* like *Fermes,* presents in epistolary form a report from an underling to a pagan emperor. It is important to establish the similarities between these letters and the *Wonders* because the perspective the letters present, a Christian view of the pagan view of the world, is also the perspective of the *Wonders* and will color the reading of that work.

The "pagan" view of the world as presented in the *Wonders* differs greatly from the Christian view of the *Physiologus* or Aldhelm's *Enigmata,* for example. The information in the *Wonders* (much like that in Pliny's *Natural History*) is limited almost exclusively to physical description and shows a great preoccupation with quantification: direction, distance, length and height. The opening passage sets the tone:

> Seo landbunes is on fruman from Antimolima Þam lande; ðæt land is on rime Þæs læssan milgetæles ðe stadia hatte fif hund, & Þæs micclan milgetæles Þe leuua hatte ðreo hund & eahta & syxtig. On ðam ealande byð micel menigeo sceapa. & Þanon is to Babilonia Þæs læssan milgetæles stadia hundteontig & eahta & syxtig, & ðæs micclan Þe leuua hatte fiftyne & hundteontig. (*Wonders* 1)

> The colony is at the beginning of the land Antimolima, which land is 500 in the tally of the lesser measurement, which are called *stadia,* and 368 of the greater, which are called *leuuae* ['leagues']. On that island there is a great multitude of sheep, and from there to Babylon it is 168 of the lesser measurement called *stadia,* and 115 in the greater measurement called *leuuae.* (trans. Orchard)

As the reader progresses through the written work, so does s/he also progress along the physical landscape: "Sum stow is ðonne mon færð to ðare Readan Sæ, Seo is gehaten Lentibelsinea . . . Hascellentia hatte Þæt land, Þonne mon to Babilonia færð, Þæt is Þonne ðæs læssan milgetæles Þe stadia hatte .IX. mila lang & brad" ("As you go towards the Red Sea there is a place called

Lentibelsinea . . . Hascellentia is the name of the land on the way to Babylon, that is in length and breadth nine of the lesser measurements called *stadia*") (*Wonders* 3, 5; trans. Orchard).

Along the way, the reader often encounters many "wonderful" people and animals which are almost always described, often in numerical terms, but are rarely judged in moral terms, despite sometimes reprehensible behavior:

> Begeondan Brixonte ðære ea, east ðanon, beoð men acende lange & micle, Þa habbað fet & sceancan twelf fota lange, sidan mid breostum seofan fota lange. Hi beoð sweartes hiwes & hi syndan Hostes nemde. Cuðlice swa hwylcne mann swa hi gefoð, Þonne fretað hi hine. (*Wonders* 13)
>
> Beyond the River Brixontes, east from there, there are people born big and tall, who have feet and shanks twelve feet long, flanks with chests seven feet long. They are of a black colour, and are called Hostes. As certainly as they catch a person they devour him. (trans. Orchard)

The author uses the same tone to describe a completely benign, if equally odd-looking, race:

> Ðanan is east ðær beoð men akenned Þa beoð awæstme fiftyne fota lange & on bræde tyn fotmæla. Hi habbað micle heafda & earan swa fann. Oþer eare hi him on niht underbredað, & mid oðran hy wreoð him. Beoð Þa earan swiðe leohte & hi beoð an lichoman swa hwite swa meolc. & gif hi hwylcne mann on ðam landum geseoð oðÞe ongytað, Þonne nimað hi heora earan on hand & feorriað hi & fleoð, swa hrædlice swa is wen Þætte hi fleogen. (*Wonders* 21)
>
> Going east from there is a place where people are born who are in size fifteen feet tall and ten broad. They have large heads and ears like fans. They spread one ear beneath them at night, and they wrap themselves with the other. Their ears are very light and their bodies are as white as milk. And if they see or perceive anyone in those lands, they take their ears in their hands and go far and flee, so swiftly one might think that they flew. (trans. Orchard)

One might expect, in the spirit of the *Physiologus,* some explanation of the significance of such behaviors or some kind of moral evaluation that would then become applicable to one's own behavior. The reader receives no such commentary. The *Wonders* narrator does, however, make a few moral judgments concerning the behaviors he claims to have witnessed, and these can tell something about the Christian perception of pagan morality.

Despite the absence of horror or even sadness at the Hostes' behavior, the *Wonders* does in fact differentiate between good and bad; it is not amoral. The *Wonders*' ideas about good are, however, not entirely Christian:

> On Þam wynstran dæle Þæt rice is Þe ða deor on beoÞ Catinos, & Þær beoð gæstliÞende menn, cyningas Þa habbað under him mænigfealde leodhatan. Heora landgemære beoð neah Þam garsecge, & Þanan fram Þam wynstran dæle syndan manege cyningas.
>
> Đis mannkynn lifað fela geara, & hi syndon fremfulle menn. & gyf hwylc mann to him cymeð Þonne gyfað hi him wif ær hi hine onweg lætan. Se macedonisca Alexander, Þa ða he him to com, Þa wæs he wundriende hyra menniscnysse, ne wolde he hi cwellan ne him nawiht laðes don. (29–30)
>
> On the left-hand side of the kingdom in which there are wild animals called Catini, there are hospitable people, kings who have subdued many tyrants. Their boundaries border on the Ocean, and from there, from the left-hand section, there are many kings.
>
> This race of people live for many years, and they are generous people. If anyone visits them they give him a woman before they let him go. When Alexander of Macedon visited them, he was amazed at their humanity, and would not kill them or cause them any harm. (trans. Orchard)

Hospitality, generosity, and a sense of fairplay and *noblesse oblige* characterize this unnamed race of people, and Christian readers would agree that these are fine traits. However, the Christian might pause uncomfortably at the example of generosity the *Wonders* provides to prove these people's goodness. While a Christian audience might even find the "gift" of a woman tempting, medieval Christians would still very probably recognize the shaky moral ground on which the gift rests. Even if the audience did not object to the possession and commodification of human flesh, the implication of the possibility of adultery and fornication on the part of the recipient of such generosity remains. It would not follow necessarily that the givers are therefore to be considered wicked, depraved, and dissolute; they still apparently have good instincts that have been inappropriately channeled. They do not lack morality, but rather a Christian framework by which to shape the admirable quality of generosity in order to avoid specifically Christian sins that would arise not out of wickedness, but from ignorance.

Whereas the *Wonders*' instincts towards good remain basically sound, the text is more ambivalent about evaluating evil. As noted above, the text passes over such behavior as cannibalism without comment. When it does claim to have discovered wickedness, its criteria for such an evaluation seems problematic:

> Đonne sindon oðre wif ða habbað eoferes tucxas & feax oð helan side, & on lendenum oxan tægl. Þa wif syndon ðreotyne fota lange & heora lic bið on marmorstanes hwitnysse. & hi habbað olfenda fet & eoferes teð. For heora unclennesse hie gefelde wurdon fram ðam mycclan macedoniscan Alexandre. Þa he hi lifiende gefon ne mihte, Þa acwealde he hi for ðam hi syndon æwisce on lichoman & unweorðe. (*Wonders* 27)
>
> Then there are other women who have boar's tusks and hair down to their heels and ox-tails on their loins. Those women are thirteen feet tall and their bodies are of the whiteness of marble. And they have camel's feet and boar's teeth. Because of their uncleanness they were killed by Alexander the Great of Macedon. He killed them because he could not capture them alive, because they have offensive and disgusting bodies. (trans. Orchard)

Granted, these women appear quite grotesque and "unclean," and their bodies may indeed be "offensive and disgusting." But mere appearance does not explain why the women deserve death. Compared to the cannibalistic Hostes, these women do not appear to have performed any unclean or offensive action that warrants Alexander's hostility. This race of women is, according to Augustine's line of reasoning, fully human and thus deserving of the consideration and respect one ought to show to all human beings:

> Verum quisquis uspiam nascitur homo, id est animal rationale mortale, quamlibet nostris inusitatam sensibus gerat corporis formam seu colorem sive motum sive sonum sive qualibet vi, qualibet parte, qualibet qualitate naturam, ex illo uno protopasto origenem ducere nullus fidelium dubitaverit. (Augustine 16.8)
>
> Yet whoever is born anywhere as a human being, that is, as a rational mortal creature, however strange he may appear to our senses in bodily form or colour or motion or utterance, or in any faculty, part or quality of his nature whatsoever, let no true believer have any doubt that such an individual is descended from the one man who was first created. (trans. Sanford and Green)

The great majority of medieval thinkers deferred to this line of reasoning, "relying in the main on the authoritative figure of Saint Augustine" (Friedman, *Monstrous Races* 183). The point here is that the *Wonders* has made yet another ethical mistake, although one that is perfectly understandable if one relies on superficialities and lacks the benefit of Christian teaching, that is, if one has a pagan perspective.

Perhaps here would be a good place to sum up the perspective of the *Wonders of the East.* First, the text proceeds in a horizontal, linear fashion from place to place and from wonder to wonder without ever giving the reader any sense of how the places fit into the physical or spiritual landscape. The text provides remarkably sparse commentary on the implications of monstrous behavior, and when it does provide a moral, never spiritual, judgment, that judgment is inevitably but understandably skewed in such a way as to be capable of being properly redirected through the introduction of Christian doctrine. The lack of any encyclopedic perspective, of any "prying" into the potential moral or spiritual meaning for the monsters and marvels, and the focus on physicality limit the *Wonders*' perspective to that of the pagan world, or more specifically, to a Christian perception of the pagan perspective. Such a pseudo-pagan perspective may accurately depict the physical world, but without the benefit of Christian doctrine, such a perspective remains limited and often mistaken. This interpretation also explains why the narrator never bothers to reject and then re-incorporate the monsters into a Christian scheme, as the clearly Christian works considered here do, until later scribes felt the urge to make the *Wonders* more obviously Christian, as we shall soon see.

This interpretation may not be immediately apparent from the text of the *Wonders* itself, but when one considers the text in conjunction with the two letters that served as source and analogue, the *Wonders*' intent becomes clearer. The very titles, *The Letter of King Premonis to the Emperor Trajan* and *The Letter of Fermes to Hadrian,* go out of the way to emphasize the purported perspective of the "writer" and the "recipient." These are fictional Roman field reports to pagan emperors and should be read as such. Once again Augustine provides a useful reference in this matter, for while *The City of God* naturally aims to represent the transcendence of Christianity, Augustine, always a reasonable man, recognizes the Roman Empire's contributions to the order of the earthly realm. When explaining the role of the Empire in Christian history, Augustine admits that the Romans'

> eagerness for praise and desire of glory, then, was that which accomplished those many wonderful things, laudable, doubtless, and glorious according to human judgment . . . for they built in very close proximity the temples of Virtue and Honour, worshipping as gods the gifts of God. Hence we can understand what they who were good thought to be the end of virtue, and to what they ultimately referred it, namely, to honour. (5.12; trans. Smith)

While giving credit where it is due, Augustine never loses sight of the limitations of the Romans and their empire, for in his "comprehensive view of human history, so trivial and evanescent a thing as the Roman empire plays little part" (O'Donnell 57). The Roman perspective reveals its flaws, in the two letters and the *Wonders,* because "Christianity gave Augustine a perspective from which to view Rome, at least in the imagination, from outside" (O'Donnell 42).

In order to appreciate the perspective of the *Wonders* more thoroughly, the reader will require a more extensive understanding of the Anglo-Saxon view of the ancient pagan, mostly Roman but also Greek, past. Contrary to what the *Liber Monstrorum* might lead one to think, classical learning did play a role in the construction of Christian Anglo-Saxon culture. That role, however, can best be characterized as ambiguous. Clearly, the most famous and influential scholars—Bede, Aldhelm, Alcuin—had intimate acquaintance with Latin poetry and prose, but individual writers varied in the degree to which they were willing to acknowledge their debt to the classics; "[c]lassical myth, history, and legend were apparently viewed with the same suspicion as literature" but the persistence of classical sources and allusions "testif[ies] to the enduring appeal of classical authors and texts in Anglo-Saxon England," according to *The Blackwell Encyclopedia of Anglo-Saxon England*'s entry on "classical learning."

This "suspicion" alludes to the fact that while Anglo-Saxon scholars recognized the genius and aesthetic appeal of classical learning, they had to reconcile this appeal with the knowledge that the authors were benighted, hell-bound heathens whose beautifully structured works were often blasphemous. Scholars achieved reconciliation by assessing classical texts purely for their theological value via reinterpretation:

> . . . a trend that is supremely characteristic of medieval education and, in particular, the medieval use of the classics . . . is the inherent bent toward a moral or moralizing interpretation of the literary texts, the use of which was ultimately justified precisely insofar as they could yield a moral lesson in a Christian key. . . . Hence the classics were accepted and welcomed but only, and this consistently and coherently, with the end of subordinating science and formal literary virtues to the absolute values of Christian formation and observance, theologically and morally. (Scaglione 350–1)

Bately's study of the Alfredian translation of Boethius' *Consolation of Philosophy* and the anonymous Anglo-Saxon translation of Orosius' *History Against the Pagans* demonstrates the ways in which classical learning could be put to use; she concentrates on showing how the translators' additions and omissions prove an extensive Anglo-Saxon familiarity with classical learning (Bately 45–78). I would add that her examples also demonstrate the ambiguous relationship of Anglo-Saxon Christianity to a pagan past that could be positively or negatively valenced in accordance with the writer's personal view and with his particular didactic and literary needs at the time.

Although the *Wonders* is not, of course, a true classical text, its sources (and it also, by extension) purport to be part of the classical tradition. The reader should thus continually remind herself that these texts imitate the pagan perspective, which is a limited one at best and whose value derives only from what spiritual use the reader can put it to. The absence of a Christian perspective limits the letters and the *Wonders* to earth-bound information about distances, physical forms and behaviors. Such reports may be accurate, but they lack any "higher meaning" or any awareness of their role in Christian history due to their earthly limitations. Although the *Wonders* does not conform to the explicit epistolary framework of *Fermes* and *Premonis,* its virtual repetition of the matter of those texts suggests a similar repetition of perspective and interpretation. And while the *Wonders* may not retain the epistolary framework in its title, as James notes, it does retain the itinerary structure that *Premonis* has lost (33–5), a structure which gestures quite clearly towards the pseudo-pagan epistles from which it derived.

While the source epistles point toward the *Wonders*' purposely skewed pagan perspective, two passages found in Tiberius B.v and Bodley 614 but not in Vitellius A.xv can aid the Christian reader in the correct understanding of this rather inscrutable text. Whereas Vitellius ends after the thirty-second wonder, Tiberius adds an additional four quite typical wonders about the east (33–36). However, Tiberius then concludes with a long atypical story that serves to redirect the reader's attention to the proper, Christian perspective. I quote it here in full:

> Her segð hu Mambres ontynde ða drylican bec his broðer Iamnes, & him geopenude Þa heagorune ðæs deofolgildes his broður. Andswarode him Iamnes saul Þyssum wordum: "Þu, broðor, ic naht unrihtlice eom dead, ac soðlice & rihtlice ic eom dead & Godes dom wið me standeð for Þam ðe ic wæs ana wisera Þonne ealle oðre dryas & ic wiðstod twam gebroðrum Moyses hatte & Aaron, Þa worhtan Þa micclan tacna & forebeacnu. For Þan ic eom dead & for Þam ic eom gelædd on helwara rice mid, Þær is seo miccle hatnys Þæs ecan wites, & Þær is se seað Þæs singales susles Þanon ne byð ænig upp adon. Nu, min broðer Mambre, beheald Þe on Þinum life Þæt ðu do wel Þinum bearnum & Þinum freondum, for Þan Þe on helle ne byð nawiht godes nemðe unrotnys &

> Þystru. & æfter Þam Þe ðu dead bist, Þonne cymst Þu to helle & betwix deadum mannum bið Þin eardungstow, niðer on eorðan, & Þin seað bið twega cubita wid & feowra lang. (*Wonders* 37)
>
> Here it says how Mambres opened the magical books of his brother Iamnes, and to him were revealed the deep mysteries of his brother's idolatry. The soul of Iamnes answered him with these words: 'Brother, I am dead not unjustly, but rightly and justly am I dead, and God's judgment stands against me because I alone was wiser than all the other sorcerers, and I withstood the two brothers called Moses and Aaron, who performed those great portents and signs. For that reason am I dead, and for this am I brought to the middle kingdom of hell, where there is the great heat of eternal punishment, and where there is the pit of perpetual torment from which no one ever ascends. Now, my brother Mambres, take care that you do well to your children and your friends, because in hell there is nothing good, only misery and darkness; and after you are dead, then you will come to hell, and your dwelling-place will be among the dead, down in the ground, and your pit will be two cubits wide and four cubits long.' (trans. Orchard)

In this, Tiberius' final and longest entry, is the very first mention of God and Christianity. It comes from the mouth of a pagan and therefore also represents a pagan perspective like the rest of the *Wonders.* However, this pagan, having gone to his reward, can see what earth-bound pagans cannot: the error of his ways and his religion, the justness of his punishment, and the power and wisdom of the One True God. Orchard posits that

> [t]he suspicion that there is a didactic or homiletic purpose to the addition of the tale of Iamnes and Mambres at the end of a catalogue of wonders is increased by the way in which the Old English version goes beyond the Latin text, by its formulaic repetition of the horrors of hell (*Þær is . . . Þær is . . . ne byð . . . ne byð*), and aligns itself with stock descriptions of Hell familiar from numerous Anglo-Saxon homiletic sources. (21)

I agree, but whereas Orchard sees this entry's primary function as warning against the specific sin of pride (21), I would suggest that by ending the litany of marvels this way, the anonymous author of the *Wonders* redirects his audience's perspective onto the true and proper path. By having a pagan speak to the audience from beyond the grave, the audience is reminded that, however titillating and intriguing this catalogue of monsters and marvels has been for the reader, such a report remains oblivious to more important issues, such as the afterlife and the prophecies of Moses, which are capable of giving meaning to the Christian reader beyond the simple report of physical realities which s/he has just read. Instead of enjoying these tabloid reports for their own sensationalist pleasures, the Christian ought to be contemplating "the middle kingdom of hell" and "eternal punishment" as this final entry so abruptly and pointedly reminds us.

In addition, I would also posit that the specific measurements of the pagan grave in the final clause—"and after you are dead, then you will come to hell, and your dwelling place will be among the dead, down in the ground, and your pit will be two cubits wide and four cubits long"—refer ironically to the painstakingly recorded measurements of distances and monstrous bodies enumerated throughout the *Wonders*. The measurements of one's pit in hell show the reader the trivial absurdity of the previous faithfully recorded heights and lengths compared to the import of one's final and eternal resting place. Of course, as Orchard points out, such measurements do correspond to "stock descriptions of hell" found in numerous Anglo-Saxon homilies. However, as Biggs and Hall have noted in their study of the Jamnes and Mambres story in Anglo-Saxon England, this ending represents an abbreviated version of the original ending: "In contrast, the Chester Beatty version [its source] apparently includes a much lengthier description of Hell" (70). Biggs and Hall characterize this new ending as a "rhetorically effective statement" (70), and I would argue its effectiveness derives in part from the way it points to the triviality of the sizes of monsters and the distances between encounters with them. The author/compiler could have continued with a "lengthier description of hell," but he chose instead to end with the only measurements in the itinerary that actually matter.

Bodley 614 does not end with the entry on Mambres and Jamnes but instead adds an additional twelve marvels (39–50). The first eleven (39–49) return to the standard list-type formula we observed throughout the first 37 entries, and ten of these (39–41 and 43–49) derive from Isidore's *Etymologies* (James 11). Bodley 614's final entry, however, functions in much the same fashion as did Tiberius B.v's final entry: it returns the reader's attention to Christian matters and perspective.

> Cernuntur et in Galliarum finibus vii mulieres chorum ducentes, humo in girum sub plantis earum decrescente, que huiusmodi cursitantes patria lingua edunt uoces. Ue mihi misere, quam male iui dum sanctum URRI commoui. Quando ueniet finis seculi? He igitur omnes sorores feruntur cum matre die quodam festo chorum duxisse, bisque prenominato presbitero ad missam parato eas corripiente, terio ut nunquam cessarent imprecante sic permansisse. Uacuum autem paret spacium quo mater se sub momento interminationis abripuit, duarum separatim

> brachiis protensis. Has estate media aliquantis diebus ab omni motu et uoce compertum est quiescere.
>
> Huiusmodi quoque mulierculárum chorum in Brittania que et Anglia uocatur esse notum est; quarum una, ab omnibus bina redargutione repulsa, presbitero qui ODO dicebatur egresso, atque ut ad diem usque iudicii ita canerent imprecanti, sententiam imprecationis reddidit, ut nec ipse loco unquam moueretur. quo fact cernitur presbiter librum ad pectus tenens solo fixus manere.
>
> Fama est etiam quibusdam easdem causa per annum imprecationis sententiam illatam. ex quarum choro cuidam sororem abstraere nitenti brachium in manibus, illa quasi non curante, remansit. post finem uero anni omnes morte defecerunt. (*Wonders* 50)
>
> There are to be seen also in the Gallic land seven women leading a dance and the soil sinking beneath their feet in the form of a circle. As they thus run round, they utter words in their native tongue: "Woe's me unhappy! what an ill way I went when I angered Saint Urri! when will the end of the world come?" Now all these are said to have been sisters, who with their mother led out a dance on a feast-day. The priest named above was about to celebrate mass, and rebuked them twice. The third time, he prayed that they might never leave off dancing, and so they have remained. One empty place is seen *in the ring* where the mother tore herself away at the moment of the curse; the two *adjoining her* have their arms stretched out, but not touching. It has been observed that at midsummer they rest for some days without movement or speech.
>
> It is well known that there is a like dance of women in Britain, otherwise called England. One of these women, when all of them had twice despised a warning, and when a priest named Odo came forth and prayed that they might continue singing like that till Doomsday, retorted the sentence of the curse upon him, *praying* that he too might never stir from that spot. Whereupon the priest is seen standing fixed to the earth, holding a book to his breast.
>
> It is also said that upon certain *others* the sentence of a curse was laid for a year for the same reason. From the dance of these *women* one man tried to detach his sister, but her arm remained in his hand—she apparently taking no note of it. At the end of the year however all of them died. (trans. James)

With this final entry the reader returns to more familiar physical ("the Gallic land" and Britain) and spiritual space. James designates this entry as "three tales of Accursed Dancers" and contends they "are plainly aetiological explanations of stone circles" (31). Beyond this explanation, however, one might ask what function this overly long, atypical, non-eastern marvel serves in Bodley 614. I would suggest that the author/compiler of this *Wonders* text concludes with this entry for essentially the same reason that the author/compiler of Tiberius B.v concludes with the tale of Mambres and Jamnes: the tale redirects the reader's attention back toward a Christian perspective. In this case, not only is the "moral" of the story quite obvious (Christian devotion supersedes merriment), but the very presence of any moral at all reminds the Christian how s/he ought to "read" all marvels. This "reading" of the marvel of the Accursed Dancers contrasts starkly with the short, unanalyzed eastern marvels that comprised the earlier entries. James remarks in addition that "[t]he midsummer repose of the dancers reminds one of the periodical rest of souls in purgatory or hell" (31). And just as Jamnes spoke directly to his brother and the audience to redirect their attention toward their ultimate reward, the dancers here also speak directly to their audience, asking a highly pertinent question with which all Christians ought to be concerned: "when will the end of the world come?" The text of the *Wonders* and MS Bodley 614 itself end with an illustration that blends all three legends recounted, leaving the reader with a visual as well as verbal impression of the wages of sin signified by the marvel.

It would be useful to know whether the original *Wonders* text incorporated one or both of the stories of Mambres and Jamnes and the Accursed Dancers or whether a later compiler or compilers, believing the original *Wonders* to be insufficiently clear in its literary and theological functions, added these stories to make the Christian perspective clearer. James believes that a *Wonders* "archetype" must once have existed and that it must have been closer to Bodley 614 than to Tiberius B.v, even though Tiberius pre-dates Bodley:

> That it [Bodley] is a direct copy of T[iberius] I am unwilling to believe: the variations in the text are too marked to allow me to think this is probable: but its archetype must have been the parent or sister of T[iberius]. That archetype must also, I feel sure, have contained the text and pictures which B[odley] has in excess of T[iberius]. (51)

Orchard, however, contends that the story of Mambres and Jamnes was definitely a later addition to the "archetype" which "demonstrates that explicitly pious material might be included in such a collection, if sufficient thematic links were perceived" (20–1). In addition, Orchard cites evidence that Bodley 614, far from representing an unpurged "archetype," actually derives straight from Tiberius B.v (22). Since it has been generally agreed and substantially demonstrated that the *Wonders* text uses the Fermes and Premonis letters as its primary source, and since neither of these pseudo-epistles includes the stories of Mambres and Jamnes and the Accursed Dancers (or even any folkloric or Germanic elements), I must concur with Orchard that these stories are later additions. In addition to seeing "sufficient thematic links" between the eastern marvels and the folkloric marvels, however, I would suggest that these additions, coming as they do at the ends of the manuscripts, serve an even larger function: to establish the proper Christian perspective in relation to the marvelous and monstrous in the reader's mind.

The last text, *Alexander the Great's Letter to Aristotle,* resembles the *Wonders* text in many ways. Its manuscript history comprises a small part of the amazingly complex history of the medieval Alexander material in general; as Ross somewhat flippantly but accurately states, "The Alexander Romance as a subject for research rather resembles the Holy Grail—once get involved with it and you tend to sink without a trace" (*Studies* preface). In an effort to avoid sinking, I will briefly summarize Ross's meticulous account. A fictional biography of Alexander the Great, known as the Pseudo-Callisthenes for the philosopher to whom it was attributed, was composed in Greek in the third century A.D. by "an Alexandrian of very mediocre intelligence" (Ross, *Alexander Historiatus* 5). Circa A.D. 320–30, Julius Valerius Alexander Polemius translated the Pseudo-Callisthenes into Latin. Then, sometime before the ninth century, a very popular condensed version of Julius Valerius appeared and came to be known as the *Zacher Epitome.* This abbreviated version was often accompanied by the *Epistola Alexandri Magni ad Aristotelem Magistrum,* as the Latin version of the *Letter of Alexander to Aristotle* is known. This fictionalized first-person account of Alexander's dealings with various nations of monsters and monstrous men while on campaign in India began to circulate independently and was translated into numerous vernaculars—Old English, Middle English, Middle Irish, Icelandic, Italian, German, Arabic, and French (*Alexander Historiatus* 5–9, 27–30). The *Letter*'s popularity soon surpassed that of both Pseudo-Callisthenes and the *Zacher Epitome;* at least a hundred and five manuscripts of the *Letter* survive from the ninth through the sixteenth centuries, as compared with sixty-eight of the *Epitome* (Ross, *Studies* 85–8).

The *Letter*'s textual history is of less concern than the more general ideas surrounding both Alexander and Aristotle in the early Middle Ages. Orchard has pointed out, correctly, that he can discern

> two quite distinct prevailing views of Alexander throughout the medieval period. . . . The first viewpoint considers Alexander in an overwhelmingly positive light as an explorer, inventor, and discoverer of many of the world's marvels. . . . The second view of Alexander is overwhelmingly hostile . . . as a megalomaniac, a tyrannical mass-murderer, a figure of extreme Pride. (117)

Cary provides a more extensive and detailed summary of medieval perceptions of Alexander (80–274). Quintus Curtius' *Gesta Alexandri Magni* served as one of the most ubiquitous and most imitated sources for medieval Alexander stories (Cary 16), and the author gave a very balanced evaluation of Alexander's virtues and vices, thereby providing fuel for both the positive and the negative traditions. Concerning Alexander's good qualities, Curtius wrote:

> Vis incredibilis animi, laboris patientia propemodum nimia, fortitudo non inter reges modo excellens, sed inter illos quoque quorum haec sola virtus fuit, liberalitas saepe maiora tribuens quam a dis petuntur, clementia in devictos . . . (10.5)
>
> He possessed incredible strength of mind, an endurance of toil which was almost excessive, a courage excelling not only among kings but among those whose sole merit it is, a generosity that often bestowed greater gifts than are asked of gods in prayer, clemency towards the vanquished . . . (trans. Rolfe)

But Curtius admitted that Alexander tended "Dis aequare se et caelestes honores accersere et talia suadentibus oraculis credere et dedignantibus venerari ipsum vehementius, quam part esset, irasci . . ." ("to equal himself with the gods and to aspire to divine honours, to trust to oracles which advised such conduct, and to be more angry than was fitting with those who refused to venerate him . . .") (10.5; trans. Rolfe). Curtius also allows that Alexander had "iracundiam et cupidinem vini" ("a bad temper and a love of wine") (10.5; my translation).

Thus this highly influential history provided ample material for both Alexander's detractors and his admirers. Orosius, for example, considered him "a ruthless, blood-thirsty conqueror fired by his insane love of glory in battle" (Cary 119). Orosius depicts the general as an indiscriminate murderer who "hienende wæs ægÞer ge his agen folc ge oÞerra cyninga, he wæs sin Þyrstende monnes blodes" ("was persecuting both his own people and other kings, he was forever thirsting for human blood") (3.9; my translation). Rhabanus Maurus, on the other hand, seems to admire his "magnitudo animi" ("great spirit") and "dignissimum" ("worthiness") (1131; my translation) and characterizes him as a tool of God, "inter pericula praeliorum Dei nutu servatus" ("contending among dangers at the command of the will of God") (1130; my translation).

While commentators on Alexander may disagree on his motivation, and even his degree of sanity, all agree that he was an excellent soldier, which leads later in the Middle Ages to the heroic Alexander of medieval romances, "the paragon of all virtue" (Cary 144). One can imagine how a warrior culture such as the Anglo-Saxon could admire the great Macedonian general, much as they admired the Geat Beowulf, for qualities that were, in Christian terms, at least problematic if not antithetical. Wormald explains how this tension between pagan and Christian virtues might have arisen:

> As the English church became "established," it tended, as church establishments have (to the anger of Christian enthusiasts, from Christianity's founder onwards), to be identified with society's ruling class. The personnel of the early medieval western church was dominated by the aristocracy. To sing, or to write, of its warrior prototypes came as naturally to them as to live in the style to which, as noblemen, they were accustomed. (10)

Clerical nobility could, then, admire a secular pagan hero provided he embodied some of the virtues of a warrior culture. However, as Wormald also points out, "nothing had much chance to survive unless it was eventually copied and kept in a church library" (10). These two facts together explain why both Orchard and I insist upon a religious interpretation of Alexander's exploits, much as critics have persisted in explaining *Beowulf* in a similar fashion (Georgianna 829–50).

In addition to his military expertise, Alexander also possessed another universally admired characteristic: "in every medieval period Alexander's education was represented as including all those subjects which the imagination of the writer considered essential to the perfect prince" (Cary 108). Gerald of Wales used Alexander as proof that "quanto litteratiores erant et eruditiores, tanto in rebus bellicis animosiores exstiterant et strenuiores. Veluti Macedonum dux Alexander egregius . . ." ("the greater they are in learning and scholarship, so much more do they stand out as more courageous and vigorous in military matters. Take, for example, the illustrious prince Alexander of Macedon . . .") (8.7; my translation). Alexander's education reflected well on his tutor Aristotle, toward whom the general medieval attitude is less easy to discern than that toward his pupil, but who appears, according to both Grant and Knowles, to have been regarded with a kind of amorphous respect that only increased after the arrival of accurate Latin translations of his works in the twelfth century. But the early Middle Ages relied on the commentaries of earlier scholars on Aristotle's work. Boethius, for example, commenting on Aristotles' *Categories,* declares that "liber est utilis" ("the book is useful") (80; my translation) and that Aristotle himself "diligentissima inquisitione vestigat" ("searches with most diligent investigation") (79; my translation). The positively valenced depiction of the relationship between Alexander and

Aristotle bolsters my contention that the *Letter,* while embodying the ambiguous and potentially contradictory attitude of Anglo-Saxons toward Alexander the Great, ultimately reflects favorably upon him while simultaneously condemning his paganism. In this sense, while still embodying the pagan perspective of the world, the *Letter* is also re-incorporated back into the Christian metanarrative as a literary endeavor. The first-person narrative presents an unenlightened and therefore un-self-aware pagan viewpoint to an enlightened and aware Christian audience who would see how Alexander could be integrated into the transcendent Christian episteme as a cautionary tale.

Orchard compares the Old English and Latin versions of *Alexander's Letter* side-by-side in order to examine how the Anglo-Saxon translator altered his copy-text to change the meaning of the Old English *Letter.* He concludes that "[i]n a number of additions and amendments to his Latin source, the Old English translator clearly undermines Alexander, and seeks to stress his cruelty and pride" (121). For Orchard, Alexander in the Old English *Letter* becomes the ultimate representative of pride, to be viewed in a mercilessly negative light. I would suggest an additional interpretation, one quite similar to that of the *Wonders* above: Alexander may well be a great soldier and explorer, and his teacher Aristotle may well be the repository of a considerable store of physical and earthly knowledge to which Alexander quite admirably seeks to contribute. However, as in the *Wonders,* this is the limit of their achievements and knowledge, which stay stubbornly earthbound, secular, and pagan. Without a Christian perspective, Alexander remains unable to explore the more important spiritual realm, and the preoccupations of and sometimes blasphemous mistakes in his *Letter* reveal the inadequacies of the pagan worldview. Yet the exercise of reading and explicating the letter didactically integrates the pagan point of view back into the Christian experience.

Alexander the Great's Letter to Aristotle, like the *Wonders of the East,* proceeds linearly across India. It reads very much like the field report it purports to be. Alexander begins by explaining to Aristotle that he is writing in order to tell his teacher about the marvels he has seen on campaign. He explains that "Seo eorðe is to wundrienne hwæt . . . Þa Þing eall Þæm monnum Þe hit geseoð & sceawigað wæron uneÞe to gewitanne for Þære missenlicnisse Þara hiowa" ("the earth is a source of wonder . . . things which are difficult to comprehend for those who look and observe because of the variety of their forms") (*Letter* 3; trans. Orchard). It is in fact Alexander's degree of comprehension of the earth's wonders that indicates his skewed perspective. The epistle then progresses geographically and chronologically. He conquers Fasiacen, the kingdom of Porus, and sets that king running. Alexander follows him through various Indian lands, whose landmarks and inhabitants, both human and bestial, are described. After Alexander's retinue suffers much hardship, the two armies finally meet, and the Macedonian emerges victorious. Alexander and Porus become friends, thus ending the first big adventure of the *Letter* (8–25).

Along this forced march, Alexander's army is almost continually harassed by monstrous animals, some real and some literary, but all equally hostile. While attempting to swim to an inhabited island, two hundred men are attacked and devoured by hippopotami (15). Later, the entire camp is plagued by two kinds of marvelous serpents (17–8), "hwite leon in fearra gelicnisse swa micle" ("white lions in the shape and size of bulls") (19; trans. Orchard), and a rhinoceros (20). Circumstances do not noticeably improve for the beleaguered army after the defeat of Porus, for two of Alexander's thegns are killed by a crocodile (27) and 500 more perish in a marvelous firestorm:

> . . . Þa eac cwoman of Þæm sweartan wolcne byrnende fyr. Þa fyr ðonne feollon on Þa eorÞan swelce byrnende Þecelle & for Þæs fyres bryne eall se feld born. Ða cwædon men Þætte hie wendon Þæt Þæt wære goda eorre Þæt usic Þær on becwome. Ða het ic eald hrægl toslitan & habban wið Þæm fyre & sceldan mid. Þa seoððan æfter Þon we hæfdon smolte niht & gode siðÞan usic Þa earfeðo forleton. (30)
>
> . . . from the dark sky there came burning fire. The fire fell to the earth like a burning torch, and the whole plain was burning from the fire's flame. Then men said that they thought it was the anger of the gods which had fallen upon us. Then I ordered old clothing to be torn up and used as a protection against the fire. After that we had a quiet and peaceful night, once our difficulties assuaged. (trans. Orchard)

My interest in this passage lies in Alexander's reaction to the firestorm and to a possible interpretation of it. No other monster or marvel in the *Letter* receives even the suggestion that it might mean something beyond its own mere existence. The attacks by monstrous animals mentioned above Alexander treats simply as bad luck or the result of treacherous guides willfully leading him astray.

The firestorm, however, opens the possibility that other forces, "the gods," are at work in the marvel, but Alexander appears not to entertain this for a minute. He reports that "men" said that they thought so, but the general himself does not embrace this interpretation, or even really consider it. He reacts like a soldier, practically and promptly, and he does not stop to consider the spiritual and/or theological implications of this particular disaster or the entire series of disasters he has encountered at the hands (paws?) of monstrous animals. Alexander's encounters with monstrous humans likewise fail to inspire contemplation. He is curious about the "ruge wifmen, & wæpned men wæron hie swa ruwe & swa gehære swa wildeor" ("shaggy women, and men who were as shaggy and hairy as beasts") (29; trans. Orchard), but only in a very physical sense. Even monstrous people who attack his troops receive remarkably little pondering:

> . . . healfhundinga micle mængeo, ða cwoman to Þon Þæt hie woldon us wundigan. & we Þa mid strælum hie scotodon, & hie sona onweg aflymdon ða hie eft on Þone wudu gewiton. Þa syððan geferdon we in Þa westenn India & we Þa Þær noht wunderlices ne mærlices gesawon. (29)
>
> . . . a great multitude of Cynocephali . . . came because they wished to wound us, and we shot them with arrows, and they soon fled away and went back into the woods. Then we went into the Indian desert, and we saw nothing marvellous or extraordinary there. (trans. Orchard)

The search for marvels, not the contemplation of their meaning or place in a spiritual sense, is the focus of Alexander's efforts. Such a seemingly innocent preoccupation with "mira" or "wundor" in fact masks a stunted spiritual development. As Bynum has pointed out, while wonder is often contrasted to prying, the former is meant to induce the latter: "the opposite of *admiratio* was in some sense the *scientia,* or knowledge, to which it led" (7). Alexander very pointedly does not pry into the meanings of the marvels he encounters and therefore fails to see evidence of the *invisibilia*—the "micelre gemynde"(*Letter* 6)—in the monstrous and marvelous *visibilia.*

Shortly after his skirmish with the hound-heads, Alexander embarks on the letter's final adventure, the search for the prophetic trees of the Sun and the Moon. He finds them and inquires three times about his earthly fate. On the third attempt, the tree of the Sun provides the most complete answer:

> . . . yb anes geares fyrst & eahta monað Þu swyltst in Babilone, nalles mid iserne acweald swa ðu wenst ac mid atre. Ðin modor gewiteð of weorulde Þurh scondlicne deað & unarlicne, & heo ligeð unbebyrged in wege fuglum to mete & wildeorum. Þine sweostor beoð longe gesæliges lifes. Ðu Þonne ðeah Þu lytle hwile lifge hweÞre ðu geweorðest an cyning & hlaford ealles middangeardes. (40)
>
> . . . in the space of one year and eight months you will die in Babylon, killed not, as you expect, with iron, but with poison. Your mother will leave the world by a shameful and lowly death, and she will lie unburied in the street as food for birds and wild beasts. Your sisters will have long

> and happy lives. And as for you, though you live but a short time you shall be sole king and lord of the whole world. (trans. Orchard)

After receiving such news, Alexander is understandably distraught, but not in the ways one might expect. First, instead of indulging in extensive soul-searching or examining his conscience or preparing himself spiritually for death, Alexander makes sure that this news spreads no further than his immediate circle, "Þy læs Þa elreordegan kyningas ðe ic ær mid nede to hyrsumnesse gedyde, Þæt hie on Þæt fægon Þæt ic swa lytle hwile lifgean moste . . . Þy læs hie for ðon ormode wæron & Þy sænran mines willan & weorðmyndo, Þæs hie mid mec to fromscipe geferan scoldon" ("in case the foreign kings that I had forcibly brought under my command should be glad that I had so little time to live . . . [and] in case they [the army] became dispirited, and more indolent concerning my will and my honour, for which they had to carry me to success") (41; trans. Orchard). Secondly, when Alexander does get around to thinking about his impending doom, he ponders not the afterlife, but his earthly life, lamenting that "[o]nd me næs se hrædlica ende mines lifes swa miclum weorce swa me wæs Þæt ic læs mærðo gefremed hæfde Þonne min willa wære" ("to me the swift ending of my life was not so much pain as the fact that I had achieved less glory than I would have wished") (41; trans. Orchard). Such a sentiment may be a commonplace of Alexander's character in the literature about him, but that does not make its reiteration here any less unchristian.

Alexander's reaction to news of his own death might appear to confirm Orchard's assertion that Alexander only functions as a representative of pride, a negative example not to be emulated by the Christian reader. I believe, however, that one can discern a slightly more complicated depiction of the character of Alexander the Great in the *Letter.* Even with the alterations that occurred from the Latin to the Anglo-Saxon, as noted at length by Orchard (121–39), Alexander as depicted here is not, in fact, morally unredeemable; he does exhibit quite a few admirable qualities, although they admittedly remain imperfectly admirable precisely because Alexander lacks the benefit of Christian teaching to direct his instincts.

Alexander begins his letter by explaining to Aristotle why he is writing these things to him, and his reason shows a profound respect for scholarship: "for Þon Þe ic Þe wiste wel getydne in wisdome, Þa geÞohte ic for Þon to Þe to writanne . . . to Þon Þæt hwæthwygo to Þære ongietenisse Þissa niura Þinga Þin gelis & gleawnis to geÞeode" ("since I know that you are well set in wisdom, I thought to write to you . . . so that your learning and knowledge might contribute to a certain extent to the understanding of these novelties") (2;

trans. Orchard). Alexander also respects and appreciates his comrades in arms, making sure to give them proper credit and gratitude: "Ic ðæs Þoncunge do greca herige & swyðost Þæm mægene Þære iuguÞe & Þæm unforswyÞdum urum weorode, for Þon on ieÞum Þingum hie me mid wæron & on Þæm earfeðum no from bugon" ("In this I give thanks to the Greek army, and especially to the strength of youth and our unconquered troop, because they were with me in the easy things and did not depart during the hardships") (5; trans. Orchard). Alexander is not merely giving lip service here, for when his army is lost in the Indian desert without water for days and one of his thegns finds and brings to him a single helmet full of water, "het ic min weorod & ealle mine duguÞe tosomne, & hit Þa beforan heora ealra onsyne niðer ageat, Þy læs ic drunce & Þone minne Þegn Þyrste & minne here & ealne Þe mid me wæs" ("I ordered together all my troop and all my trusted band and poured it away in the sight of them all, so that I should not drink and leave thirsty my thegn and my army, and all who were with me") (12; trans. Orchard). Although possibly foolhardy, such a gesture surely demonstrates a conscience touched by loyalty and generosity and unselfishly willing to share a possibly ignoble fate with his men (as well as a crafty intelligence that sees the loyalty-inspiring possibilities of such a theatrical performance). Alexander even seems to sense the hand of God in creation, even if he cannot quite explain it. He recognizes that "[s]eo eorðe is to wundrienne" ("[t]he earth is a source of wonder") (3; trans. Orchard) and that "ðing eall ne magon elcor beon buton micelre gemynde swa geendebyrded & fore stihtod" ("all these things cannot be otherwise than so arranged and foreordained by a great intelligence") (6; trans. Orchard).

I would characterize the portrait of Alexander that emerges from the *Letter* as that of a curious, basically good man with solid theological instincts but lacking the necessary Christian framework to guide them. Still, Orchard points out quite correctly that Alexander's desire for personal glory, his relentless ambition and concern for his earthly reputation do indicate that the audience is to read him as an exemplum of pride and condemn him as such. However, I would also argue that the specific terms by which the *Letter* imparts this impression to the reader indicate that Alexander's fault derives directly from a lack of Christian perspective and not merely from a cruel and megalomaniacal nature. For example, Alexander's most obvious fault consists, as Orchard notes, of desire for personal and earthly glory. As mentioned above, Alexander regrets his early death for the specifically earthly reason that he has not had time to fulfill his potential for glory. After expressing such regret, he goes on to ponder the legacy he will leave, and his concerns in this matter show a similarly non-spiritual bent:

> Ond eac swelce ecelice min gemynd stonde & hleouige oðrum eorðcyningum to bysne, ðæt hie witen Þy gearwor Þæt min Þrym & min weorðmynd maran wæron, Þonne ealra oÞra kyninga Þe in middangearde æfre wæron. *Finit.* (41)

> And also my memory shall forever stand and tower as an example for other earthly kings, so that they know the more readily that my power and my honour were greater than those of all the other kings who have ever lived in the world. *Finit.* (trans. Orchard)

As the final word of this passage indicates, the *Letter* concludes with this expression of self-importance and pride. A Christian reader would no doubt note that, such egomanaical assertions notwithstanding, Alexander's legacy as he depicts it would not stand him in good stead in the next world, which is imminent. The example he provides for earthly monarchs is in many ways a negative one, especially in Christian terms, as it emphasizes personal exaltation and glory instead of humility and good governance. Such a Christian interpretation is obvious, and it is the one Orchard adopts when he stresses the evils of pride in his reading of this text as well as his reading of *Beowulf.* I would suggest that the *Letter*'s structure imparts a message even more specific and explicitly Christian than this.

Early in the *Letter* the reader encounters an even greater example of Alexander's egocentricity than that found at its end. After giving his thanks to his army for sticking by him, Alexander tells the reader the results of their loyalty: "[a]c hie on Þære geÞylde mid me a wunedon Þæt ic wæs nemned ealra kyninga kyning" ("but with patience they bore with me always so that I was called king of all kings") (5; trans. Orchard). This passage is not part of those additions in the Anglo-Saxon that Orchard cites as evidence for the translator's agenda; the Latin text reads, "ut rex regum appellarer" (Orchard 205). Upon encountering this assertion, the Christian reader may well feel scandalized, for the phrase "king of kings," in whatever language, inevitably recalls the Biblical references to Christ which used exactly this phrase: 1 Timothy 6:15; Revelation 17:14; and Revelation 19:16. This last verse is most pertinent to this discussion, as it demonstrates how tragically and blasphemously mistaken Alexander has been: "And he [Christ] hath on his garment, and on his thigh written: KING OF KINGS, AND LORD OF LORDS" (Apoc. 19:16).

I cannot believe that the author or the translator of the *Letter* put this phrase into Alexander's mouth by accident. According to the *Oxford Latin Dictionary*'s entry on "rex," the phrase has its origin in antiquity when it referred to Agamemnon and the kings of Persia and Parthia, and in this sense, the term could apply to Alexander. However, by the time of the *Letter's* composition, the phrase appears to have been appropriated exclusively as a title for Christ. I can find no post-classical secular use of the Latin term, and in his *Lexicon Latinitatis Medii Aevi,* Blaise has gone so far as to define the phrase exclusively in religious terms, "en parl. du Christ." The same appears to hold true in the vernacular, for I can find no nonreligious Anglo-Saxon use of the phrase "cyninga cyning." The *Anglo-Saxon Poetic Records* lists eleven occurrences of the phrase, all of which use it to designate either Christ or (less frequently) God (Bessinger). The *Middle English Dictionary's* entry on "king" does list three instances of "king of kings" being used to refer to earthly rulers, the earliest of which comes from Chaucer, circa 1375: "Nabugodonosor . . . This kyng of kynges proud was and elat." However, the fact that only three out of several dozen examples refer specifically to this phrase being used in a secular way and that all three examples come from the late fourteenth century or later leads me to conclude that the secular usage developed late in the medieval period; in Anglo-Saxon times "king of kings" referred to Christ, and Alexander's appropriation of this title for himself has implications beyond the reflection of his pride.

Coming as it does as the beginning of the *Letter,* the phrase underscores Alexander's fundamentally mistaken perception not only of his place in world history, but also of the function of history itself. If the author of the Latin original knew of the classical definition of the term, then his use of it in this context is even more pointed: Alexander might rightly see himself as the worthy heir to Agamemnon, but he is tragically unaware that the title he seeks to assume has been usurped by Christ. Alexander has no knowledge of the true king of kings and therefore mistakes himself for such. His warped view reveals the absence of a framework by which to structure his knowledge, both of himself and of the world around him, and thereby plants suspicion in the reader's mind that s/he is not to take Alexander's interpretation of events at face value.

Scrutiny of the letter's intended recipient may bolster my contention. Above, I briefly outlined the pre-twelfth-century perception of Aristotle as an important, if incompletely understood, authority on strictly earthly matters. The medieval interpretation of Aristotle's relationship to Alexander reflects this judgment. Cary states that the example of their relationship illustrated "the importance of a tutor to a king . . . the necessity, if a prince is to preserve his fame, that he shall surround himself with a circle of learned writers . . . [and] praise of Alexander as a learned prince, and one who encouraged learning in other men" (Cary 106). The reader can learn from the epistolary format some indication as to how to "read" Alexander, for his positively valenced relationship with Aristotle is foregrounded. Whereas the writer might have chosen another fictional recipient, such as Alexander's mother or sister, he instead emphasized one of Alexander's indisputably good attributes, his respect for learning, in, I would argue, an attempt to predispose the reader charitably toward the protagonist. This maneuver puts the reader in a position to interpret Alexander's words in the way I have outlined here: as the geographically and physically true report of a learned man with some good instincts who, regrettably, lacks the religious paradigm to make spiritual sense of the physical world. Thus an apparently limited pagan point of view becomes part of a larger Christian literary project.

What has all this to do with monsters and marvels? As mentioned above, Alexander's accounts of monsters are straightforward and uninterpreted. He seeks to find and observe wonders but not to ponder them. His involvement with them remains stubbornly rooted in observation, as he says:

> Þa ic Þe write & cyÞe, & æghwylc Þara is wyrðe synderlice in gemyndum to habbanne æfter Þære wisan Þe ic hit oferseah. . . . Seo eorðe is to wundrienne hwæt heo ærest oÞÞe godra Þinga cenne, oððe eft Þara yfelra, Þe heo Þæm sceawigendum is æteowed. Hio is cennende Þa fulcuÞan wildeora & wæstma & wecga oran, & wunderlice wyhta, Þa Þing eall Þæm monnum Þe hit geseoð & sceawigað wæron uneÞe to gewitanne for Þære missenlicnisse Þara hiowa. (3)
>
> These things I write and tell you, and each of them is individually worth bearing in mind exactly as I observed it. . . . The earth is a source of wonder first for the good things she brings forth, and then for the evil, through which she is revealed to observers. She is the producer of well-known wild beasts, and plants, and stones and metal-ore, and of wondrous creatures, all those things which are difficult to comprehend for those who look and observe because of the variety of their forms. (trans. Orchard)

Alexander finds these "wondrous creatures . . . difficult to comprehend" precisely because, as a pagan, he can only observe. When he says "exactly as I observed it," he cuts himself, and Aristotle, off from all avenues of comprehension that are not strictly physical observation. For this reason he cannot divine the spiritual meaning behind the marvelous firestorm and leaves the monstrous creatures he encounters, and the suffering they inflict on him, uninterpreted. This same limitation causes him to mistake himself for "king of kings," for he is surely a great and powerful conqueror, if the criteria are entirely earthly. So the monsters and marvels as depicted in the *Letter* function, as in the *Wonders of the East,* to demonstrate the linear, geographical limitation of the pagan perspective and by extension to privilege Christian literary and religious interpretations and uses of monsters, such as those observed in Aldhelm and the *Physiologus*.

Like their pictorial counterparts on medieval mappaemundi, the monsters of these early works remain on the edge of the textual world, certainly a part of the world and even defining its boundaries, but not the chief object of interest. On medieval mappaemundi such as the Ebstorf map,[3] Jerusalem appears at the center of the world, and Christ's body, splayed across the globe's surface, is the central object of contemplation. The authors of Christian texts studied here employed a similar strategy in their written works, for the ultimate point of their texts is spiritual contemplation, not monstrous voyeurism. They may use this strategy explicitly, as in the *Physiologus*, or quite subtly, as *The Letter of Alexander to Aristotle*. They may depict a Christianized encyclopedic and interconnected view of the monstrous, as in Aldhelm's *Enigmata*, or a fabricated pagan and therefore linear view, as in the *Wonders of the East*. Yet even those works which appear to conform to the Plinian model in fact work to re-incorporate that model back into the Christian symbolic on a literary level. While purporting to be purely pagan, and therefore rejected as models for Christian understanding, the *Wonders* and the *Letter* in fact function as negative pagan examples within Christian didacticism.

The realization of divine transcendence and interconnectedness and of the role the monstrous signifier plays in this process results, as Bynum has put it, from "prying" into the "wonder" initially induced by the reader's encounter with the monstrous (7). Later medieval texts also used monsters as objects of spiritual contemplation, but by the twelfth century such texts were beginning to expand the signification of the monstrous beyond the spiritual realm into the areas of simple, everyday morality and even purely secular concerns. Such splintering in a sense undermines the transcendent nature of the Anglo-Saxon monster since the focus comes to be placed on particular moralities rather than on the all-encompassing nature of Christianity. One of the best texts in which to find this expansion of potential avenues of signification is the *Bestiary*, to which this study now turns.

Chapter Three
The *Bestiary*

This chapter and the one following will compare two previously analyzed texts from the Anglo-Saxon period with two later works that resemble them in form. The differences in substance that will become apparent can perhaps reveal something about the changes that occurred in the twelfth century that made things from the Anglo-Saxon age substantively different from those in the later Middle Ages. I will be making comparisons between the *Liber Monstrorum* and the *Bestiary* in this chapter and between *Alexander's Letter to Aristotle* and *Mandeville's Travels* in chapter four. The former are both "lists" of monsters, some real and some fanciful, while the latter are both fictional journeys purporting to be true first-person narratives of travels that encounter fabulous beasts and marvels. The popularity of these texts attests to the concerns, preoccupations and associations of the "popular" mindset or worldview and can thus perhaps offer the reader insights into the general epistemological trend from the Anglo-Saxon age to the later Middle Ages.

The *Bestiary* was a highly popular work, especially in the twelfth and thirteenth centuries, and a very large number of manuscripts survive. Clark and McMunn provide the most current and exhaustive list of surviving copies in the appendix to their study of the *Bestiary*. By their count, ninety-one Latin bestiaries remain extant, along with thirty-five French bestiaries, eleven Italian bestiaries, five Catalan bestiaries, and one Middle English bestiary, making a total of 143 (Clark and McMunn 197–203), of which forty are of English provenance (Hassig 2).

The final total swells even further if, in fact, we do consider the Middle English version a proper bestiary. Its most recent editor refers to it as *The Middle English Physiologus* because, she explains, it is basically an English translation of the Latin verse *Physiologus* of Theobald, a popular medieval school text that does not meet the criteria (outlined below) for a bestiary (Wirtjes lxxvi–lxxix). Other scholars, however, disagree and maintain

Theobald's schoolbook is, in fact, a bestiary (McCulloch 40–1). If the Theobald version does qualify as a bestiary, then the ranks of extant bestiaries swell significantly, as Wirtjes counts sixty-four extant copies of the Latin verse Theobald (lxxvi). The time frame within which the *Bestiary* falls ranges from the early twelfth- through the fifteenth centuries, with production peaking in the late twelfth and early thirteenth centuries (Clark and McMunn 4; McCulloch 34; Hassig 2).

The confusion engendered by the question of whether or not the Theobald text is a *Bestiary* or a *Physiologus* should give some idea of the extremely close relationship between the two works. Hassig refers to the *Physiologus* as "the core text of the Latin prose bestiaries" (5). Clark and McMunn attempt to locate the moment at which a *Physiologus* metamorphoses into a *Bestiary:*

> When significant numbers of new chapters and new animals are added to the traditional *Physiologus* chapters, and when material is interpolated into existing chapters from sources such as St. Ambrose's *Hexameron* and Isidore's *Etymologies,* the resulting compilation can safely be considered a bestiary. (3)

They go on to explain the substantive differences that also distinguish the two works:

> . . . the bestiary differs in tone and emphasis from the *Physiologus.* The animal interpretations in the *Physiologus* tend to be moral theological, that is, "mystical," while the bestiary expands the moral-ethical content considerably, making the work more obviously didactic than its predecessor. (3)

In addition, the organizational method of the *Bestiary* differs from that of the *Physiologus.* The animals, both mundane and fabulous, are rearranged into "a logical sequence of beasts, birds, and reptiles" (Diekstra 146), and this reorganization reflects mostly Isidore's arrangements in book 12 of his *Etymologies* (Wirtjes lxxiii). Although the addition of the Isidorian material occurred sometime in the tenth century, the reorganization and the shift in emphasis from "mystical" to moral both took place in the twelfth century, thereby giving rise to a new kind of work quite different from the *Physiologus,* a genuine *Bestiary* (Diekstra 146; Wirtjes lxxiii).

McCulloch's study charts exhaustively the descent from the *Physiologus* to the *Bestiary,* and here I will attempt to summarize and simplify her admirable work. The *Physiologus* version known as versio B, while not as close to the

Greek original as the longer versio Y, gave rise to the majority of European Latin bestiaries and also enjoyed greater popularity than any other version of the *Physiologus.* Versio B spawned another generation of *Physiologus* known as the B-Is version for its incorporation of additions from Isidore's *Etymologies,* a practice which was continued in the twelfth century when the *Bestiary* proper came into being. This new entity more than doubled its content of animals, added more material from Isidore and adopted the classification system he used in book 12 of his *Etymologies,* and added, in some versions, material from Rhabanus Maurus, Solinus, and Ambrose's *Hexameron* (McCulloch 22–38). The following study will employ as exemplar a typical member of this group, what M.R. James has referred to as the Second Family of manuscripts: Aberdeen University Library MS 24, of the late twelfth century.

Before proceeding any further, the question of the bestiary's readership or audience must be addressed, if not resolved. If the enormous number of extant manuscripts testifies to the *Bestiary*'s popularity, its various avenues of influence reflect both popularity and a remarkably diverse audience. McCulloch sees in the *Bestiary*'s translation from Latin into several vernaculars evidence of its appeal to and consumption by "an even larger public than those whose reading was largely in Latin" (44). This does not imply that the *Bestiary* became a purely popular text in the modern sense of the word; ample evidence exists for its use by professional religious as "a popular source for sermon writers . . . [and] as a monastic teaching text" (Clark and McMunn 3–4). Preachers used its easily recalled examples of animal behavior often verbatim in "an attempt to instruct the laity in the Christian life by impressing relevant images on the memory" (Rowland 16), but they also employed bestiary material in a more fluid way, not necessarily quoting from it, but incorporating its matter into sermons (Morson 146–70). On occasion, a preacher would even take the attributes of the animal and reverse their moral signification as it appeared in the *Bestiary* in order to make his information conform to the lesson he wished to impart (Spencer 343–5). Baxter's impressive study of the production, consumption, and classification of the *Bestiary* in the twelfth and thirteenth centuries concludes that it was primarily a sermon sourcebook (83–228), although he does allow that "no single answer" can be given to the question, "what were bestiaries?" (183). Thus through preaching, bestiary lore became available and even widespread among a vast lay, and very probably illiterate, audience. Indeed, the use of the *Bestiary* for sermon material even helps explain its "diversity of forms, each answering different needs" (Baxter 83), as opposed to the single-minded intent of its source, the *Physiologus.*

Apparently not only the "lewed" could benefit from bestiary examples, for the *Bestiary* was used as a teaching text as well. Theobald's *Bestiary* (or

Physiologus—its problematic status is mentioned above) "acquired an extraordinary significance as a schoolbook" (Diekstra 147) in its Latin version and quite possibly in vernacular versions as well. The sixty-four extant Latin manuscripts of Theobald contain no pictures, testifying to the necessity that its audience be literate. At least one critic has implied that works like the *Bestiary* provided instruction not only to pupils in monastic orders but also to "literate laymen curious to know more about the natural world" (Friedman, "Peacocks and Preachers" 182). Laymen not necessarily curious about nature but merely consigned to the schoolroom also encountered it, "since it was widely read in many a medieval grammar school" (Houwen 79n). Basically, the *Bestiary* was "more of a reference book and less of a lecture script" (Baxter 209) than its source, the *Physiologus.*

In addition to "literate laymen," scholars have identified at least two specific categories of the secular audience that show signs of having been directly influenced by the *Bestiary:* romance writers and the authors of hunting manuals. McMunn has documented at length bestiary influences in two medieval romances, the *Chevalerie de Judas Macabe* and the *Roman de Kanor* (McMunn 134–50). In addition, Ziolkowski has suggested a potential connection between beast lore, such as that found in the *Bestiary,* and *William of Palerne* and *Melusine* (2–3). McNelis has noted how *Bestiary* influences repeatedly assert themselves in hunting manuals in the form of fictional narratives and descriptions of animal behaviors and qualities. Most surprising is the tendency of "even master huntsmen" to assign "qualities and behaviours to [the animals] which the authors well knew they did not, and even could not, possess" (McNelis 75) because the authority of the bestiary tradition surpassed the authority of the huntsman's own firsthand experience. McNelis suggests this apparently nonsensical tendency indicates that "both genres [the *Bestiary* and the hunting manual] may have occupied a shared space—jumbled and contradictory though it may appear to be—in the intellectual framework of their authors and contemporary readers" (76). McNelis' conclusion, along with the abundance of evidence for a myriad of uses, both secular and religious, for the *Bestiary,* suggests widespread dissemination and familiarity with bestiary material on the part of a vast cross section of medieval society. This abundant availability provided "lessons in ethical behavior and Christian spirituality for both religious and lay audiences" (Clark and McMunn 4).

If the works with which it is bound are any indication, the *Bestiary*'s functions and audience were quite multifaceted. Although one hesitates to derive any definitive conclusions from its manuscript associations, it perhaps may be worthwhile to consider the types of works that appeared alongside the *Bestiary.* Of the twenty-eight bestiary manuscripts of English provenance listed by Hassig in the appendix to her work, eight contain only the *Bestiary.* Three contain a bestiary and a lapidary only, while four others contain a bestiary and a lapidary bound with other works (Hassig 183–7). The *Bestiary*'s association with lapidaries should come as no surprise, especially since many bestiaries contain entries on the fire rocks as well as on beasts. Beyond its association with lapidaries, however, the *Bestiary* does not appear to be associated with any other particular kind of work. Sometimes the *Bestiary* is bound with a variety of purely religious texts; Harley 3244 contains Alain de Lille's *Liber penitentialis,* Robert Grosseteste's *Templum Domini,* and a treatise on biblical names among other religious works (Hassig 184). One also finds the *Bestiary* alongside historical texts, as in Laud. Misc. 247, which contains histories of the Vandals, the Lombards, Alexander the Great, and Apollonius (Hassig 185). And sometimes one finds a *Bestiary* amongst a jumble of political, scientific, and administrative texts. C.U.L. Kk.4.25 houses religious texts, a history of Alexander the Great, excerpts from John of Salisbury's *Policraticus,* Seneca's philosophical dialogues, an herbal, and an astronomical treatise (Hassig 187). St. John's 178 collects together extracts from Aristotle's *Tractatus de quatuor humoribus,* Alexander Neckham's *Libellus de figuris rhetorices,* a judicial directory, and a variety of grammatical, numerical and philosophical treatises (Hassig 186). Royal 12.C.XIX binds the *Bestiary* with medical recipes in both French and Latin (Hassig 186). If the company the *Bestiary* keeps is any indication, as a literary work it may defy categorization or, alternately, it may be seen as "part of a genre which is broad" as well as apparently "jumbled and contradictory," yet well within "the intellectual framework of their authors and contemporary readers"(McNelis 76).

The *Bestiary,* like the *Physiologus,* consists of a compilation of animals, both real and imaginary. First, the animal's name is given, often followed by an etymological explanation linking the name to the animal's behavior. Then the animal's physical appearance and behavior are described. Lastly, as in the *Physiologus,* the *Bestiary* derives a moral from the animal's behavior, but unlike the *Physiologus,* this moral is not necessarily a spiritual one in the sense that it tells the reader something about God or scripture. Of course, the moral may be based on scripture, but just as often the moral applies equally to secular concerns, even if it has its basis in scripture and spirituality. Hassig suggests that bestiary animals both "facilitated understanding of doctrine that remained otherwise problematic" and also

> provided lessons on morality from which their readers were expected to profit: the stag demonstrated the value of friendship, the beaver taught the lesson of chastity, and the hoopoe illustrated filial piety, whereas the fox reminded all beholders of the constant threat of deception. (171)

Although Hassig does not use the term "allegory," it is quite a useful one for thinking about the *Bestiary*'s various levels of meaning. St. Thomas Aquinas explained these levels in particularly lucid fashion:

> Illa ergo prima significatio qua voces significant res pertinet ad primum sensum, qui est sensus historicus vel litteralis. Illa vero signification qua res significatae per voces iterum res alias significant dicitur sensus spiritualis; qui super litteralem fundatur et eum supponit.
>
> Hic autem sensus spiritualis trifariam dividitur. . . .
>
> Secundum ergo quod ea quae sunt veteris legis significant ea quae sunt novae legis est sensus allegoricus; secundum vero quod ea quae in Christo sunt facta vel in his quae Christum significant sum signa eorum quae nos agere debemus est sensus moralis; prout vero significant ea quae sunt in aeterna gloria est sensus anagogicus. (Aquinas 1a.1.10)
>
> That first meaning whereby the words signify things belongs to the sense first-mentioned, namely the historical or literal. That meaning, however, whereby the things signified by the words in their turn also signify other things is called the spiritual sense; it is based on and presupposes the literal sense.
>
> Now this spiritual sense is divided into three. . . .
>
> Well then, the allegorical sense is brought into play when the things of the Old Law signify the things of the New Law; the moral sense when the things done in Christ and in those who prefigured him are signs of what we should carry out; and the anagogical sense when the things that lie ahead in eternal glory are signified. (trans. Gilby)

What Aquinas calls allegorical can also be called typological, and I will refer to it in this way to avoid confusion with the more general meaning of allegory. Of greater interest is what Aquinas calls moral, also known as tropological. He places this type firmly under the larger category of "spiritual sense," which argues that, for him, lessons about behavior necessarily derive from and refer back to religious issues. But the phenomenon developing in the *Bestiary* involves lessons in morality that can, although they rarely do, exist independently from an immediately religious subtext. One cannot, then, categorize such lessons as strictly tropological; I would suggest the term *secular morality* and note that such morals can and do occur alongside more traditional spiritual interpretations without either discourse losing its claim to validity.

The *Bestiary* is not unique in its capacity to encompass and present several different kinds of morality simultaneously. One can observe an analogous process taking place in the twelfth-century romance. Vance has documented how, in the works of Chretien de Troyes, "symbols became movable, acting as 'shifters' between different systems and discourses (the psychic, the social, the religious)" (80). Such mobility "presupposed a new sense of freedom, nurtured by logic, of his art from the claims of ontological truth" (Vance 80–1). Likewise the lessons of the *Bestiary,* while never questioning the validity of ontological truth, are freed from the overt and explicit connection between revealed cosmology and a didactic exercise. As a result of this new mobility in the romances, "multiple codes compet[e] with each other to determine reality within [a] culture" (Vance 78), and while I would hesitate to suggest that they are in competition in the *Bestiary,* the evidence for "multiple codes" of morality is abundant. Vance even remarks how a *Bestiary* creature, the lion, functions as "a symbol whose polyvalence will mark [Chretien's] text as a shifter between multiple discourses" (84) within the romance structure.

Hanning sees this phenomenon in the romance as part of a larger cultural change taking place in the twelfth century: "Along with other texts of the twelfth-century Renaissance, the romances manifest a desire to portray human experience from an individual as well as (or instead of) a corporate or an ideologically exemplary point of view" (17). I would suggest that the *Bestiary* participates in that same dynamic. The multiplication of points of view in the romance corresponds to the *Bestiary*'s construction of individual and independent moralities distinct from the lessons in universal and eternal truth as offered in the *Liber Monstrorum* or the *Physiologus.* Even the structure of the romance parallels that of the *Bestiary:*

> [A] story of the adventures of one or two knights and their ladies is presented as a series of juxtaposed episodes, each one a complete, miniature action. The relation between each episode and the ones before and after it is not always progressive, or even evident, as there is no larger, overarching historic or epic action that unifies and frames all separate deeds. . . . (Hanning 61)

Such a description aptly characterizes the separate and independent *Bestiary* entries as well. Thus the *Bestiary* and the romances occupy a rather odd place on the literary landscape where human experience is both individual and corporate, and moral conduct is compatible with religion yet not necessarily divinely inspired. These twelfth-century texts differ from what came before, which was universally and ontologically valid (or "epic" as Bloch and Hanning would have it), and from what will follow, in which meaning will be subject entirely to human agendas and ingenuity. I would therefore characterize this odd, awkward and sometimes inscrutable text as in some way transitional. A closer look at individual entries will bolster my point.

The reader can derive both spiritual and secular morals from a typical, if lengthy, entry on the most familiar of all domestic animals, the dog:

> Canis nomen Latinum Grecam ethimologiam habere videtur. Greco enim cenos dicitur, licet quidem a canore latratus appellatum existiment, eo quod insonat unde et canere dicitur. Nihil sagatius canibus plus enim sensus ceteris animalibus habent, nam soli sua nomina cognoscunt, dominos suos diligunt. Canum sunt plurima genera, alii ad capiendum investigant feras silvarum, alii ab infestationibus luporum, vigilando greges custodiunt ovium, alii custodes domorum, substantiam dominorum suorum custodiunt ne forte rapiatur, in nocte a latronibus et pro dominos suos se morti obiciunt, voluntarie ad predam cum domino currunt, corpus domini sui etiam mortuum custodiunt, et non linqunt. Quorum posttremo nature est, extra hominem esse non posse. . . . Cani vero ubi vestigium leporis cervive reppererit, atque ad diverticulum semite venerit, et quoddam viarum compitum, quod partes in plurimas scinditur, obiciens singularum semitarum exordia tacitus secum ipse pertractat, velud sillogisticam vocem, sagacitatem colligendi odoris emittens. Aut in hanc partem, inquid deflexit aut in illam, aut certe in hunc se anfractum contulit. Sepe etiam necis illate evidentia canes ad redarguendos reos indicia prodiderunt, ut muto eorum testimonio plerumque sit creditum. . . . Victus eius admodum modicus esse fertur. Catuli denique lingua vulneratorum solet esse saluti intestinorum. Natura eius est ut ad vomitum suum revertatur iterumque comedat. Cumque fluvium transnataverit carnem vel aliquid tale in ore tenens, cum viderit umbram os suum aperit, atque dum properat aliam carnem sumere, ipsam quam tenet amittit. (*Aberdeen Bestiary*)

> The Latin name for the dog, *canis,* seems to have a Greek origin. For in Greek it is called *cenos,* and some think that it is called after the musical sound, *canor,* of its barking, because when it howls, it is said to sing, *canere.* No creature is more intelligent than the dog, for they have more understanding than other animals; they alone recognise their names and love their masters. There are many kinds of dogs: some track down wild beasts of the forests to catch them; others with vigilance guard flocks of sheep from the attacks of wolves; others as watch-dogs in the home guard the property of their masters lest it be stolen by thieves at night and sacrifice their lives for their master; they willingly go after game with their master; they guard his body even when he is dead and do not leave. Finally, their nature is that they cannot exist without man. . . . When a dog picks up the track of a hare or a deer, and comes

> to a place where the trail divides or to a junction splitting into several directions, it goes to the beginning of each path and silently reasons with itself as if by syllogism, on the basis of its keen sense of smell. "Either the animal went off in this direction," he says, "or that, or certainly it took this turning." Often, also, when a murder has been committed, dogs have produced clear evidence of the guilt of the accused, with the result that their unspoken testimony is for the most part believed. . . . A dog's tongue, licking a wound, heals it. A dog's way of life is said to be wholly temperate. A puppy's tongue is generally a cure for internal injuries. It is characteristic of a dog that it returns to its vomit and eats it again. If a dog swims across a river carrying a piece of meat or anything of that sort in its mouth, and sees its shadow, it opens its mouth and in hastening to seize the other piece of meat, it loses the one it was carrying. (trans. McLaren)

The passage goes on to explain the various lessons the reader is to take from the dog's behavior. First, "[c]uius figuram in quibusdam rebus predicatores habent" ("in some ways preachers are like dogs"), a rather straightforward metaphor, and "[l]ingua canis dum lingit vulnus curat. Quia peccorum vulnera cum in confessione nudantur, sacerdotum correctione mundantur" ("a dog's tongue, licking a wound, heals it the way that sinners, laid bare in confession, are cleansed by the correction of the priest") (*Aberdeen Bestiary;* trans. McLaren). Obviously, the comparison and the lesson derived from it are entirely religious. But the entry continues by explaining the dog's temperance: "Modicus admodum victus canis dicitur esse, quia qui preest aliis, sapientie studiis invigilat, crapulamque omnimodis vitare debet" ("As the dog is said to be temperate in its ways, the man who is set over others diligently studies wisdom and must avoid drunkenness and gluttony in every way") (*Aberdeen Bestiary;* trans. McLaren). This moral could be interpreted tropologically, as the entry goes on to imply it should: "nam in saturitate panis Sodoma periit" ("for Sodom perished in a surfeit of food") (*Aberdeen Bestiary;* trans. McLaren). However, this passage could be equally well interpreted according to secular morality, for "the man who is set over others" might refer to anyone in authority, kings or nobles as well as clerics. And overeating and drunkenness, besides being sins, also damage one's health and can lead to foolish and self-destructive behavior. The bestiarist makes no attempt to explicate the dog's temperate behavior anagogically, and the warning relates to the very physical functions of eating and drinking, practical behaviors in which everyone engages every day.

The last lesson of this entry demonstrates moral lesson that appears almost entirely secular:

> Quod carnem in flumine propter concupitam umbram relinquid, significat stultos homines propter ambicionem ignote rei, id sepe quod proprii iuris est relinquere. Unde fit, ut dum non valent adipisci id quod cupiunt, perdere frustra norunt id quod reliquerunt. (*Aberdeen Bestiary*)
>
> The dog leaving its meat behind in the river, out of desire for its shadow, signifies foolish men who often forsake what is theirs by right out of desire for some unknown object; with the result that, while they are unable to obtain the object of their desire, they needlessly lose what they have given up. (trans. McLaren)

The lack of good judgment demonstrated by the dog seems to apply to the acts of "foolish men" in the secular world. A strictly tropological moral, such as a warning against covetousness, has not been ruled out, but it has not been made explicit as it was earlier in the passage. "[S]ome unknown object" and "the object of their desire" remain sufficiently ambiguous that the reader could insert any desire in their place. And although the image of lost food might recall the particular sin of gluttony, its association here with the dog seems to imply something more along the lines of one's greatest pleasure, since dogs are notoriously fond of their food. This ambiguity demonstrates that, whereas the *Bestiary* undoubtedly can trace its origins back to the *Physiologus,* by the twelfth century it has expanded not only its content of animals, but also its possible avenue of instruction from purely religious allegory into what I would call secular morality.

Such expansion is also evident, if more subtly executed, in the passage on an animal that, unlike the dog, has a direct source in the *Physiologus.* The ant, both the *Bestiary* and the *Physiologus* agree, has three natures: each ant contributes to the food hoard of the colony; ants store away a portion of their food in case of emergency; and ants discriminate between barley and wheat, rejecting the former in favor of the latter. The *Bestiary* reproduces the religious moralities explicated by the *Physiologus* in the second and third characteristics, and while it does not utilize as many scriptural quotations as the *Physiologus,* it does refer directly to Corinthians and Job respectively (*Aberdeen Bestiary; Physiologus* 22–4 [versio B]). Concerning the second and third natures of the ant, the *Bestiary* does not alter its source in any meaningful way. However, the changes it makes to the first nature of the ant are of more interest, for the *Bestiary* has shortened this part of the *Physiologus* entry significantly and in such a way as to alter its meaning. The *Bestiary*'s entry on the ant reads as follows:

> Formica tres naturas habet. Prima natura est ut ordinate ambulent, et unaqueque earum granum baiulet in ore suo. Et he que vacue sunt, non dicunt date nobis de granis vestris, sed vadunt per vestigia priorum usque

> ad locum ubi frumentum inveniunt et afferunt frumentum in cubile suum. Habet ad prudentium significationem dicta sufficiant, quia sicut formice congregant unde remunerentur in futuro. (*Aberdeen Bestiary*)

> The ant has three characteristics. The first is that they march in line, each one carrying a grain of corn in its mouth. Those who have none do not say to the others: 'Give us some of your grain,' but follow the tracks of those who first went out to the place where they find the corn and carry it off to their nest. Let this description serve to signify sensible men, who, like the ants, act in unity, as a result of which they will be rewarded in the future. (trans. McLaren)

As the *Bestiary* entry stands here, the lesson to be learned from the ants is one of prudence and cooperation. No mention is made of any religious or scriptural connection to the ant's behavior in spite of the fact that "give us some of your grain" comes from Matthew 25:8 (Curley 20).

This stands in contrast to the way the *Bestiary*'s source applies the moral of the first nature of the ant, and the reader can observe the important conceptual change that has taken place in this adaptation through what the *Bestiary* has added to the *Physiologus* and through what has been omitted. *Physiologus* begins with a quote from Solomon about ants which the *Bestiary* has not kept: "De formica Salomon dicit: Uade ad formicam, o piger, meditare eam; quae cum sit uiribus infirmior multum per aestatem frumentum sibi reponit" ("Concerning the ant, Solomon said: Go to the ant, o lazy one, to reflect on him; he, though weaker than man, through the summer puts away much grain for himself") (*Physiologus* 22 [versio B]; my translation). In addition, the *Physiologus* contains a long passage which the *Bestiary* has not reproduced explicating the ant's behavior with specific reference to the five foolish virgins of Matthew 25 who wasted the oil in their lamps (*Physiologus* 23 [versio B]). Lastly, the *Bestiary* adds a short but telling moral not found in its source when it informs the reader that ants represent sensible and cooperative people who will be rewarded for their foresight. The *Bestiary* makes no attempt to relate such sensible behavior to any specifically religious issue, and the ant stands as an example of sound, everyday, secular hard work and planning. The fact that the *Bestiary* specifically omits material that could give the message a religious slant indicates that the author was fashioning a purposefully secular moral to stand alongside the religious significations that the ant's second and third natures provide.

Critical opinion has not always looked favorably on the *Bestiary* and its strategy of moral instruction. As recently as 1991 a critic could feel the need to defend it as "far from being an ignorant collection of moralities and old wives' tales, as has usually been assumed by scholars" (George and Yapp 1). In recent years, however, it has enjoyed renewed critical interest which has revealed its noble and entertaining, if popular, instructional purpose. Clark and McMunn see the *Bestiary* as an attempt to demonstrate the functioning of Augustine's dictum that "Creation was a mirror of the Creator, a means of revealing his nature and his intentions for the life and salvation of the Christian believer . . . in an easily comprehended, indeed appealing manner to a broad audience" (Clark and McMunn 5–6). Salisbury reveals the *Bestiary*'s harshest critics' lack of historical understanding when she explains that "medieval thinkers moved rapidly and comfortably from the practical to the allegoric and back again" (*The Medieval World of Nature* xi-xii), a habit which would obviously make the structure of the *Bestiary* ideal for the moral instruction of the masses in spite of the fact that the majority of English bestiaries are written in Latin. Rowland has explained how the *Bestiary* might have been adapted for various audiences:

> Of course, the milieu of the bestiary varied but the overall function of the illustrations probably remained unaltered. In a noble household, the wealthy patron and his ladies would remember the Christian story by studying the brilliant illuminations while the text was read aloud; in various theological schools that possessed bestiaries . . . the illustrations would assist in the moral and spiritual edification of lay brothers or provide preachers with easily remembered allegories for their sermons. (18)

But while it may certainly be the case that the *Bestiary* was intended for popular instruction, as testified by its use as a school text and a source of sermon exempla, it does not follow that the *Bestiary*'s structure and strategy are somehow simplistic, worthy only of "moralities and old wives' tales." As this chapter will show, the *Bestiary*'s moralities often exhibit a sophisticated multilayer effect indicative of the late medieval expansion of potential meanings.

In its expansion of potential meanings, the *Bestiary* obviously differs vastly from its early medieval counterpart, the *Liber Monstrorum,* which, the reader will recall, functioned as an exercise in piety and *auctoritas.* In doing so, the *Liber Monstrorum* had to be taken in its entirety; what was to be believed about monsters and beasts depended on the source for each passage, specifically on whether the source were Christian or pagan. The former were reliable and to be believed; the latter were liars and to be discounted; and the pattern revealed by the complete work was one of regression from a majority of Christian sources in book one to a majority of pagan ones in book three. This imitated the metaphor of the little sea girl with her head of reason and barbarous tail, the head of reason obviously symbolizing Christian authority.

But the reader could not know any of this unless s/he had studied the entire work and actually puzzled through what was to be believed and what was not. The moral lesson of the *Liber Monstrorum* resided in its whole, as it were, as opposed to its parts as in the *Bestiary*, in which any single entry can not only function independently of the rest of the work, but can also reveal a multiplicity of truths, both religious and secular.

This multiplicity of moral truths remains evident not only in entries on everyday animals such as the dog, but also in entries on spectacular animals in which the reader might expect to find a more sensationalist interpretation. Granted, some of the entries on monsters, such as the manitcore, the leucrota and the griffin, do seem to be included in the *Bestiary* merely for sensational effect as the text provides no moral implication for their appearance and behavior; however, some perfectly ordinary animals, like the sheep and the cat, are also included without moral explication. But when a monster or unusual creature does communicate one or more morals, these lessons do not differ substantially from those derived from ordinary animals.[1] Observe the entry on the phoenix:

> Fenix Arabie avis dicta quod colorem feniceum habeat, vel quod sit in toto orbe singularis et unica. Hec quingentos ultra annos vivens, dum se viderit senuisse, collectis aromatum virgultis, rogum sibi instruit, et conversa ad radium solis alarum plausu voluntarium sibi incendium nutrit, seque urit. postea vero die nona avis de cineribus suis surgit. (*Aberdeen Bestiary*)

> The phoenix is a bird of Arabia, so called either because its colouring is Phoenician purple, or because there is only one of its kind in the whole world. It lives for upwards of five hundred years, and when it observes that it has grown old, it erects a funeral pyre for itself from small branches of aromatic plants, and having turned to face the rays of the sun, beating its wings, it deliberately fans the flames for itself to be consumed in the fire. But on the ninth day after that, the bird rises from its own ashes. (trans. McLaren)

The text goes on to explain that the phoenix's life cycle symbolizes how Christ died on the cross and rose again from the dead, saying explicitly that "[h]uius figuram gerit dominus noster Jesus Christus" ("our Lord Jesus Christ displays the features of this bird") (*Aberdeen Bestiary;* trans. McLaren). The entry, however, does not stop here; it continues to ruminate on the example of the phoenix as it applies to mankind as well as to Christ, comparing the very human St. Paul to the phoenix, and declaring that "[d]oceat nos igitur hec avis vel exemplo sui resurrectionem credere" ("let this bird teach us, therefore, by its own example to believe in the resurrection of the body") (*Aberdeen Bestiary;* trans. McLaren). Thus the example of the phoenix applies not only to Christ's resurrection but also, as Hassig points out, "would have been perceived by medieval readers as support for the dogma of the resurrection of the flesh, in line with contemporary theological opinion, and concomitantly would have assuaged fears concerning the fate of the human body after its deposit in the grave" (81).

This distinction may appear to be a fine one, but it is nevertheless an important one. The *Physiologus* limits its interpretation to Christ's resurrection and concentrates on the significance of Christ's incarnation, citing three different scriptural references (*Physiologus* 20–1 [versio B]). The *Bestiary* entry of course includes this interpretation, but it also extends the application of the phoenix's significance into the physical world of mankind, speaking at one point of "odoribus . . . funeris" ("the stench of death") (*Aberdeen Bestiary;* trans. McLaren) that the phoenix's perfumed odor obliterates. It also urges the reader directly "[c]ognosce ergo diem mortis tue" ("to know therefore the day of your death") so that "possint ossa tua pinguescere, et sint sicut ortus ebrius" ("your bones may be fertile; let them be like a well-watered garden") (*Aberdeen Bestiary;* trans. McLaren). This physical detail and reassurance to earthly inhabitants about the ultimate fate of their bodies seems, as Hassig says, to be designed to placate the very human fear of physical deterioration in the grave. Whereas both interpretations are to a great extent religious, only the first, copied from the *Physiologus,* is spiritually sophisticated, concerned with theological conundrums like Christ's dual nature; the second concerns itself much more with the real fears and questions of everyday people, albeit fears and questions of a religious nature. Both interpretations remain simultaneously valid, but the *Bestiary* has added a level of meaning to the material of the original *Physiologus* that is not merely additional but also substantively different.

Comparison of the phoenix entry with the entry on the dog shows some profound similarities. Both are concerned with religious issues and with how those issues affect the lives of people in the world: the priest is a watchdog over his parishoners' souls, and the phoenix assures mortal people of the ultimate fate of their physical bodies. In both cases the moral is certainly religious but not quite typological or anagogical, being concerned more with the function of Christians in the physical world than with contemplating the nature of Christ Himself. The first part of the phoenix entry, of course, does have an anagogical component (Christ's resurrection and the coming resurrection of all bodies), and the curative powers of a dog's lick as illustrative of the function of the priest during confession is almost tropological in its explanation of the sacrament. The phoenix does not, however, provide any moral lesson that might be interpreted as secular, as the entry on the dog does. Perhaps the fact that the dog does not even appear in the *Physiologus* can explain the lack of any strictly allegorical component and the presence of potentially secular moralities, for as a later addition the composition of the entry would have reflected the particular concerns of the era in which it was written without also having to take into account the allegorical baggage of an esteemed source like the *Physiologus.* The dog does not seem to have made an appearance in the *Physiologus/Bestiary* family of texts until the 12th-century pseudo-Hugo of St. Victor's *De bestiis et allis rebus* (McCulloch 78–80, 110–11). Yet the intrusion of a new interest in secular morality has penetrated the *Bestiary* to the extent that the ant entry has refashioned a religious moral into a secular one. And while the entry on the phoenix does not extend its significance into purely secular matters, it does go so far as to acquire a physical function beyond the issue of Christ's resurrection. The *Bestiary* adds a worldly, human-centered message that its source passage lacks; both the entry on the phoenix and that on the dog provide not just one moral or one type of moral, but a variety and plurality of morals; and the entries do not differ substantially from each other in tone or presentation, even though medieval readers would have regarded one as a remarkable and fabulous monster and the other as remarkably and fabulously ordinary.

In contrast, the *Liber Monstrorum,* which resembles the *Bestiary* in that it is comprised of a list of animals and monsters, concerns itself almost exclusively with the distinction between ordinary and fabulous, that is, between truth and falsehood. One might argue that this is not surprising since the *Liber Monstrorum* is interested mostly in the idea of authority, a concern that the *Bestiary* does not appear to share, but that is precisely my point. In the *Liber Monstrorum* one finds one issue—revealed cosmology—and one authority for interpretation—the Christian church. The *Bestiary,* in contrast, has almost eliminated authority; even the authority of physiologus has for the most part been eliminated. Such lack of authority allows for a plurality of interpretations and categories of meaning, but this plurality is to some extent still bound to the general area of the moral, either in the ethical sense or in a "moral-of-the-story" sense, i.e., as a lesson. Meaning and interpretation have not yet become a matter of arbitrary personal whim, as they later will. This is why, I would argue, the *Bestiary* can be characterized as a transitional text.

The narrator of the *Liber Monstrorum* begins his treatise by protesting that he would have thought belief in the monsters depicted in the lying fables of poets and philosophers had thankfully vanished (*Liber Monstrorum* prologue). However, he implies in the prologue, and at various other points throughout the work, that the very function of the pack of lies he is repeating is to force the reader to uncover the nature of truth for him- or herself: "Quaedam tantum in ipsis mirabilibus uera esse creduntur . . . et sequentem historiam sibi quisque discernat" ("Only some things in the marvels themselves are believed to be true . . . and let each judge for himself the following material") (*Liber Monstrorum* prologue; trans. Orchard). The epilogue to book three, on serpents, ends the *Liber Monstrorum* on a similar note: "In his namque serpentibus quos superius descripsimus, quaedam uera, quaedam namque omni ueritate carentia reperiuntur" ("Now, among these serpents which we have described above, some true things are found, and some lacking all truth") (trans. Orchard). But the narrator does not obliquely state which things are true and which are lacking; to do so would have violated the entire spirit of his treatise, the reader's search for truth through reliable authority as outlined in chapter two above. So whereas "real" animals and monsters exist alongside each other in the *Liber Monstrorum* as they do in the *Bestiary*, the latter seems not to care for the distinction between real and imaginary at all, whereas this distinction becomes a major component of the former's didactic function.

The narrator announces that he is beginning his book of monsters "quae leuiore discretu ab humano genere distant" ("with those things which differ by a rather trifling amount from humankind") (*Liber Monstrorum* prologue; trans. Orchard), and book one's entries do consist of human monsters and human hybrids. The first group is composed mostly of grotesque human specimens such as hermaphrodites, giants, Cyclops, people with extra arms and legs, and other clearly human-shaped beings, and the narrator refers to them as humans or people. The hermaphrodite, for example, is "hominem . . . utriusque sexus" ("a person of both sexes") (*Liber Monstrorum* 1.1; trans. Orchard), and a race with their heads on their chests, known in Plinian language as Blemmyae and in the *Liber Monstrorum* as Epifugi, are "homines . . . qui absque capitibus nascuntur" ("men who are born without heads") (*Liber Monstrorum* 1.24; trans. Orchard). Hybrids, on the other hand, are usually shown clearly to be not human, precisely because their association with the animal world precludes their membership in the human race. Fauns, for example, are described as being human to the navel and goat from belly to feet. After describing them, the narrator then notes that fauns "ad Orphei liram, cum innumerosis ferarum generibus, cantu deductos cecinit" ("along with countless other kinds of wild animals, were drawn to the lyre of Orpheus by his song") (*Liber Monstrorum* 1.5; trans. Orchard). Thus, without actually saying so, the narrator clearly differentiates fauns from real humans by implying their membership in the category "ferarum generibus." Occasionally, he is more overt about his categorical divisions, as when he tells us that

Cynocephali, or dog-heads, "omne uerbum quod loquuntur intermixtis corrumpunt latratibus, et non homines, crudam carnem manducando, sed ipsas imitantur bestias" ("spoil every word they say with mingled barks, and do not imitate humans but the beasts themselves in eating raw flesh") ") (*Liber Monstrorum* 1.16; trans. Orchard). Clearly, since Cynocephali have no human language and apparently no human culinary skill or discernment, they are not human, but beasts. In spite of apparent hybridization in both these and other entries, human-animal ambiguity is depicted as necessarily animal because not fully human. Augustine's explanation of the monstrous races epitomized this view in that "he was certain that there was no ambiguity between the species; one was either animal or human" (Salisbury, *The Beast Within* 148). The treatise implies in addition that they must be monstrous by including them in a book of monsters.

The *Liber Monstrorum* is almost as insistent about separating beasts from ordinary animals as it is about separating animals from humans. In the opening to book two, the narrator defines a beast or monster ("belua") as "quidquid in terris aut in gurgite in horrendi corporis ignota et metuenda reperitur forma" ("whatever is found on land or in the sea of unknown and fearsome form of terrible bodily appearance") (2. prologue; trans. Orchard). Many of the creatures that appear in book two are *bestia, belua,* or *monstruosa,* but some are not, and the narrator takes pains to point this out. Wild asses, for example, "animalia sunt, non bestiae" ("are animals, not beasts") (*Liber Monstrorum* 2.3; trans. Orchard), and tigers "sunt ferae horrendae animositatis" ("are wild animals of fearsome hostility") (*Liber Monstrorum* 2.4; trans. Orchard). While this may seem like hair-splitting to the modern reader, to the narrator of the *Liber Monstrorum* these distinctions are quite a serious matter as they operate as signposts along the way to determining what is and what is not to be believed in his treatise. Observe the words he uses to describe the chimaera:

> Chimaeram Graeci scribunt quandam fuisse bestiam triplicis monstruosa corporis foeditate terribilem quam flammis dicunt armatam, eo quod tria capita ignem habuisset uomentia. (*Liber Monstrorum* 2.11)
>
> The Greeks write that the chimaera was formerly a certain terrible beast of triple body with monstrous hideousness, which they say was armed with flames, in that it had three heads spewing fire. (trans. Orchard)

As the narrator makes clear elsewhere, those poetic lying Greeks are not to be trusted, and here the terminology he uses about the chimaera corresponds in its excess to the degree of believability of the source.[2]

So while the clearly divided books of the *Liber Monstrorum* might appear to base their division on species differences, this is not the only, or even the primary, division. Far more important is the separation between truth and falsehood as determined by reliable Christianity and lying paganism, and in fact the subdivisions amongst animals, beasts, and monsters function in service to the religious distinction. Such a strategy contrasts sharply with that of the *Bestiary* where not only does the physical truth and source of the animal/monster in question appear irrelevant, but each separate entry operates independently of the scheme of the whole work. Better to observe these differences and what the reader can learn from them, the remainder of this section will compare and contrast entries from both the *Liber Monstrorum* and the *Bestiary* about the same creatures: the lion, the viper, and the siren.

The *Liber Monstrorum*'s entry on the lion fails to offer the kind of respect typically afforded that animal in, for example, the *Physiologus:*

> Leonem, quem regem esse bestiarum, ob metum eius et nimiam fortitudinem poetae et oratores cum phisicis fingunt, in frontem beluarum horribilium ponimus. Qui fiunt generaliter colore fuluo, sed tamen albos cum ingentibus iubis leones et in taurini corporis magnitudine habuisse Indus fertur. Et ipse uastissimae leo formae describitur quem Hercules sub rupe Nemeaei montis occidit. (2.1)
>
> We place in the forefront of fearsome beasts the lion, which because of his dread and excessive strength poets and orators, as well as scientists, imagine to be the king of the beasts. They are generally of a tawny colour, but the Indus, however, is said to have had white lions with huge manes and bodies as large as bulls. And the same kind of lion of the most enormous size is described, which Hercules slew under the rock of the Nemean mountain. (trans. Orchard)

Here the lion is simply an animal imagined ("fingunt") to be the king of beasts, and the author sees no moral significance in this fact, even though the phrase "king of the beasts" seems to imply that he knew of the traditional interpretation. If he did know of it, he obviously places no store in it or in those "poets and orators, as well as scientists" who fancifully imagined such a thing. The reader can further surmise the author's opinion on this subject through his sources, the questionable *Alexander the Great's Letter to Aristotle* (Orchard 319), notably not a reliable Christian source, and through the reference to Hercules, the pagan subject of the lying fables of unreliable Greeks and Romans. So while the author does not seem to question the existence of an animal called a lion, he sees no possibility of deriving a moral from it and clearly disagrees with those who "imagine" it as worthy of moral contemplation and literary significance.

The *Liber Monstrorum*'s attitude contrasts sharply with the *Bestiary*'s lengthy and respectful treatment of the king of beasts. First, the *Bestiary* author gives the etymology of "leo," then a physical and psychological description. Next, the lion's three natures are given along with their scriptural correspondences; this section follows very closely the lion's entry in the *Physiologus*. However, the *Bestiary* goes much further with its moral lessons than does the *Physiologus:*

> Circa hominem leonum natura est ut nisi lesi nequant irasci. Ad cuius exemplum rationabiles homines respicere debent, qui non lesi irascuntur, et innocentes opprimunt, cum iubeat Christiana lex noxios dimittere liberos. Patet enim leonum misericordia exemplis assiduis, prostratis enim parcunt, captivos obvios repatriare permittunt. In viros potius quam in feminas seviunt. Infantes non nisi in magna fame perimunt. Pariter omnes parcunt a sagina. . . . (*Aberdeen Bestiary*)
>
> Where men are concerned, it is the nature of lions not to grow angry unless they are harmed. An example which thoughtful men should heed; for men grow angry even when they have not been harmed and they oppress the innocent, although Christian law bids them set even the guilty free. The compassion of lions is apparent from endless examples. They spare those whom they have brought down. They allow captives whom they encounter to return home. They vent their rage on men rather than women. They do not kill children except in time of great hunger. Equally, lions refrain from over-feeding. . . .) (trans. McLaren)

Isidore's *Etymologies* serves as the source for most of this new information about the lion's mercy and lack of temper (12.2.3–6), but the explicit link between such behavior and its applicability to man has been inserted by the bestiarist, as have the details about sparing women and children. Although the author does not apply all the lion's admirable traits to human behavior, he obviously could, for "thoughtful men" ought to follow the lion's examples of compassion and temperance, as the text implies. The text also refers to a scriptural source for the moral of the lion's behavior in "Christian law," but the specific scriptural source is not dwelt upon as it was in the *Physiologus*. The virtues of mercy, compassion, and temperance apply quite well to everyday secular behaviors and are, in fact, not of the same variety of moral as the traditional allegorical explication of the lion's three chief characteristics that constitute the *Physiologus* and are recounted earlier in the *Bestiary* entry. The latter has gone significantly beyond the former by including the addition of secular morals to be derived from the lion's behavior without nullifying the spiritual lessons also to be learned.

The viper offers another opportunity to see the contrasting concerns of the *Liber Monstrorum* and the *Bestiary:*

> Vipera autem, eo quod ui pariat, ita nuncupatur, de qua scribunt phisici quod ignotum genus quoddam humanae formae simillimum usque ad umbilicum habeat, et semen ore concipiat et fracto latere moriens pariat. (*Liber Monstrorum* 3.18)
>
> But the viper is so called because it gives birth by violence. About which scientists write that they have a certain unknown kind most like the human form down to the navel, which receives seed in the mouth and in death gives birth through its split side. (trans. Orchard)

If the author of the *Liber Monstrorum* is not as skeptical about the information he presents about the viper as he is about, for example, the lion, this is perhaps because his source, Isidore of Seville, is a more reliable (i.e., Christian) one (Orchard 320). Instead of having his scientists "imagine" their information, as they apparently did about the lion, here the author observes more objectively that this is what they have written, and he does not call their validity into question by associating the scientists with "lying" poets and orators. The reader should also note that the viper here is somewhat monstrous due to its apparent hybridization. However, the author never implies it is partially human; it is merely "humanae formae simillimum," but not part human by virtue of this similarity.

The *Bestiary* does something quite new and interesting in its entry on the viper that distinguishes it not only from the *Liber Monstrorum* but also from earlier sources. The *Bestiary* viper begins by recounting basically what the *Liber Monstrorum* has to say, omitting the reference to the scientific source and adding that the male dies during conception when the female bites off his head. Then is recounted information attributed to St. Ambrose that the male viper, when feeling particularly lustful, has been known to copulate with the female lamprey, who never fails to accommodate him in this cross-species abomination. The *Bestiary* author then explains the somewhat surprising moral:

> Quid sibi sermo huius modi vult nisi ferendos esse mores coniugum, et si absens est eius comperienda presentia? Sit licet asper, fallax, inconditus lubricus, temulentus, quid peius veneno quod in coniuge murena non refugit, vocata non deest, et serpentis lubricum sedula caritate complectitur. Ille tua mala portat et levitatis feminee facilitatem, tu

> virum tuum non potes mulier sustinere. . . . Sed etiam tu vir, possumus enim etiam sic accipere, depone tumorem cordis, asperitatem morum cum tibi sedula uxor occurrit, propelle indignationem cum blanda coniux ad caritatem provocat. Non es dominus sed maritus, non ancillam sortitus es, sed uxorem. Gubernatorem te deus voluit esse sexus inferioris, non prepotentem. Redde vicem studio, redde amori gratiam. Vipera venenum suum fundit, tu non potes duriciam mentis deponere? Si habes naturalem rigorem, debes temperare eum contemplatione coniugii, et reverentia coniunctionis deponere animi feritatem. (*Aberdeen Bestiary*)

> What should these words signify to us if not that we should put up with the behaviour of our partner, and even if his whereabouts cannot be discovered, we are to behave as if he were present? Let him be harsh, deceitful, uncouth, unreliable, drunken: are any of these things worse than the poison from which the lamprey, in intercourse, does not shrink? When she is invited, she is not found wanting and embraces the slimy snake with sincere affection. The man puts up with your mischief and your feminine tendency towards triviality. Can you, o woman, not stand by your man? . . . But you too, o man, for we can also bring you into the discussion, set aside the passion in your heart and the roughness of your manner when your loving wife comes to meet you. Get rid of your ill-humour when your wife sweetly rouses you to express your love. You are not her master but her husband, you have gained not a maidservant but a wife. God wished you to govern the weaker sex, not rule it absolutely. Return her care with attention; return her love with grace. The viper pours out its poison, can you not get rid of your harsh attitude? If you are severe by nature, you should moderate your manner in consideration of your married state and set aside your harshness out of regard for your relationship. (trans. McLaren)

This is a remarkable and almost entirely secular moral. With the exception of two nearly incidental asides not quoted here about Adam and Eve as the model of a married couple, the entry's advice about marriage is almost entirely of a practical, not spiritual, variety; the author gives excellent and even-handed advice that can easily be applied in everyday situations to both husbands and wives. Such a practical moral appears even more astounding when compared with the *Physiologus*' entry on the viper in which Christ likens the Pharisees to the viper and no parallel is made to the marital state (*Physiologus* 15–6 [versio Y]).[3] Such a long entry given over entirely to the subject of marriage also indicates that the *Bestiary*'s intended audience was composed at least partially of the secular public who were most likely reached through sermons based on the *Bestiary* material.

The final comparison between the *Liber Monstrorum* and the *Bestiary* involves a truly monstrous monster, as opposed to a beast or serpent, the siren. The *Liber Monstrorum* has this to say about these female human hybrids:

> Sirenae sunt marinae puellae, quae nauigantes pulcherrima forma et cantu dulcedinis decipiunt, et a capite usque ad umbilicum sunt corpore uirginali et humano generi simillimae, squamosas tamen piscium caudas habent, quibus semper in gurgite latent. (1.6)
>
> Sirens are sea-girls, who deceive sailors with the outstanding beauty of their appearance and the sweetness of their song, and are most like human beings from the head to the navel, with the body of a maiden, but have scaly fishes' tails, with which they always lurk in the sea. (trans. Orchard)

The sources for this information remain unknown, but there is reason to believe that the author found them reliable. First, he makes no mention of lying poets or credulous scientists; in fact, he makes no attempt at all to blame another for perpetuating misinformation as he so often does, especially in cases where the existence of a creature is unlikely. Instead, he simply states that "Sirenae *sunt* marinae puellae" without equivocation. Secondly, although the source for this information has not been reliably traced, this entry appears at the beginning of the *Liber Monstrorum* which, representing the "head of reason" in the prologue, contains mostly reliable, i.e., Christian, sources. The sources for entries one through eight (of which the siren is sixth) are as follows: Augustine, unknown, Jerome, Augustine, Isidore, unknown, Jerome, and Augustine (Orchard 318–9); one notices a marked decline in "reliable" Christian sources in the second half of the entries to book one thus representing the scaly "tales" of the prologue. Lastly, the fact that the siren or sea-girl does appear in the prologue as a metaphor for truth perhaps implies that, in spite of her scaly tail/tale, there is some kernel of truth to be derived from her. Interestingly, the author does not comment on the deceit with which the siren tricks sailors. If the sea-girl moral had anything to do with her actual behavior, which involves both deceit and lust, the author would not use her here where she stands as his metaphor for the truth that is to be extracted from his collection of facts and fables. The moral of the sea-girl here has nothing to do with her actual behavior, but rather with the reliability of the information about her revealed not by empirical evidence but by the religious status of her source and the fact that her head, if not her tail/tale, is reasonable.

The *Bestiary*'s entry on the siren provides slightly different information and a moral to be derived from her. (I cite the *Cambridge Bestiary* (C.U.L.

II.4.26) here instead of the *Aberdeen Bestiary* because the latter's entry on the siren is atypical.)

> The sirenae, so Physiologus says, are deadly creatures who are made like human beings from the head to the navel, while their lower parts down to the feet are winged.[4] They give forth musical songs in a melodious manner, which songs are very lovely, and thus they charm the ears of sailormen and allure them to themselves. They entice the hearing of these poor chaps by a wonderful sweetness of rhythm, and put them to sleep. At last, when they see that the sailors are deeply slumbering, they pounce upon them and tear them to bits. That's the way in which ignorant and incautious human beings get tricked by pretty voices, when they are charmed by indelicacies, ostentations and pleasures, or when they become licentious with comedies, tragedies and various ditties. They lose their whole mental vigour, as if in a deep sleep, and suddenly the reaving pounce of the Enemy is upon them. (trans. White)[5]

It appears that the entry on the siren conforms, like that of the lion or the viper, to the theory of the *Bestiary* I have been propounding here: description, spiritual moral and then secular moral, the last of which is something entirely new and unseen in the source material. However, in this case the information provided by the *Bestiary* corresponds almost verbatim to the much earlier *Physiologus* entry on the same monster, with the exception that the latter does quote Isaiah on the subject of the siren's habitat in Babylonia (*Physiologus* 25 [versio B]). The sins of the siren about which the reader is warned begin in a secular way, citing the evils of the theater, but this is done to show how the theater makes one vulnerable to the "pounce of the Enemy," i.e., Satan; thus, ultimately, the moral is at least mostly spiritual in nature. However, just because the *Bestiary* reproduces the text of the *Physiologus* on this entry does not necessarily mean that the siren has not acquired some secularized subtext of which the reader would be aware and, thereby, forewarned by the *Bestiary.*

Hassig's book, *Medieval Bestiaries: Text, Image, Ideology,* can help us come to a more complete understanding of the new secularized function of the sirens in the *Bestiary.* Hassig devotes an entire chapter to the siren, in which she convincingly argues that the female monster's contemporary social function was to recall and warn the reader against the allure of the prostitute. Hassig's argument rests on contextual and pictorial evidence, since the entry on the siren itself, as noted above, varies very little from its ancient source. First, the bestiary illustrations often depict the siren as clutching a mirror and a comb, traditional signifiers of female vanity and specific accessories of Venus, who in turn symbolized the sin of *luxuria* (Hassig 107). In addition, the siren is often depicted nude, suggesting, as Hassig puts it, "[a] certain preoccupation with female anatomy" (108). The nudity of the siren is neither arbitrary nor incidental, but, considering the derogatory social meanings attached to nakedness at this time, pointedly and specifically refers to "powerlessness and passivity . . . sin, sexual lust, and dangerous evil" (Hassig 109). Moreover, the specific and graphic preoccupation with the sirens' breasts as well as the ever-present commentary on, and often depiction of, their lust for sailors would plainly suggest to the reader that the siren entry was meant as a warning against prostitutes; even when the illustrator does clothe the sirens, their dress corresponds to that of contemporary prostitutes (Hassig 109–10). All these contextual and pictorial associations combine in such a way as to suggest that the sirens, as well as other animals like the lion and the viper, "were endowed with new significance as a result of what can be viewed as a shift in interpretation from the realm of the strictly religious and moral into the world of contemporary social and political interests" (Hassig 174). Thus the *Bestiary* goes beyond its source materials in expressing not just spiritual concern with the abstract concept of lust, but also contemporary anxiety over the ever-present temptation of the public woman in the medieval world. Once again, the *Bestiary* moral differs from that in the *Liber Monstrorum* not only in its multiple layers of meaning but also in its independence from any authority for at least one of its interpretations.

Whereas Hassig traces this "shift" in the bestiary's illustrations, I would like to examine the literary evidence for such a claim. Another sea-going monster demonstrates this change in perspective in a specifically verbal fashion. The serra, or flying-fish or sawfish or swordfish, depending on which authority one consults, may not readily appear to be monstrous, but the *Bestiary,* following the *Physiologus,* very specifically labels it a "belua in mari" ("a sea monster") (*Aberdeen Bestiary;* trans. McLaren). In fact, the *Bestiary* follows the *Physiologus* almost verbatim concerning what it has to say about the serra. Its tendency to follow ships for a few miles and then give up is moralized in a very religious way:

> Hec belua figuram habet seculi. Navis vero iustorum habet exemplum, qui sine periculo et naufragio fidei transierunt per medias huius mundi procellas et tempestates. Serra vero id est belua illa que non valuit velificare cum navi, figuram illorum gerit, qui in inicio ceperunt bonis operibus insistere, postea non permanentes in eis, victi sunt diversis viciorum generibus que illos tanquam fluctuantes maris unde mergunt usque ad inferos. (*Aberdeen Bestiary*)
>
> The flying-fish represents this world. The ship symbolises the righteous, who sail through its storms and tempests without putting their faith in

> danger or at risk of shipwreck. But the flying-fish, which could not keep up with the ship, represents those who at the start apply themselves to good works, but do not afterwards persevere with them and yield to all sorts of vice, which carry them, like the restless waves of the sea, down to hell. (trans. McLaren)

This moral exactly reflects that in its source, except that the *Physiologus* adds a list of specific vices—"cupiditate, superbia, ebrietate, luxuria" (*Physiologus* 15 [versio B])—before the generalized "diversis viciorum."

This monstrous fish would be of no interest to this study were it not for the change that has taken place in the final sentence to the entry on the serra. The *Physiologus* sums up the moral of the serra in this way: "Qui uero perseuerauerit usque in finem, hic saluus erit" ("Truly, whoever persists all the way to the end, he is saved") (*Physiologus* 15 [versio B]; my translation). This moral is lifted directly from Matthew 24:13, which reads in the Vulgate, "qui autem permanserit usque in finem hic salvus erit" ("but whoever holds out all the way to the end, he is saved") (*ARTFL Project;* my translation). Now let us observe how the *Bestiary* has altered this sentence: "Non enim incipientibus sed perseverantibus premium promittitur" ("Indeed, the prize is given not to those who begin but to those who persevere") (*Aberdeen Bestiary;* my translation). At first glance, the reader may not find any significance in the change that has taken place; the sense of the two sentences may appear virtually the same. However, two very important issues show that the *Bestiary* has been altered in a profoundly secular direction that expands the potential lesson to be learned from the entry without negating the original religious message.

First, one must question why the bestiarist has altered this single sentence so significantly while leaving the rest of the entry virtually intact. A word-by-word comparison of the *Bestiary* with the *Physiologus* shows a remarkable, almost verbatim, similarity between the two except for this final sentence. One can only conclude that the bestiarist must have had some specific meaning he was trying to impart to the reader through the change. In order to access what that meaning may be, one must look at the connotations of the words rejected and the words substituted, especially "salvus" and "premium."

The *Physiologus,* following Matthew, concludes "hic saluus erit" ("he is saved"). "Salvus" has a specific religious meaning in ecclesiastical Latin according to *Harper's Latin Dictionary:* "saved from sin, saved by Christ." The use of "salvus" is thus commensurate with the *Physiologus*' strictly religious moralizing, but the *Bestiary* alters the wording, and thus the meaning, of this sentence significantly: "premium promittitur" ("the prize is given [to him]"). "Premium" has no specific spiritual connotation when used alone; according to a search of the *ARTFL Project* database of the Latin Vulgate, it is not found at all in the New Testament, which seems to favor "merces" to connote spiritual reward. *Harper's Latin Dictionary* indicates, in fact, that it is very earthbound, implying "profit, reward" or sometimes even "bribe" or "booty."

While I doubt that the bestiarist had the latter meanings in mind, the fact remains that "profit" and "reward" differ markedly from "salvation." Of course, spiritual salvation can be the reward or prize for religious perseverence in the face of earthly temptation. Blaise's *Lexicon Latinitatis Medii Aevi* records several instances of "premium" being used in a spiritual sense, but the word is never used alone and is always accompanied by adjectives that make its religious connotation clear: "praemium caeleste," "aeternae beatitudinis praemia," "salutis aeternae praemia." Aquinas used "praemium" to describe "the reward which consists of eternal happiness," but once again adjectives are used to distinguish such a spiritual reward from the ordinary use of the term, and Aquinas' usage is almost technical jargon (Defarrari 828). Aquinas' term is "praemium beatitudinis," which he further divides into "praemium accidentale" and "praemium essentiale." Aquinas also uses the term "retributio praemii" to refer to a category of "retributio." "Retributio praemii" is clearly distinguished from "retributio gloriae," which is the reward of eternal glory (Defarrari 922). The substitution of "premium," without qualifying adjectives or any indication it is being used in a technical theological sense, for "salvus" must call into question the exclusively spiritual implications of the moral of the serra. If one removes the *Bestiary* moral from its immediate context, the moral it promotes—the prize is given not to those who begin but to those who persevere—can be interpreted as a perfectly valid secular lesson on the profit ("premium") to be gained from persistence in any endeavor. The moral has become both religious and secular.

This "shift in interpretation," which I would argue reflects a larger shift in the medieval episteme, begins with the birth of the *Bestiary* from the parent *Physiologus* "sometime during the twelfth century" (McCulloch 34) and becomes solidified by the middle of the thirteenth century, as we will see. McCulloch sees this change as being "not beyond recognition . . . but the transformation is still very great" (34). She documents that "[t]he number of chapters . . . is far more than doubled . . . [including] many chapters with no moral or spiritual exposition" (34–5). While the inclusion of unmoralized animals and monsters might appear to undermine the argument set forth here, in fact the lack of moralization supports the idea that ways of knowing and types of knowledge to be derived from examination of a single entity multiplied in a hitherto unseen way in the twelfth century. Hassig explains how this might work:

> The lack of moralizations for so many of the new creatures also might be related to the general interest in Aristotle and empirical observation popular in England during the thirteenth century. However, even scholars such as Albert the Great and Thomas of Cantimpre, who are most often cited as pioneers of medieval empiricism, were interested in scientific accuracy not primarily for its own sake but rather as a tool for better interpreting the Scriptures: their first order of business remained service to the Church. This is not to suggest that their observations were contrived, but rather to guard against an interpretation of the bestiaries as "scientific" at any point during the Middle Ages. (173)

Thus the change consists of a multiplication of potential ways of looking at beasts and monsters. These ways are not infinite and are always compatible with Christianity, but clearly the possible interpretations are multiple. (Hugh of Fouilloy [d. 1172?] goes so far as to distinguish "mystice" from "moraliter" in his interpretation of birds.) The *Physiologus* method, which was almost always carried into the *Bestiary* entries, involved a spiritual or even mystical way of knowing the animal world. The *Bestiary* expanded this into the separate but related world of everyday social and moral concerns, and then went even further with its unmoralized entries, which document the physical world empirically. Such unmoralized entries, while they may resemble the pseudo-pagan observations of monsters in the *Wonders* and *Alexander's Letter,* cannot function in the same way as the monsters in those works, for their presence in a text that does make explicitly Christian interpretations negates this possibility.

Karen Jolly explains this multiplication in terms of the bigger picture of the development of western civilization:

> . . . in the early medieval use of the Latin word *scientia* (knowledge), there was no distinction between knowledge by revelation or knowledge through human reason: it either was of God or was not. The post-twelfth-century view of this term, as science, has evolved to the point today of eliminating revelation altogether, relying entirely on human reason. The whole faith-reason debate, and its consequences in Western history, was a product of the intellectual climate of the twelfth century; prior to that, knowledge was explored within a different framework, in which knowing was based on an authoritative, revealed cosmology governed by spiritual entities not directly perceived by the senses but understood through the imagination. (240)

In this sense, then, the *Bestiary* is a transitional text between the world of authoritative cosmology and its splintering into separate and mostly independent ways of knowing, including literary caprice and empirical observation,[6] for it utilizes all methods of knowing, sometimes within the same entry. Jolly's assertion might appear to exclude the possibility of such a text, for she seems to imply that *scientia* is either divine or it is not. However, it is the "post-twelfth-century" view, not the twelfth-century view, that has made the inviolable distinction between revelation and reason. The transitional view itself can be found in the twelfth-century change as documented by the bestiaries of that era and the one closely following upon it. As Baxter has put it, "[t]his is not to say that the moral didacticism of the *Physiologus* was abandoned at a stroke . . . The additions to the text and the stripping of the image point to no more than a change of emphasis. The process begun here was to go much further" (86).

The *Bestiary* entries themselves resist efforts at this sort of either/or classification. The lion exemplifies the possibility for knowing in several different ways, for it is described and its behaviors sometimes have a moral and sometimes simply are. In addition, authoritative knowledge has expanded from the purely spiritual realm (lion as Christ) to the realm of secular morality (compassion, temperance, control of anger). I would suggest that it is the peculiar fate of the *Bestiary* to become the epitome of the transition from an authoritative to an idiosyncratic mindset due to its wonderfully adaptive nature and the fortunate survival of the original *Physiologus* material into this particular time frame. I might also suggest that much of the confusion about the *Bestiary*'s merits and function could arise out of a misunderstanding of its transitional nature. Baxter has pointed out that "we no longer possess the medieval category into which Bestiaries fell" (213) and that "changes in the content of the book were dictated by changing conditions of use" (183). Although Baxter concludes that bestiaries were primarily used as sermon exempla, which explains their didactic focus, his analysis demonstrates the potential adaptability of the *Bestiary* entries to particular religious and secular concerns in a way unseen in the *Physiologus*. For example, he shows how the behavior of the badger in Bodley 764 justifies a rigid and potentially abusive class system (Baxter 199–201).

While it would be quite difficult, if not impossible, to pin-point the exact beginning and ending of this transition, as McCulloch points out, the beginning of a monumental change started sometime in the twelfth century. The transition ended by the middle of the thirteenth century when a new kind of *Bestiary* appeared, Richard de Fournival's *Bestaire d'amour*, whose arrival "point[s] to an entirely new and secular function for the bestiary in line with contemporary interest in the literary conventions of chivalry and courtly love" (Hassig 27). Fournival's work, a love complaint to a *belle dame sans merci*, presents the bestiary animals as "figures of various aspects of profane love" (Hassig 177), instead of the spiritual, brotherly, or even marital love one might find in the traditional *Bestiary.* In doing so, Fournival's purpose was obviously satiric, pointing as it did to the animalistic nature of supposedly lofty amorous sentiments and functioning as "a challenge to the Platonic idealism of contemporary love literature" (J. Beer, Preface xv). Fournival's *Bestiary* begins by invoking Aristotle, that exemplar of empiricism, and his *Metaphysics* with the quotation "All men naturally desire knowledge" (J. Beer, Preface ix), an assertion that might belong more comfortably in the realm of authoritative certitude but that is here used to justify the apparently bizarre application of a traditionally religious and moral genre to a treatise that is an exercise in relativism and arbitrariness.

Observing how Fournival alters a traditional *Bestiary* entry can help illuminate how radical this epistemic shift was. The siren, whose *Bestiary* entry is analyzed above, provides a suitable example:

> There are three sorts of siren: two are half woman and half fish, and the third is half woman and half bird. All three make music . . . Their melody is so pleasing that, however far away, no man hears them without being forced to approach. When he is near, he falls asleep, and when the siren finds him asleep, she kills him. And it seems to me that the siren has much guilt for her treacherous killing of him, but the man also has much guilt for trusting himself to her. And I am dead through such a killing, in which you and I are guilty. But I do not dare to accuse you of treachery, I shall take full blame upon myself, and shall say that I killed myself. (10–11; trans. J. Beer)

Here the reader finds no warning against lust or prostitutes; the metaphor is not only entirely secular but also completely arbitrary. With the exception of the description of the siren, this entry bears no resemblance at all to the traditional *Physiologus* and *Bestiary* entries which strive to establish a universal moral, whether spiritual or secular, through their explanations of the monster.

Although it may appear that Fournival is merely adapting the allegory in much the same way as the authors of the *Roman de la Rose,* familiarity with that work should not blind the reader to the radical nature of Fournival's revision, which preceded the *Roman* by many years; as Hassig notes, "it represents an entirely new interpretation of traditional bestiary lore" (8) that indicates a "new and secular function for the bestiary" (27). The adaptation of a moral catalogue to a treatise on profane love "involved more than a mere transposition of metaphors. The juxtaposition of the two known traditions was a provocation to both, for *Les Bestiaire d'amour* transcended all conventions by its ambivalence" (J. Beer, *Duel of Bestiaries* 96). Beer explains the profound implications of this change:

> *Le Bestaire d'amour* was sustained metaphor, the complete transference of a given set of Christianized symbols to the alien context of profane love. . . . The inferences were clear, and the forced redirection of the bestiary's symbolism was cataclysmic. Originally the function of that symbolism had been unequivocal, its possible interpretations had been finite. Now fixed symbolism acquired idiosyncratic application. From that moment it was capable of infinite variation at the hands of any enterprising expositor. (*Duel of Bestiaries* 97)

By the time Fournival composed his *Bestaire d'amour,* the authoritative and revealed cosmology of early medieval thought had given way to an "infinite variation" of meaning, and it is this "infinite variation," and not the scandalous and sometimes repulsive "morals" themselves, that is significant. Not only was the symbolism of the siren no longer "fixed" in its particulars, but it was also no longer necessarily attached to moral discourse at all. Its range of potential meanings now corresponded to a increasing variety of ways of knowing the world which rely on observation and idiosyncratic personal application of knowledge as well as an omniscient spiritual authority; indeed, the *Bestiaire*'s irreverent cooption and revision of a traditionally moral and/or spiritual genre implies that there are subject areas in which the final authority resides not in revealed truth but in humankind's imagination.

Thus the changes undergone by the *Bestiary* from the twelfth through the thirteenth centuries heralded a larger change, a branching off of kinds of knowledge—religious-moral, secular-moral, idiosyncratic, and proto-scientific-empirical—from the tree of revealed and authoritative cosmology. Jolly's argument can help chart this process:

> This "nature mysticism" of the early medieval period reveals the existence of holistic worldviews lacking the fundamental distinctions of natural-supernatural and reason-revelation . . . microcosm and macrocosm were interconnected through God, and everything was alive with the presence of God. . . . (224)

Just such a system defines the discourse of the *Physiologus,* in which the "natural" behavior of beasts and monsters reveals a "supernatural" characteristic of the Creator precisely because the two were inseparable to begin with. But in the discourse after "this twelfth-century revolution in epistemology" (Jolly 225) as epitomized by the *Bestiaire d'amour,* one finds that the lesson (no longer "moral") derived from the natural world has become divorced from supernatural authority, let alone any supernatural or divine component. This new kind of lesson is arbitrary and governed not by an omniscient and benevolent authority but by the very earthbound caprice of human fancy and ingenuity. Such a change does not necessarily appear radical in retrospect since "the modern Western perception of nature is rooted in a post-twelfth-century world view that has developed rigidly defined categories" (Jolly 224) to differentiate between empirical and intuitive ways of knowing. Looking backward, as the reader must, "earlier views of nature therefore appear 'mystical' because nature and supernature were not differentiated" (Jolly 225).

The *Bestiary,* an awkward yet pervasive product of that century of change, thus occupies an uncomfortable transitional space in the "progress" from "mysticism" to "science" in regards to beasts, birds, snakes, fish, and monsters. While the *Bestiary* has retained some of the "mystical" component of the *Physiologus* and has added some "scientific"—that is, objective or Aristotelian—entries, it is also permeated by creatures with multiple meanings, many of them not of a necessarily spiritual nature. A beast can be used to contemplate a moral or truth that has been established or affirmed by a Higher Authority, but this moral or truth does not necessarily partake of the essence of the Higher Authority himself and is therefore not part of the "supernatural." But as awkward as the *Bestiary* may be, it paves the way for even more awkward and complex beasts and monsters in a clearly earthbound text, the *Travels of Sir John Mandeville.*

Chapter Four
Mandeville's Travels

In order to evaluate the changes in the way monsters signified over the course of the medieval period, this chapter will examine the multifaceted functions of the monstrous in one of the most popular works of the later Middle Ages, *The Travels of Sir John Mandeville,* and will then compare Mandevillean monsters to the monsters of the Old English *Letter of Alexander the Great to Aristotle.* I base the rationale for a comparison of the Old English *Letter* and the Middle English *Mandeville's Travels* on the obvious similarities between the two works. Both are manufactured, fictitious treatises that in their narrative structures purport to be true, eye-witness, first-person accounts of journeys through exotic eastern lands; in this regard, they seem ideal sources for information about changes that may have occurred during the four centuries that separate them. However, certain profound differences between them also exist which will affect their interpretation: the narrator of the *Letter* is a pagan, while that of the *Travels* is a Christian, and the latter journeys through the Holy Land as well as India, China, and Russia, while the former confines his journey mostly to India and its environs. Nevertheless, with these *caveats* in mind, the reader may still uncover certain differences in interpretive methods that may provide insights into perceptual changes that took place between the Anglo-Saxon age and the Late Middle Ages. Unfortunately, the complex and controversial nature of the *Travels* necessitates lengthy scrutiny of its focus and organization before proceeding to an examination of how monsters and marvels function within the work itself.

The reader may find useful at this point a brief review of how an earlier chapter interpreted the *Letter of Alexander the Great to Aristotle.* The *Letter,* much like the *Wonders of the East,* depicts a linear, horizontal and physical world only, a world that has no higher spiritual meanings but only earthbound facts; this is a Christian perception of the pagan view of the world. The narrator Alexander's lack of a Christian point of view leads repeatedly to mistakes in his interpretation of earthly phenomenon (as when he dubs himself "king of kings" based on his successful pursuit of earthly glory), or to complete rejection of interpretive possibilities (as when he refuses to consider that his army's hardships may be a sign of divine disapproval). With this limited point of view, Alexander leaves the monsters and marvels he encounters uninterpreted; in a pagan landscape, such things are merely spectacular, not meaningful. Even so, Alexander himself is not completely without redeeming values: he is loyal, he respects scholarship, and he senses that some sort of deity must have created such a diverse and interesting universe. By implication, the *Letter* seems to say, what Alexander the pagan lacks is not good character or instincts or intelligence, but simply the revealed and authoritative Christian cosmology by which to make sense of the many earthly signs of God's intent.

Sir John Mandeville, the narrator of *Mandeville's Travels,* suffers from no such perceptual limitations and, as will become apparent, sees a variety of interpretive possibilities in all his surroundings. The manuscript history of the *Travels* is less clear but can be summarized succinctly for our purposes here. *Mandeville's Travels* was written around 1356/7 in French and probably in France by an unknown author claiming to be an English knight from St. Albans by the name of Sir John Mandeville (Seymour, *Sir John Mandeville* 1,5). Despite extensive investigation of (Bennet) and somewhat farfetched conclusions about (Hamelius 1–13) Sir John, he remains anonymous and possibly even non-existent; modern critical opinion has it that not only may "Sir John Mandeville" be an alias but that the author may have forged the entire piece while safely at home at his writing desk (Seymour, *Sir John Mandeville* 1–2). Critical opinion, however, is by no means unanimous on this point (Moseley 9–18).

The contention that the only traveling "Mandeville" did was to the nearest library is supported by the large number of sources to which many of the details in the *Travels* can be traced. The author used, at minimum, fourteen well-known books as sources for the adventures he recounts, including the works of Jacques de Vitry, Vincent of Beauvais, John of Plano Carpini, Odoric of Pordenone, Hetoum (or Hayton) of Armenia, and the anonymous (and ubiquitous) *Letter of Prester John;* considering the variety of sources, it has been suggested that "Mandeville" was a cleric or at least had access to one of the great ecclesiastical libraries (Seymour, *Sir John Mandeville* 8–10). For our purposes, the author's identity and research methods are of much less importance than the book's popularity, which cannot be denied, and the public's uncritical reception of it. The remarkable number of surviving manuscripts, approximately 250 (Seymour, *Mandeville's Travels* xiii), attests not only to popularity but also to believability, for the *Travels'* veracity was "universally accepted" (Seymour, *Sir John Mandeville* 1) well into the Renaissance. Hakluyt included it in the first edition of his *Principall Navigations* (although not in the second) and praised the book's scholarship (Moseley 30). Christopher Columbus was also undoubtedly familiar with the *Travels* and appears to have considered it an authoritative work (Moseley 9). Of importance here is neither the identity of "Mandeville" himself nor the blameworthiness of his plagiarism but rather the incredible popularity and authority the *Travels* enjoyed, which indicates something important about the constitution of the late medieval mindset.

The manuscript used here will be B.L. Cotton Titus C.xvi, an early fifteenth-century manuscript (c. 1410–20) of the insular tradition (Hamelius 19). As its editor points out, its mistranslations and slavish and unidiomatic translation of the French testify "to the wants and shortcomings of his fourteenth-century readers" (Hamelius 17), which are of more importance here than poetic rendering of the original. Cotton Titus also has the advantage of being a relatively early English manuscript and of being "closer to the French original than the once prominent 'Defective Version'" (Campbell 125n). Higgins describes Cotton Titus' adaptations as "infrequent and minor, making the rendering quite a good proxy for the authorial version" (24). In addition to being close to the authorial version, Cotton Titus has the advantage of being a good example of the Insular form of the *Travels*, "which represents the dominant form of the book" (Seymour, *Sir John Mandeville* 37).

Cotton Titus is divided into chapters by titles, but these chapters are unnumbered; the editor provides numbering and counts thirty-five chapters. He also divides the work into two parts: part one, chapters 1–16, concentrates on the Holy Land and the Near East, while part two, chapters 17–35, recounts Mandeville's journey to the Far East, designated by the editor as "The Countries Beyond the Holy Land." This ethnocentric designation is actually quite appropriate for the work at hand, for what Mandeville often found important was the relationship of the outer limits of the world to Christianity and Christendom. Since "the expanded East resulting from *The Book*'s move beyond the Holy Land is anything but a turning away from Jerusalem" (Higgins 51), it is not surprising to find the editor also referring to rich and important civilizations of the Far East purely through their relationship to Christian Europe. Beyond this kind of compartmentalized organization, the reader will find it difficult to discern any familiar narrative structure, as critics have noted:

> The tight categorical and proportional structuring of narrative, where everything relates to everything else, where balanced structure is an important clue to meaning, that we find in, for example, Dante, Gower or Chaucer, is largely lacking. There are, however, certain topics Mandeville refers to frequently—the insistence on Christians' unworthiness to possess Palestine, the corruption and complacency of the Western Church, the goodness in works of non-Christians. These could be said to be the thematic keys of the work. (Moseley 16)

In this regard, the *Travels* greatly resembles *Alexander's Letter,* for both are of the linear and descriptive variety of narrative whose meaning resides less in the tightly structured unfolding of events than in certain thematic recurrences within the work, a trait they share with many medieval works.

On the other hand, *Mandeville's Travels* differs from *Alexander's Letter* in this respect as well, for whereas *Alexander's Letter* takes as its single focal point the folly of pagan rejection of Christianity, the *Travels* considers many and various aspects of Christianity and paganism and how they coexist and even intermingle. Thus, Christianity plays almost as large a role in Part Two of the *Travels* as it does in Part One. For example, when recounting the history of the rise of the Great Khans, Mandeville implies that the founder, Changuys (Genghis), was almost Christian. In a dream, Changuys is visited by a white knight who tells him: "the Inmortall god hath sent me to Þe & it is his wille Þat Þou go to the vij lynages & seye to hem Þat Þou schalt ben here Emperour" (*Mandeville's Travels* 147). After Changuys is elected emperor, his first decree is that all his people worship "god Inmortall Þat is allmyghty" (*Mandeville's Travels* 147). Changuys' descendents Mango Khan and Kublai Khan are described as "gode cristene m[e]n & baptyzed" (*Mandeville's Travels* 150). Of the most recent Khan, Mandeville laments, "Wherfore it is gret harm Þat he beleueth not feithfully in god. And natheles he wil gladly here speke of god And he suffreth wel Þat cristene men dwell in his lordschipe & Þat men of his feith ben made cristene men" (*Mandeville's Travels* 162), implying both that a non-Christian can be instinctively good and that the Tartars are ripe for some timely Christian evangelization.

In addition, Mandeville can describe a Christian land in terms that have little to do with religion. He says of the islands governed by Prester John that "this lond is full gode & ryche, but not so riche as is the lond of the grete Chane. For the marchauntes comen not thider so comounly for to bye marchandises as Þei don in the lond of the gret Chane, for it is to fer to trauaylle to" (*Mandeville's Travels* 179). The implication here has little to do with the spread of Christianity and much to do with the rise of trade, both current, as in the Khan's kingdom, and potential, as in the kingdom of Prester

John. The reader can observe the new emphasis on trade best by comparing Mandeville's rendering with that of his major source, Odoric of Pordenone's *Travels*. Friar Odoric, a Franciscan, journeyed in the land of the Mongols from 1316/18 until his return to Italy in 1330; he dictated his experiences shortly before his death in 1331 (Cordier 9–13). Odoric has only this to say about the land of Prester John:

> Departing from that land of Cathay and travelling westward for fifty days through many cities and towns, I arrived at the country of Prester John; but as regards him not one hundredth part is true of what is told of him as if it were undeniable. His principal city is called Tozan, and chief city though it is, Vicenza would be reckoned its superior. He has, however, many other cities under him, and by a standing compact always receives to wife the Great Khan's daughter. (Odoric of Pordenone 244–6; trans. Yule)

While Odoric remains unimpressed, he does bring up another interesting source Mandeville used for information about Prester John. "[W]hat is told of him as if it were undeniable" refers to *The Letter of Prester John,* a late twelfth-century (circa 1165) forgery purporting to be from the legendary eastern Christian emperor (Silverberg 40). The original letter as reconstructed by Friedrich Zarncke does detail quite an impressive list of riches: "emeralds, sapphires, carbuncles, topazes, chrysolites, onyxes, beryls, sardonyxes, and many other precious stones"; "For gold, silver, precious stones, beasts of every kind, and the number of our people, we believe that we are unequaled under heaven"; "The greater gates of the palace are of sardonyx inlaid with the horn of the serpent cerastes, . . . the lesser gates are of ebony; the windows are of crystal. The tables at which our court dines are some of gold and some of amethyst; the columns supporting them are of ivory" (*The Letter of Prester John* 41–5; trans. Silverberg). However, notably absent from both *The Letter* and Odoric's *Travels* is any mention of trade, as well as any comparison to the realm of the Khans. The preoccupation with trade and "marchaundise" alongside religious and political/military issues is the *Mandeville*-author's innovation. The point to be made here is that in *Mandeville's Travels* the east does not function as just another physical place waiting to be "read" (by Christians) or misinterpreted (by Alexander the Great) but rather as a multi-thematic venue full of potential meanings—religious, mercantile, and political.

Perhaps more astounding to modern readers than the "stroke of literary imagination on Mandeville's part to combine a tale of pilgrimage . . . with one of an Oriental expedition" (Howard 62) is the fact that Mandeville's fictional account was believed well into the Age of Discovery while the veracity of

Marco Polo's *Divisament dou Monde,* a nonfiction report of the writer's experiences in the east, was doubted. Critics have attempted to account for the dismissal of Polo's work by arguing that while "Marco's account is [stylistically] traditional and beyond suspicion . . . he was considered a liar mainly because he contradicted the traditional image of the Mongols" (Gosman 76) as belligerent, immoral and unclean. In contrast, supposedly, "John of Mandeville was well aware of how people thought. He composed a very intelligent 'travel account' in accordance with current European perceptions of the Middle and the Far East" (Gosman 77). This interpretation unfortunately must be rejected if the reader looks closely at what Mandeville actually says. Whereas Mandeville does note of the Mongols that "of sotyltee & of malice . . . Þei passen all men vnder heuene" (*Mandeville's Travels* 143), he also mentions their material wealth and luxury (152–3), the smooth functioning of the government bureaucracy in ruling the provinces and operating the postal service (160), and the Khan's willingness to tolerate Christianity and his eagerness to find out more about it. Mandeville does this not merely to humanize Eastern people and encourage relations with them, although this, too, is one of his aims. But he is also providing overt and covert lessons to readers, "employ[ing] . . . pagans to teach proper behavior . . . Mandeville's tolerant accounts of religious and social diversity are taken from fourteenth-century travel narratives that use the information to prove a society's pestiferous or abominable behavior: he consistently omits or reverses the prejudices and criticism of his sources" (Westrem 71–3). Mandeville's admiration for the Mongol civilization at least equals that of Marco Polo, but his admiration serves a thematic purpose perhaps absent from or less apparent in Polo's account.

In addition, Mandeville finds many good things to say about other non-European and even heathen peoples. The Bragmen, for example, while "Þei ben not cristned ne haue no perfyt lawe" (*Mandeville's Travels* 194) are virtuous and peaceful and therefore "this folk . . . ben so trewe & so feythfull, Þat god loueth hem" (*Mandeville's Travels* 197) in spite of their doctrinal shortcomings. Even more surprising is Mandeville's attitude toward the Cynocephali or Hound-heads who "ben full resonable & of gode vnderstondynge, saf Þat Þei worschipen an ox for here god" and that they cannibalize the bodies of their enemies (*Mandeville's Travels* 130). One might expect a Christian writer to condemn idolatry and cannibalism in no uncertain terms, as many earlier writers have done; Odoric, for example, refers to cannibalism as one of many "preposterous and abominable customs" (254; trans. Yule) even when it is meant as a sign of respect. Mandeville, instead, finds plenty to admire. Not only are Hound-heads reasonable, but their king is also "full riche & full myghty & right deuout after his lawe" (*Mandeville's Travels* 130).

He "is so rightfull & of equytee in his doomes Þat men may go sykerlych Þorghout all his contree & bere with him what him list, Þat noman schall ben hardy to robben him" (*Mandeville's Travels* 131), not only indicating that even a cannibalistic idolater can run a country justly, but also ascribing to that idolater one of the traditional virtues of Prester John.[1] One can see from the examples of the Mongols, the Bragmen and the Cynocephali that Mandeville did not, in fact, indulge in the prejudices of medieval Europe of which he has been accused and which would explain the popular reception of the *Travels;* if anything, Mandeville extended the evenhanded treatment Marco Polo afforded the Mongols to other races that his readers would find even more foreign and threatening.

One of the first and more surprising features the reader notices in *Mandeville's Travels* involves the interaction between Christian and non-Christian. Not only are these interactions not always, or even often, hostile, but in very many cases, the Christian and/or Christianity does not compare favorably with the non-Christian. One of the more famous examples from the *Travels,* the sultan for whom Mandeville worked, proves this point. Mandeville served the sultan, apparently of his own free will, and was favored by him for his service. Mandeville seems to admire the sultan in certain respects, speaking glowingly of his army and government and of the custom that "no straungere cometh before him but Þat he maketh him sum promys & graunt of Þat the sowdan asketh resonabely beso it be not aȝenst his lawe" (*Mandeville's Travels* 24). Mandeville's evenhanded treatment of Saracens contrasts sharply with his sources' disdain and often hatred for the "heretics" (Odoric of Pordenone 117; trans. Yule) and the "evil seed of Mohammed" (Hetoum 19; trans. Pynson). Higgins has described how the hateful diatribe of Mandeville's main source for this passage, William of Boldensele's *Liber de quibusdam ultramarinis partibus,* "disappears," to be replaced by "a lengthy, dispassionate, ethnohistorical account of the Mamluk sultanate" in which "the current Sultan is depicted almost positively" (98).

Knowing that the sultan is basically a good man and a competent ruler makes all the more shocking his long and well-known speech condemning the behavior of Christians. At one point the sultan inquires of Mandeville how Christians govern themselves, and Mandeville replies that they do very well. The sultan disagrees:

> . . . & he seyde me treulych nay,. . . for ȝee scholde ȝeuen ensample to the lewed peple for to do wel & ȝee ȝeuen hem ensample to don euyll. for the comownes vpon festyfull dayes whan Þei scholden gon to chirche to serue god, Þan gon Þei to tauernes & ben Þere in glotony all Þe day. . . .

> And also the cristene men enforcen hem in all maneres Þat Þei mowen for to fighten & for to desceyuen Þat on Þat other . . . Ihesu was in whom Þei trowe, but Þei ben all the contrarie & euere enclyned to the euyll & to don euyll. And Þei ben so coueytous Þat for a lytyll syluer Þei sellen here doughtres, here sustres & here owne wyfes to putten hem to leccherie . . . Þei defoulen here lawe Þat Ihesu crist betook hem to kepe for here saluacioun. And Þus for here synnes han Þei lost all this lond Þat wee holden. (*Mandeville's Travels* 88–9)

The obvious motive for putting such a speech in a Saracen's mouth is, of course, to provoke the Christian reader into changing his/her ways by shaming him/her, and the narrator Mandeville readily sees this (*Mandeville's Travels* 89–90). But whatever the motive may be, it remains true that the reader has here been presented with a case in which the Saracen is not evil by virtue of his religion, nor are Christians necessarily good by virtue of theirs. This contrasts sharply, for example, with the narrative Odoric relates of an encounter between Christian friars and followers of Islam in the city of Tana. This encounter, which leads eventually to the friars' martyrdom, depicts the Christians and Muslims in simplistic, even caricatured terms (Odoric of Pordenone 117–32). Likewise, the Armenian nobleman Hetoum in his *La Fleur des histoires de la terre d'Orient* cannot seem to mention the Saracens without invoking his contempt for the "false law of Mohammed" (22; trans. Pynson) and his indignation for their alleged conquests of eastern Christian lands. But in Mandeville's world, the interaction between Christian and non-Christian is neither simplistic nor one-sided, and the message itself (that Christians need to reform and Saracens are not inherently bad just because they worship Allah) is complex and multilayered, unlike the single-minded intent of *Alexander's Letter,* Hetoum's chronicle, and, as will become apparent below, John of Plano Carpini's *History of the Mongols.*

Not only does Mandeville declare that "the sarazines ben gode & feythfull" (90) but also that Christians habitually fail to live up to their own professed ideals. Christians peddle false relics, sell benefices, and behave in such reprehensible ways as to become unworthy of holding the Holy Land, thereby allowing it to be seized by unbelievers (*Mandeville's Travels* 6; 12; 49; 51–2). This refrain does not originate with Mandeville, of course, but his open-mindedness with regards to Saracen moral stature goes a bit beyond what is necessary to provoke shame and rehabilitation in the Christian conscience. Mandeville also sees great similarities between Christians and Saracens and believes the latter could be easily converted to the true faith (86–7), an idea that further implies the need for a greater Christian presence in Islamic lands. Interestingly, the same idea applies to many of the other races Mandeville encounters, including the Mongols, the Bragmen and the Cynocephali:

> And ȝȝee schull vndirstonde Þat of all Þeise contrees & of all Þeise yles & of all the dyuerse folk Þat I haue spoken of before & of dyuerse lawes & of dyuerse beleeves Þat Þei han, ȝit is Þere non of hem alle but Þat Þei han sum resoun within hem & understonynge, but ȝif it be the fewere, & Þat han certeyn Articles of oure feith & summe gode poyntes of our beleeve. (*Mandeville's Travels* 208)

That Mandeville uses virtuous Saracen behavior to provoke better behavior in Christians is neither new nor surprising, but that he also extends the potential for admirable behavior and spiritual fulfillment to much more distant and unfamiliar people points to a world view that is kinder and more open-minded than critics such as Gosman have allowed.

The reader can observe how truly astounding Mandeville's attitude is by comparing his treatment of the Hound-headed king's rosary to the treatment given him in the source. Odoric reports that "the king of that country weareth round his neck a string of three hundred very big pearls, for that he maketh to his gods daily three hundred prayers" (169; trans. Yule). Mandeville expands on Odoric:

> And he hath abouten his nekke ccc perles oryent god & grete & knotted as PATER NOSTRES here of Amber. And in maner as wee seyn oure PATER NOSTRE & oure AUE MARIA, cowntynge the PATER NOSTRES, right so this kyng seyth euery day deuoutly ccc preyeres to his god or Þat he ete. (130)

The connection between the Hound-head's prayer beads and Christian prayer beads apparently did not occur to Odoric, or, if it did, he rejected the comparison.[2] Mandeville has taken the same information and implied not only that a monstrous pagan can be as devout as any Christian but also perhaps a universal human connection within this devotion between the monstrous pagan and the average European telling his rosary beads. And such benevolent connection between Christian and non-Christian remains only one of a multitude of complex functions found in the *Travels*.

The third notable feature in *Mandeville's Travels* involves the way the scriptural and religious world interconnects with the contemporary and physical world. An excellent example of this phenomenon is found in chapter five on Cyprus and the road to Jerusalem. One often encounters contemporary geography serving almost exclusively as a prompt for recounting the spiritual or scriptural significance of the place in early pilgrim narratives. Odoric's account of the martyrdom of the friars at the hands of Muslims mentioned above was prompted by his own travel through the city of Tana. And for once Margery Kempe conforms to the practice of her time when sacred places in the Holy Land inspire "contemplacyon in Þe sygth of hir sowle," as when the physical sight of Calvary makes it appear "as yf Crist had hangyn befor hir bodily eye in hys manhode" (Kempe 70). In *Mandeville's Travels,* geography reminds the narrator not only of religiously significant details, but also of secular stories, local customs, and generally useful travel and mercantile information. Chapter five opens with a description of Cypriot wine, followed by a local legend of how necrophilia once caused the demise of an entire city, a demographic description of Cyprus, and then a more traditional account of religiously significant details inspired by the geography: the cross of the good thief and the shrines of St. Zenomyne and St. Hillary. Then, where one might expect introspective contemplation of these religious details, the chapter instead immediately proceeds to describe how the people of Cyprus use leopards instead of hounds to hunt (*Mandeville's Travels* 16–7).

The narrative then resumes a more traditional course with a description of Tyre, the first port on the passage to Jerusalem, and its religious association. The account continues in this way through many cities, such as Jaffa, Acre, and Carmel, with many religious references and the occasional local legend, and ends with practical advice about obtaining a license from the sultan to pilgrimage to Sinai and the ease with which a pilgrim can find good food and lodging (*Mandeville's Travels* 18–20). Mandeville gives a good bit of physical detail about the journey, but he also periodically digresses to recount the spiritual importance of a place, as when he links the story of Samson and Delilah to his account of Gaza (20). He also digresses to give the reader some potentially interesting trade information:

> And Þere nygh is the Foss of Mennon Þat is all round & it is an hundred cubytes of largeness & it is all full of grauell schynynge brighte of the whiche men maken faire verres & clere. And men comen fro fer by watre in schippes & be londe with cartes for to fetten of Þat grauell And Þough Þere be neuere so meche taken awey Þere of on the day at morwe it is as full aȝen as euere it was. . . . (*Mandeville's Travels* 19)

This might be considered merely yet another account of a marvel were it not for the mention of how men in ships come to harvest the gravel which is then used to make a commodity, glass; the implication of this detail makes the information clearly of the mercantile variety. *The Letter of Prester John* describes the sea itself but omits the harvesting of the gravel or any practical purpose it may serve, presenting the sea simply as a wonder (42–3).

Thus the reader finds all mixed together in this single chapter information on geography, local legend, tourism and trade intermingled with religion. Such intermingling would not be all that surprising unless one also considered the standard format for travel writing that came before the *Travels*. Early Christian travel writing consisted almost entirely of only religious matters. The narrator/traveler would identify his/her location, cite its religious associations (as a place of martyrdom or a location of importance in the Bible), and then indulge in spiritual introspection not necessarily about the place, but about the moral to be derived from the story associated with the place. Critics have lamented this strictly spiritual interest in early travelogues:

> A modern reader can . . . but regret that the reverend lady's [Abbess Etheria] interests were so exclusively spiritual. . . . a little more interest in things secular is what we should like to find in her. . . . Only rarely she permits herself to comment on the beautiful scenery in some spot or on the fine vineyards and orchards that she saw on her journeys. . . . (Laistner 31–2)

Laistner goes on to complain that "[a]s in the itineraries of pilgrims, so in the accounts of the ecclesiastical historians, scarcely any geographical information is given" (33). This is presumably the rule in early travel writing because the importance of the physical world was to be denied in favor of contemplation of the spiritual implications it inspired. "More interest in things secular" would constitute the sin of *curiositas* against which pilgrims were repeatedly warned and to which many must have succumbed, judging by the numerous polemics against it one finds in a variety of medieval genres (Zacher 42–59).

Perusal of his sources can illuminate to some extent Mandeville's departure from the religious and political format of medieval travel writing. Many of his sources, however, are not strictly Christian travelogues even when they are composed, as they often are, by professional religious; the priest or monk inevitably has another motive, usually because he is on a political as well as religious mission. Therefore, it is not surprising to find many of these accounts wandering from the original early format, yet it remains illuminating to see how the *Travels* departs from their concerns and narrative structures.

Odoric's digressions, like the one about the martyrdom of the friars already mentioned, are sometimes of a religious nature. His departure from the present to recount a past devotional lesson acted out in the place through which he is traveling conforms to the general early scheme employed by Abbess Etheria. Of perhaps greater interest is the way in which he addresses one of Mandeville's chief preoccupations, trade. While he does on occasion notice merchants and merchandise, he tends not to dwell on their particulars or on how the goods were obtained. Odoric generalizes items as "costly wares" (112; trans. Yule) or "any species of goods" (104; trans. Yule) with the notable exception of food. What kind of food is available and its cost preoccupy him to some extent, which I believe can be explained as due to the uncertain day-to-day subsistence of a wandering and, as it turned out, ill-provisioned friar.

Hetoum's account of the east differs from that of the *Travels* in fascinating and revealing ways. Hetoum does mention trade and consumer goods, but in a very perfunctory fashion:

> They [the Persians] lyue moost on marchaundyses and tyllyng of the grounde; armour nor warre they meddyll nat gladly, at this tyme vnconstrayned. In auncyent tyme they worshipped ydols, but namesly thei honoured the fyre for theyr god; but sith tyme that the wicked and false sect of Mahomet spredynge abrode came into those parties, the Persyens haue all ben Sarasyns and beleue in the false lawe of Mahumet. (13; trans. Pynson)

This passage is typical of most of Hetoum's accounts of eastern Saracens and helps reveal his true motives in writing his "histoires": to present both a survey of Saracen strongholds and the best ways to oppose them militarily and an argument for enlisting the Mongols' help in this endeavor. When Hetoum mentions Saracen mercantile activity, he does so merely in order to give a complete military report on Saracen urban strongholds.

Hetoum's depiction of the Mongols themselves also fails to give trade and merchandise the extended treatment they find in the *Travels*. His description of Tartary mentions "good cytees and ryche" (9; trans. Pynson), but what sort of activity has given rise to these riches is omitted. Riches and "treasoure" do play a role in the history of the Mongols, but this is most often a military role. Treasure serves as the reward of conquest, not trade (Hetoum 25), or even as the source of a military downfall, as when the caliph of Baldach is forced to yield his city to Tartar forces because he refused to part with his treasure to finance the necessary defenses his city required (Hetoum 39–40). Yet in spite of Hetoum's preoccupation with military matters, when it comes to his descriptions of locations of importance to Christianity, he conforms to the traditional pilgrimage model. His representative description of the "realme of Caldee" recalls two cities of Biblical importance:

> This Ninyue is the cytie of the which the Holy Scripture speketh and in the which was Ionas the Profet sende to prech the commaundement of God . . . The grettest cyte in the realme of Calde is called Babylone. In this lande Nagabudonosor brought {ȝanthetinoysonȝ} the Chyldren of Israell whan he toke Iherusalem. (15–6; trans. Pynson)

Even the *Letter of Prester John* conforms to some extent with the early travel narrative pattern. Although it describes a land that does not actually exist and its narrator is not traveling, the *Letter* still manages in one instance to use geographical description to recall Biblical and religious issues:

> Our magnificence dominates the Three Indias, and extends to Farther India, where the body of St. Thomas the Apostle rests. It reaches through the desert toward the place of the rising of the sun, and continues through the valley of deserted Babylon close by the Tower of Babel. (42; trans. Silverberg)

Prester John, like Mandeville, frequently mentions valuable consumer and luxury items, generalized "treasure" as well as particularized precious stones, cloth, wood, and balsam. However, any traffic in these items is depicted as a result of the emperor's largesse, not as a capitalist enterprise: "you [any Christian visitor] shall go laden with treasures. . . . I am a devout Christian and everywhere protect the Christians of our empire, nourishing them with alms" (*Letter of Prester John* 42; trans. Silverberg).

John of Plano Carpini's account of his own mission to the Mongol court mirrors Odoric's and Hetoum's accounts in mercantile matters. John notices costly items, but he sees them only in the context of gifts to the khan; there is no indication that he envisions any trading between East and West in regard to these riches:

> So many gifts were bestowed by the envoys there that it was marvellous to behold—gifts of silk, samite, velvet, brocade, girdles of silk threaded with gold, choice furs and other presents. . . . A certain governor of a province brought a number of camels for him, decked with brocade . . . he also brought many horses and mules covered with trappings or armour made of leather or of iron. We in our turn were asked if we wished to present any gifts, but we had by now used up practically everything, so had nothing to give him. (John of Plano Carpini 64; trans. a nun of Stanbrook Abbey)

Merchandise not only remains in the realm of gifts but also, in fact, becomes a stumbling block to John's mission since, as he repeatedly points out in exasperation, every Mongol in authority with whom he must deal expects to receive an expensive present before speaking with the Christian envoys. John's exasperation with and pointed tendency to ignore potential objects of trade most likely grows out of the fact that trade plays no part in the role he is playing as papal envoy and no part in the vision he sees of future Mongol relations with the West, which will be inevitably hostile:

> Since there is no country on earth which they fear with the exception of Christendom, they are preparing to make war on us. . . . it is their object to overthrow the whole world and reduce it to slavery—a slavery, as has already been said, unbearable for men of our race. (44–5; trans. a nun of Stanbrook Abbey)

Throughout his *History*, John displays exactly this single-minded attitude not only in his report about his mission but also in his observations of daily Mongol life, for he is interested only in discovering "how to wage war against them" (43; trans. a nun of Stanbrook Abbey). John's concerns appear to be in direct opposition to those of Hetoum, who sees the Mongols as potential allies against the Saracens, but in fact John and Hetoum differ only in their substance; the forms their arguments take resemble each other greatly, as each is very narrowly focused. Everything each man observes about the Mongols relates directly back to his vision of western religio-political relations with them, and, unlike Mandeville, neither can see beyond this vision into any other potential form of relations, nor apparently can they see the Mongols, or any other race, as an autonomous, functioning nation independent of their relations with Western Christianity.

The other side of this argument can help explain the geographical and physical preoccupations of *Alexander the Great's Letter to Aristotle* in which, in direct contrast to early Anglo-Saxon travelogues, the reader finds virtually no introspection and outright rejection of the spiritual significance of what the narrator observes. That is, the Christian perspective concentrates on spiritual insight and religious connections while providing only minimal physical description, and such description operates mostly as a spur to spiritual introspection; by extension, the pagan perspective as represented by *Alexander's Letter* would naturally concentrate only on the visible, physical world, for this is the only world the narrator, a pagan, can experience. But here in *Mandeville's Travels* one finds something profoundly different from early Christian accounts of the Holy Land, papal envoys' reports from Asia, and fictionalized pagan accounts like *Alexander's Letter*. In the *Travels* the scriptural and religious worlds intertwine in a Christian narrative to suggest that now the writer and presumably his audience would have a place in their worldview for multiple significances—religious, secular, geographical, and mercantile—derived from basically the same information or information about the same place, and Mandeville extracts these multiple meanings from sources that tend to be oblivious to matters not immediately and directly related to their own narrowly focused concerns.

The *Travels'* fourth notable feature, one mentioned in passing already, is the recurrent theme of trade and merchandise. The self-renewing gravel pit from which men take shiploads of gravel has already been examined. Numerous other examples are found in the *Travels* as well, one of the most alluring being the description of the variety of diamonds to be found in the east. Chapter eighteen begins religiously enough with the story of Job, although the text opens with a curious foreshadowing of things to come when it describes the Land of Job as "a full fair contree & a plentyfous of all godes" (*Mandeville's Travels* 100). After a description of Job's trials, the text describes several other less scripturally grounded lands, such as the land of the Amazons, Ethiopia, and India. This last country serves as a starting point for a discussion of diamonds, for Mandeville contends that India is the best country in the world for finding them. Indeed, Mandeville is so enamored of diamonds that he spends 3 1/3 manuscript pages discussing them. He describes the different kinds of diamonds that may be found in different countries, such as Araby, Macedonia and Cyprus, and the range of their quality; how they are formed; and their benefits to the wearer, including courage and health, protection from evil, and a cure for demonic possession (105–6).

One of Mandeville's chief concerns about diamonds, however, is of even greater interest here, for it is a purely mercantile digression. One might also consider the places to buy the best diamonds also of commercial concern, but the narrator does not make this explicit in the text. Toward the end of the chapter, however, Mandeville makes a point of providing clearly mercantile information:

> I schal speke a litill more of the dyamandes all þough I tarye my matere for a tyme, to þat ende þat þei þat knowen hem not be not disceyued be gabberes þat gon be the contree þat sellen hem. For whoso wil bye the dyamand, it is nedefull to him þat he knowe hem be cause þat men counterfeten hem often of cristall þat is ȝalow. (106–7)

The narrator then describes ways for the buyer to avoid being taken advantage of, and the text closes with a warning that a good diamond can lose its beneficial properties if its owner sins excessively.

The digression on diamonds demonstrates the integration of commercial endeavors into what has on occasion been described as a pilgrim narrative or a marvel book. The fact that the religious and the mercantile can here be intermingled without either subject losing its force points to multiple concerns by the fourteenth century. That Mandeville apparently suffered some indecision about which discourse, commercial or religious, should dominate "presents in sharp outline the conflict between the traditional goal of the pilgrim and the multitude of worldly goals sought by the wandering, questioning explorer" (Zacher 5). Mandeville's choice to intertwine them, both in this final warning and in their use against demonic possession, can be seen as an act of reconciliation between these two ways of thinking about diamonds and, by extension, about the world in general. The religious thus does not negate the mercantile, or worldly, way of thinking, nor does the world necessarily jeopardize religion; they are individualized, yet capable of interacting.

An almost identical episode takes place in chapter seven concerning the properties and acquisition of a certain type of balm. In Egypt, Mandeville tells the reader, one can find the most magnificent balm, which can be grown only by Christians as Saracens have had no success in its cultivation (32). But while the narrator does mention this Saracen shortcoming and that they "countrefeten it be sotyltee of craft for to disceyuen the cristene men" (33), he does not dwell on Saracen deception itself or even seem much interested in the religion of the deceiver. Instead, he concentrates on ways to assure the potential merchant of the quality of his balm: "And wyte ȝee wel Þat a man oughte to take gode kepe for to bye bawme but ȝif he cone knowe it right wel, for he may right lyghtly ben disceyued" (32). He describes several ways that "the marchauntes & the Apotecaries countrefeten it" and then offers "[b]ut ȝif it lyke ȝou I schall schewe how ȝee schull knowe & preue to the ende Þat ȝee schull not ben disceyued" (33). As with the passage on diamonds, Mandeville seems far more concerned with encouraging commerce in a valuable commodity than with using the opportunity to present a diatribe against Saracen deception.

It might be argued that the concentration on mercantilism at the expense of religious and moral contemplation derives from the fact that the diamonds and the balm come from areas where Christian landmarks and associations are lacking and thus the author has no spur to the kind of religious reflection one finds in the early Christian travelogues. However, a curious passage on Damascus, its road, and St. Paul's vision calls such a rationale into question. Chapter fifteen details the city of Damascus and the three ways to Jerusalem, an itinerary that, one would think, would give the writer ample opportunity for spiritual reflection. However, this is not how Mandeville begins; instead, he gives the reader some interesting commercial details:

> Damasce Þat is a full fayr cytee & full noble & full of all marchandises And a iij iorneyes long fro the see & a v iorneyes fro Ierusalem. But vpon Camaylles / mules / hors / dromedaries & oÞer bestes men caryen here marchandise thider, And thider comen the marchauntes with marchandise be see from ynde, persee, Caldee, Ermonye & of manye oÞere kyngdomes. (81)

Mandeville then describes Damascus' physical beauties before proceeding to perhaps its most important association, St. Paul's vision on the road to Damascus. This is recounted as matter-of-factly as the information on trade:

> And neere beside damasce was he conuerted & after his conuersioun he duelte in Þat cytee iij dayes withouten sight & withouten mete or drinke And in Þo iij dayes he was ravisscht to heuene & Þere he saugh many preuytees of oure lord. (82)

The rest of the chapter has nothing to add on the subjects of trade and St. Paul. What the reader notices here is how Mandeville attaches the same tone and, apparently, the same degree of importance to both religious and mercantile subject matter. But, as these passages show, the subject of trade is a recurring and apparently important one which is not found in, for example, *Alexander's Letter to Aristotle* or the *Wonders of the East,* in spite of the presence of gold-digging ants in the latter (9). Its presence in the *Travels* suggests not just an increase in actual real-world trade, but also a new place for the idea of trade in an ostensibly religious and personal travelogue.

Despite the author's attempt to gloss over the conflict between pagan and Christian in trade matters in the passage about the Egyptian balm, he does seem to realize that he must address the issue of Christian commerce with the spiritual enemy. One tactic he uses, which has already been touched upon, is to portray both Saracen and Mongol as moral and upright, even almost Christian, lacking only a little Christian evangelization to push them to full conversion. This resembles Hetoum's depiction of the Mongols as monotheistic and noble, but whereas Hetoum had a very specific reason for his depiction—to make the Mongols seem suitable Christian allies against the Saracens (Hetoum 26–30)—Mandeville's intent remains less obviously political. A side benefit of advocating evangelism, of course, would be that trade would undoubtedly follow, but this is never made explicit. Another tactic Mandeville uses in his effort to encourage trade between Christian and pagan involves depicting the harmony that already exists between Christians and non-Christians in these eastern countries. The vast riches of the Khan's lands have already been enumerated to some extent, and Mandeville claims he found them "more excellent & ricchere & more merueyllous Þan euer we herde speke offe" (144). This contrasts sharply with, for example, John of Plano Carpini's characterization of Tartary as "more wretched than I can possibly say"(6). To account for such riches, the narrator cleverly explains Mongol wealth by comparison in the chapter on the land of Prester John:

> And this lond is full gode & ryche, but not so riche as is the lond of the grete CHANE. For the marchauntes comen not thider so comounly for to bye marchandises as Þei don in the lond of the gret CHANE . . . (*Mandeville's Travels* 179)

To assuage possible Christian guilt over preferring to trade with the Mongols rather than with fellow Christians, Mandeville notes not only that the land of Prester John "is to fer to trauaylle to" (179), but also that the Khan is tolerant of Christianity and almost Christian himself. Thus the peace that Mandeville documents between Christian and Mongol paves the way for harmonious trading relationships, and vice versa.

He employs a similar tactic when dealing with Saracen-Christian relationships, although in this case the rationale often appears in what seem to be almost incidental, throwaway lines. When describing the busy harbor of Famagosta, "on of the princypall hauenes of the see" (17), in Cyprus, Mandeville notes that "Þere arryuen cristene men & sarazynes & men of all nacyons" (17), thereby emphasizing the good relations that can and do exist between Christians and non-Christians in a busy trading port. A similar situation exists in the realm of the emperor of Persia, whose cities the narrator describes in glowing terms. Tauris is

> . . . a full fair cytee & a gret & on of the beste Þat is in the world for marchandise. Þider comen all marchauntes . . . And men seyn Þat the Emperour taketh more gode in Þat cytee for custom of marchandise Þan doth the ricchest cristene kyng of all his reme Þat lyueth; For the toll & the custom of his marchantes is withouten estymacyoun to ben nombred. (*Mandeville's Travels* 99)

In nearby Soldania one finds "god ryueres berynge schippes" (99), and further down the road is Cassan, "a full noble cytee & a plentyfous of cornes & wynes & of all oÞer godes" (100). Amidst all this mercantile and monetary praise for the Persian empire, Mandeville offhandedly notes, "Þere duellen many cristene men vndir tribute of Sarrazines" (99). Unlike Hetoum, who laments that the Saracen Turks "haue taken the lordship of the sayd lande of the [Christian] Grekes" (17; trans. Pynson) who must now live in subjection to the heretics, Mandeville does not comment further on what might be considered such a shameful state of affairs; it does not seem to bother him that Christians live under Saracen rule, as they do not appear to be persecuted or prevented from worshipping as they please. In fact, Mandeville implies that in such a rich and well-ordered realm, Christian and Saracen can coexist and, at least in the commercial realm, benefit one another. The inclusion of the great wealth of the Persian emperor here does not seem intended to provoke Christian outrage but rather to quantify to some degree the vast amount of wealth available because of trade and to encourage Christian partaking thereof.

The radical nature of Mandeville's intentions becomes pointedly apparent when the reader considers his sources' motivations. Hetoum, very obviously, wishes to enlist Mongol help in overthrowing the Saracens and conquering the Holy Land; he even goes so far as to assert, in what must be one of history's greatest displays of willful naiveté, that "all the landes that they [the Mongols] shulde conquere vpon the Sarasins, that with a gode wyl they shulde gyue them in kepyng to the Christen men" (80; trans. Pynson). John of Plano Carpini sounds a warning to all Christendom about the military threat of the Mongols and offers practical advice for doing battle against them. Odoric simply sets out to depict all non-Christians as mistaken, backward, and sometimes evil, classifying Nestorian Christians as "schismatics and heretics" (117; trans. Yule). But in the *Travels,* the digressions into purely mercantile matters, the intermingling of Christianity and trade in the anecdotes, and the rationalizations put forth for trading with the religious enemy all function in service to the fostering of trade relations in a narrative that, at least on the surface, appears more concerned with religious issues and tabloid spectacles. I do not contend that "marchaundise" is the "real" hidden subtext of the work, but rather that the *Travels* offers its audience a variety of ways of meaning intermingled, and that commercial issues comprise merely one path of signification among many in contrast to the single paths one finds in Mandeville's sources. Monsters and marvels, as will become apparent, constitute mere vehicles for meaning along these many paths, having shed their necessarily moral and didactic significance and having become subservient to meanings that may be moral or religious but that may also be entirely secular and amoral.

One of these many paths includes, paradoxically, a warning about the perils of material greed. The *Travels* devotes three manuscript pages to a description of the Vale Perilous, a plain near the land of Prester John which acts in the narrative as a kind of testing ground for the sin of greed:

> This vale is all full of deueles & hath ben allweys. And men seyn Þere Þat it is on of the entrees of helle. In Þat vale is gret plentee of gold & syluer, Wherfore many mysbeleuynge men & manye cristene men also gon in oftentyme for to haue of the thresoure Þat Þere is, But fewe comen aȝen & namely of the mysbeleevynge men, ne of the cristene men nouÞer, for anon Þei ben strangled of deueles. (187)

The obvious lure of the Vale Perilous is the treasure therein, and this passage reminds the reader that the sin of greed and subsequent punishment do not discriminate between Christian and non-Christian, much as the virtue of trade also failed to differentiate between religions. Mandeville goes on to tell the reader how he and thirteen others, after carefully preparing themselves through hearing mass and being shriven, entered the Vale Perilous, but only nine of them came out. Mandeville places the responsibility for his own successful return upon his refusal to touch the "gold & syluer & precious stones & riche jewelles gret plentee . . . because Þat I wolde not ben put out of my deuocioun" (188). He recognizes the link between the sin of greed and the punishment of death in the Vale Perilous when, commenting on the number of bodies in Christian clothing that he saw therein, he says, "I trowe wel Þat it weren of suche Þat wenten in for couetyse of the thresoure Þat was Þere" (189).

The inclusion of the episode of the Vale Perilous might seem to contradict the encouragement to trade that the rest of the *Travels* appears to endorse wholeheartedly. However, this apparent contradiction of values—trade is good but materialism is evil—reinforces the idea presented here, that a religious and moral text is no longer necessarily unilateral in its meaning but can function in an entirely different way than its Anglo-Saxon counterparts and its own sources. Mandeville has adapted his source for this passage, Odoric, in an intriguing and subtle way. Whereas Mandeville claims that both "mysbeluynge men & manye cristene men also" are fatally tempted by the treasure in the Vale Perilous, Odoric allows that only "any unbeliever" (264; trans. Yule) is in danger from such temptation.[3] In addition, whereas Mandeville refuses the treasure himself because "I wolde not ben put out of my deuovioun," Odoric at first conceals some of the treasure in his robe, but "lest it should be a snare to hinder my escape, I cast it all down again to the ground" (265; trans. Yule). Mandeville's first adjustment of Odoric makes Christians as well as pagans subject to the sin of greed, a reflection of the radical egalitarianism found throughout the *Travels.* The second adaptation seemingly subverts this very idea, for whereas Odoric appears to have been tempted by the treasure and to have discarded it based entirely on survival instinct, Mandeville eschews it purely because of his Christian "deuocioun," which argues for the superiority of adhering to a religious—and Christian—point of view in the effort to avoid sin and death. This episode illustrates the *Travels'* confusing and often dumbfounding basis: a text can present a variety of subjects and views on these subjects, with and without the connections between them, and even apparent contradictions within a subject, thereby giving the reader—in contrast to "the ethnographic bareness that preceded Mandeville" (Campbell 150)—a more complex and therefore, in some sense, more complete view of the world s/he inhabits, if not literally then at least symbolically. In this sense, *Mandeville's Travels* is, as Campbell points out, "determined to be encyclopedic" (151). But this encyclopedic viewpoint is "eidetic, contributing enormously to our overall sense of being presented with an 'image of truth'" (Campbell 151), and as with most intuitive knowledge, overlap, plenitude, and contradiction reside together, sometimes comfortably, in this "image of truth," which is "more amenable to interpretation than simple belief" (Campbell 151).

Higgins refers to such an encyclopedic amalgam as "synthetic scholarship" whose final result is

> a new kind of work that attempts to entertain, instruct, persuade, chastise, challenge, and console its imagined audience by providing an even more comprehensive and "theologically correct" vernacular account of the world than Polo had done half a century earlier—which makes the *Mandeville*-author an entertainer, teacher, moralist, and geographer, as well as a trickster and an artist. (13)

Higgins concludes that such synthesis makes "charity, prejudice, hatred, piety, and tolerance—no less than entertainment, instruction, self-criticism and propaganda—. . . perfectly compatible with each other" (81). Howard concurs that "Mandeville was trying to write a new kind of work" that "combined the pilgrimage to the Holy Land with the missionary or mercantile voyage into the Orient; and combined the curious and vicarious intentions of some such works with the thoughtful and devotional intentions of others" (58). *Mandeville's Travels* presents the reader with various themes—the intermingling of the scriptural and religious world with the contemporary and physical one, interaction between Christian and non-Christian, the importance of merchandise, and the almost contradictory emphasis on the evils of greed—that, throughout the work, sometimes appear to stand alone and at other times appear to act upon each other. Such diversity presents difficulties to the reader attempting to classify the text, for it could be designated a pilgrim narrative, a merchant's guide, evangelical propaganda, "an anti-Papal pamphlet in disguise" (Hamelius 15), a wonder book, or even a very early attempt at multiculturalism. But as Higgins and Howard point out, the *Travels* is actually all these things at once, a synthesis dictated by an increasingly literate public who desired a "mixture of the pious, the informative, and the diverting, as well as the popular and the learned" (Higgins 268). Even more complex than the *Bestiary*, the *Travels* functions in many ways and on many levels: it addresses both religious and secular morality (and their potential conflicts, such as the thin line between commercialism and greed) as well as subjects, such as ethnography and geography, that sometimes resist moral implications. A further examination of the role of the monstrous in *Mandeville's Travels* will substantiate and bolster this view.

The monsters of the *Travels* are ubiquitous and various, but by no means uniform in their functions and meanings. Like the rest of the text, the monsters potentially have multiple meanings—religious and secular—and occasionally have no "meaning" or signification at all. Some monsters, like their ancestors in the *Physiologus,* function only spiritually; we see this in the very traditional depiction and interpretation of the phoenix. The text tells the basic story of the solitary phoenix of Heliopolis, its five hundred year lifespan, its self-immolation, and its rejuvenation after three days. An explanation of the bird's symbolism follows:

> And so Þere is no mo briddes of Þat kynde in all the world but it allone & treuly Þat is a gret myracle of god. And men may wel lykne Þat byrd vnto god be cause Þat Þere nys no god but on And also Þat oure lord aroos from deth to lyue the thridde day. (*Mandeville's Travels* 30)

The reader sees nothing new in the *Travels'* account of the phoenix; in fact, this rendering is less complex than that of the *Bestiary,* as it does not appear to address the fate of the human body after death. Aside from the phoenix's potential function as a marvelous spectacle, it seems to serve only a spiritual and religious function here.

The passage immediately preceding the phoenix appears also only to demonstrate the mystery and goodness of God through a monster, which of course also demonstrates that monsters are capable of positive symbolic meaning. This passage also has the virtue of defining the word "monster" for the reader:

> NOTA OF A MERUEYLE. At the desertes of Egypte was a worthi man Þat was an holy heremyte & Þere mette with him a Monstre Þat is to seyne a monstre is a Þing difformed aȝen kynde bothe of man or of best or of ony Þing elles & Þat is cleped a Monstre. And this monstre Þat mette with this holy heremyte was as it hadde ben a man Þat hadde ij. hornes trenchant on his forhede & he hadde a body lyk a man vnto Þe navele And benethe he hadde the body lych a goot & the heremyte asked him what he was. And the monstre answerde him & seyde he was a dedly creature such as god hadde formed & duelled in Þo desertes in purchacynge his sustynance, & besoughte the heremyte Þat he wolde preye god for him the whiche Þat cam from heuene for to sauen all mankynde & was born of a mayden & suffred passioun & deth as wee wel knowen, be whom wee lyuen & ben. And ȝit is the hede with the ij. hornes of Þat monstre at Alisandre for a merueyle. (*Mandeville's Travels* 30)

The satyr's behavior and plea to some extent recall St. Augustine's dictum that all sensible beings are human, no matter their odd shape. More generally, the passage reminds the reader that even a sensational marvel, the disembodied head of a satyr at Alexandria, can serve as religious instruction not only about doctrine (for surely all Mandeville's readers would know the essence of the creed that the satyr utters), but also implicitly about the brotherhood of all Christians, no matter their geography or physiology. In this regard Mandeville goes beyond his source, a passage in Isidore of Seville's *Etymologies*, in which the satyr functions only as a sign of heathen error but is not himself a potential member of the Christian community:

> Satyri homunciones sunt aduncis naribus; cornua in frontibus, et caprarum pedibus similes, qualem in solitudine Antonius sanctus vidit. Qui etiam interrogatus Dei servo respondisse fertur dicens: "Mortalis ego sum unus ex accolis heremi, quos vario delusa errore gentilitas Faunos Satyrosque colit." (11.2.21)

> Satyrs are poor creatures with upturned noses; they have horns on their foreheads, and are goat-footed, such as the one St. Anthony saw in the desert. And he, being questioned, is said to have answered the servant of God, saying: "I am mortal, one of the inhabitants of the waste, whom the heathen, misled by error, worship as the Fauns and Satyrs." (trans. Brehaut)

Whereas the phoenix and the satyr may communicate only explicitly religious messages, other monsters branch off into the area of secular morality as well. The Cynocephali, or Hound-heads, exemplify both good secular behavior and religious devotion. The reader may recall that the land of the Hound-heads is considered well-governed and the inhabitants reasonable and intelligent, in spite of their penchant for cannibalizing their enemies (*Mandeville's Travels* 130). In these details, the Hound-heads and their king represent a prosperous and orderly state, "a gret yle & good & fayr" (130), a description notably absent in Mandeville's source (Odoric of Pordenone 168–70). Their religious convictions are a bit more problematic. Mandeville says the Hound-heads are "resonable & of god vnderstondynge, saf Þat Þei worschipen an ox for here god" and their king is "right deuout after his lawe" (130). This seems a bit confusing, for while religious conviction is of course a good thing, Mandeville as a European Christian must recognize the heathen error of such religious convictions and thus cannot possibly endorse this particular form of devotion.

One might ask what the text is doing here. Let us return for a moment to the passage about the Hound-headed king's rosary, discussed above. Mandeville reports that the king "hath abouten his nekke ccc perles oryent gode & grete & knotted as PATER NOSTRES here of Amber. And in maner as wee seyn oure PATER NOSTRES. . . . right so this kyng seyth euery day deuoutly ccc preyeres to his god" (130). Earlier I argued that the significance of this passage was that the devotion and good governance of these people, who lack the inspired truth of Christianity, should, like the Saracens' devotion, inspire shame, self-rebuke, and reform of Christian behavior, for if these benighted pagans can govern well and behave devoutly, how scandalous it is that Christians cannot. But it may also be the case that Mandeville is insinuating that the Hound-heads' religion to some degree resembles Christianity, at least in its form, if not its content, and the similarities between their religion and ours are great enough that conversion could be achieved, given sufficient missionary impetus. Westrem points out:

> Mandeville's tolerant accounts of religious and social diversity are taken from fourteenth-century travel narratives that use the information to prove a society's pestiferous or abominable behavior: he consistently omits or reverses the prejudices and criticism of his sources. (73)

The reader must ask why Mandeville would operate in this way. Fortunately, Mandeville says himself, after a long passage detailing the similarities between Islam and Christianity, that "Þei ben lyghtly conuerted to cristene lawe whan men preche hem And schewen hem distynctly the lawe of Ijesu crist" (87). Later, he similarly laments that "it is gret harm Þat he [the Khan] beleueth not feithfully in god" (162). One may easily conclude that Mandeville's pointed emphasis on the similarity between the Hound-headed king's necklace and the Christian rosary serves as yet another reminder to his readers of the need for and potential success of Christian evangelism in Eastern lands.

If Mandeville's monsters can be positively valenced religious signifiers or simultaneously positively valenced religious and secular signifiers, then it should come as no surprise that they also sometimes only signify on the secular plane. The Pygmies are a fine example of this method of meaning. The reader learns that the Pygmies are inherently benign from the narrator's description:

> Þat ryuere goth Þorgh the lond of PIGMANS, where Þat the folk ben of lityll stature Þat ben but iij span long and Þei ben right faire & gentyll after here quantytees bothe the men & the wommen. . . . And all be it Þat the Pygmeyes ben lytyll ȝit Þei ben full resonable after here age. (138–9)

Although the reader learns nothing of the Pygmies' religious convictions, if they have any, s/he does learn that they are "reasonable" and "gentle," and certainly not representative of evil. In fact, they also represent something quite desirable: "Þeise men ben the beste worcheres of gold, syluer, coutoun, sylk & of all such thinges of ony oÞer Þat ben in the world" (138). This is high praise, but it is praise for those talents that are of commercial use in the physical world. The Pygmies exemplify good qualities, but these are qualities that are of use specifically on the secular realm; religion and morality are not disdained but are merely not taken into account. By comparison, Mandeville's source, Odoric, allows that "they do greater work in cotton, as it is called, than any people in the world" (207; trans. Yule) but omits any mention of gold, silver, and silk.

Interestingly, Odoric does address the pygmies' spiritual state very briefly when he declares that "they have rational souls like ourselves" (209; trans. Yule), a statement that Mandeville has changed to "full resonable." This translates Odoric's Latin phrase, "animam rationalem" (316n7), fairly accurately, but not exactly. The Middle English "resonable" has separate religious and secular meanings, and, according to the *Middle English Dictionary*, a common example of the former is the phrase "resonable soule," a phrase Mandeville did not use, choosing instead the more open-ended adjective. To be sure, as the *Dictionary of Medieval Latin from British Sources* explains, the Latin word "anima" also has several meanings, some of which are secular, but Odoric chose to use a phrase, "animam rationalem," whose connotation is clearly and only spiritual, although it does contain a element of "reson" as well. My point is that Odoric used a phrase that was clearly intended spiritually, and Mandeville translated the phrase with a word that has both spiritual and secular meanings even though a clearly spiritual alternative phrase, "resonable soule," was available to him. The contrast between Mandeville and Odoric in their treatments of the Pygmies is so pointed as to have led one critic to "wonder if Mandeville's text is at open war with its source" (Campbell 156).

If the Pygmies symbolize secular virtue, then a race of Cannibals symbolizes the potential evils to be derived from religious conviction. The Cannibals of Lamary profess Christianity and walk around naked because that is how Adam and Eve behaved. Were their strangeness to end here, perhaps the religious implications would be insignificant, for Mandeville's source says almost exactly the same thing:

> And in that country the heat is so excessive that all the folk there, both men and women, go naked, not clothing themselves in any wise. And they mocked much at me on this matter, saying that God made Adam naked, but I must needs go against His will and wear clothes. (Odoric of Pordenone 147; trans. Yule)

Odoric goes on to enumerate other distasteful customs of the Cannibals, but he does not indicate that they attempted to justify any behavior other than nudity with scripture.

> Now, in that country all the women be in common; and no one there can say, this is my wife, or this is my husband! But when a woman beareth a boy or a girl she giveth the child to whom she listeth of those with whom she hath consorted, and calleth him the father. (147–8; trans. Yule)

Let us observe how Mandeville expands on the information provided by Odoric:

> In Þat lond is full gret hete & the custom Þere is such Þat men & wommen gon all naked. And Þei scornen whan thei seen ony strange folk goynge clothed And Þei sayn Þat god made ADAM & EUE all naked And Þat noman scholde schame him to schewen him such as god made him . . . And Þei sayn Þat Þei beleeuen in god Þat formed the world & Þat made ADAM & EUE & all oÞer Þinges. & Þei wedden Þere no wyfes, for all the wommen Þere ben comoun & Þei forsake noman. And Þei seyn Þei synnen ȝif Þei refusen ony man, And so god commanded to ADAM & EUE & to all Þat comen of him, whan he seyde: CRESCITE ET MULTIPLICAMINI ET REPLETE TERRAM. And Þerfore may noman in Þat contree seyn: this is my wyf, ne no womman may seye: this is myn husbonde. And whan Þei han children Þei may ȝeven hem to what man Þei wole Þat hath companyed with hem. (118–9)

The reader does not find in Mandeville's version any indication that the Cannibals taunted the author with this perverse twist on Christianity as they supposedly taunted Odoric. Mandeville adds that they sincerely believe in the Christian god and has them justify not just nudity but also promiscuity with Christian theology; they even quote scripture.

The reader knows that the Cannibals are not merely sadly mistaken about scripture but are genuinely evil because they specially import children in order to eat them, a gruesome detail also found in Odoric (*Mandeville's Travels* 119; Odoric of Pordenone 148–9). Mandeville's elaboration on his source implies a lesson to be learned from the Cannibals' extensive and patently wrong interpretation of scripture: what is ordinarily a virtuous practice, the reading of the Bible and the application of its examples to one's own life, has the potential to become quite dangerous, not only to the individual, but also to the entire community. The episode thus functions as a cautionary tale about the potentially evil excesses of an inherently benign devotional activity as well as of the difficulty of constructing societal guidelines from Biblical principles.

In contrast to the symbolically heavy interpretations I have detailed here, sometimes Mandeville simply depicts a monster or monstrous race as evil, pure and simple, and makes no attempt to help the reader interpret them.

For example, a race of headless people, sometimes known as Blemmyae as in Isidore's *Etymologies,* are described in this way:

> And in anoÞer yle toward the south duellen folk of foul stature & of cursed kynde, Þat han non hedes & here eyen ben in here scholdres And here mouth is croked as an hors schoo & Þat is in the myddes of here brest. (133)

Mandeville offers no explanation why this monstrous race is "cursed." The reader may hazard a guess that this constitutes a holdover from the earlier source material, such as the *Wonders of the East,* in which an odd physical shape was sufficient to imply an equally hideous soul. While this tendency may be at work to some degree here, the reader should also remember that Mandeville takes great pains elsewhere to debunk the earlier criteria and to present monstrous-looking people as potential Christians and trading partners.

A possible explanation for Mandeville's uninterpreted monsters resides in a process I would term the secularization of Augustinian superabundance. The reader may recall that in *The City of God* St. Augustine proposed that monsters as a group exist to show "the various elements from whose likenesses and diversities he [God] contrives the beautiful fabric of the universe" (16.8; trans. Sanford and Green). They demonstrate the great expanse of His vision of the world and the variety of forms He can imagine and create—His wonderful superabundance of creation. Much later during the time of the rise of the bestiary as a form, several unmoralized, nonsymbolic monsters and animals are assimilated into the bestiary as a result of, one scholar suggests, "the general interest in Aristotle and empirical observation popular in England during the thirteenth century" (Hassig 173). These two passages taken together may suggest an explanation for Mandeville's unmoralized monsters: they are Augustine's superabundance of creation secularized into Aristotelian empiricism. If true, one might surmise that such empiricism became yet another way of looking at the world, an (almost modern) encyclopedic view, that Mandeville had to include in order to give his readers "an image of truth."

In many places Mandeville depicts monstrous races as yet another race of people, neither good nor bad nor symbolic of anything, but just there.

> And in anoÞer yle ben folk Þat han grete eres & longe, Þat hangen doun to here knees. And in anoÞer yle ben folk Þat han hors feet & Þei ben stronge & myghty and swift renneres. . . . And in anoÞer yle ben folk Þat gon vpon hire hondes & on hire feet as bestes & Þei ben all skynned & fedred & Þei wole lepen as lightly into trees & fro tree to tree as it were squyrelles or apes. . . . Many oÞer dyuerse folk of dyuerse natures ben

> Þere in oÞer yles abouten, of the whiche it were to longe to tell & Þerfore I passe ouer schortly. (134–5)

Hamelius helpfully mentions that at this point in the narrative "Odoric is abandoned" as the major source and Vincent of Beauvais' *Speculum Historiale,* an encyclopedia, is taken up (109). This may help explain some of the monsters' lack of moral explication. As Westrem has pointed out, "Mandeville's taste for 'dyverse schappes of men' enabled him to be encyclopedic in the *Travels*" (70). Higgins goes even further, arguing that Mandeville's encyclopedic intent was to make "a vision of the 'universal world': an overarching scheme within which the East's marvelous abundance of customs, manners, and diversities can be contained, made sense of, and contemplated" (79). An encyclopedia must contain not only a multitude of things, i.e., monsters, but also a multitude of ways of speaking about those things. When Mandeville fails to explain a monster, and in fact lifts his information virtually verbatim from his source, he reflects one way of speaking about them. The monsters in this case become "his 'data,' part of the total but till now fragmented image of the world he had set out to make coherent and redemptively significant" (Campbell 157). Williams has noted that while of course the monstrous was ripe for symbolic interpretation, one should not therefore assume "that what has been called the 'symbolic universe' of the mediaeval mind excluded the literal and the concrete" (11). Uninterpreted monsters, then, may constitute the literal and concrete "data" of Mandeville's East; they may be uninterpreted but not uninterpretable, not without potential symbolic meaning that remains unarticulated.

Mandeville hints at one way the reader should consider these odd races of "folk" in a passage on the Antipodes, the race of people who live on the opposite side of the planet from his European readers. In words strangely prescient of Montaigne's thoughts in *Of Cannibals,*[4] Mandeville explains the ethnocentric perspective of most people:

> For fro what partie of the erthe Þat man duell ouÞer abouen or benethen it semeth alweys to hem Þat duellen Þat Þei gon more right Þan ony oÞer folk And right as it semeth to vs Þat Þei ben vnder vs, right so it semeth hem Þat wee ben vnder hem. (123)

In contrast to his symbolic monsters, Mandeville implies here that it is entirely natural for every race of people, monstrous or European, to think of itself as "normal" while considering any deviation from its standard as abnormal. But while this response may be natural, Mandeville's purpose in pointing this out appears as an effort to unveil how arbitrary such "normality" is. Williams has explained that this was, in fact, one of the principal functions of the monster:

"Thus the monstrosity . . . functions to upset the mental expectations about the relation of the sign to what it is supposed to signify and to underscore the element of the arbitrary in the relation of the two" (5). In this light, Mandeville's uses for the monstrous in his narrative seem even more multifaceted and multi-purposeful, going beyond the merely symbolic into the realm of medieval multiculturalism and towards a truly encyclopedic nature.

The reader discovers in *Mandeville's Travels* quite a diversity of "meanings" for monsters, a diversity that reflects the myriad of subjects Mandeville addresses through the course of his work and the multiple, sometimes conflicting, opinions he has about his subjects. Monsters, like people, governments, religions, and commercial activities, can be either good or bad, symbolically religious or secular, some paradoxical combination of these categories, or determinedly non-symbolic, that is, only encyclopedic. Such a confusion and multiplicity of meanings go beyond the expansion of meanings found in the twelfth-century phenomenon of the *Bestiary,* but how might the strategies of *Mandeville's Travels* compare with a work such as *Alexander the Great's Letter to Aristotle,* a piece that, at least on a surface level, appears to have more in common with the *Travels* than with many of its own contemporaries? The contrast between the monsters of the *Travels* and those of *Alexander's Letter* makes palpable the changes that have occurred not only in thinking about the monstrous, but also in thinking generally, from the Anglo-Saxon age to the later Middle Ages.

The Cynocephali once again provide a convenient example for illustrating the shift in thinking that occurred between *Alexander's Letter* and *Mandeville's Travels.* Mandeville's Hound-heads, it will be recalled, were basically admirable creatures who exemplified good governance and religious devotion; Mandeville implies that western Christians could learn something from them. But in the *Letter,* Alexander finds a far different purpose for the Cynocephali he encounters:

> Þa æfter Þon gesawon we betweoh Þa wudu bearwas & Þa treo healfhundinga micle mængeo, Þa cwoman to Þon Þæt hie woldon us wundigan. & we Þa mid strælum hie scotodon, & hie sona onweg aflymdon Þa hie eft on Þone wudu gewiton. (29)

> After that we saw amongst the wooded groves and trees a great multitude of Cynocephali who came because they wished to wound us, and we shot them with arrows, and they soon fled away and went back into the woods. (trans. Orchard)

Alexander's Cynocephali serve no symbolic or metaphoric purpose; they merely exist as yet another kind of creature for Alexander's army to shoot. This coincides with Alexander's attitude toward symbolism in general, in that he rejects or ignores the possibility of it. Symbolic meaning has no place in his world. This rejection of higher symbolic meaning is the "moral" of the whole story, for it is Alexander's materialistic paganism that brings about such rejection.

Thus the differences that exist between *Alexander's Letter* and *Mandeville's Travels* can be perceived most easily and obviously in their respective uses of the monstrous. Alexander rejects them, or anything else, as symbolic of any higher meaning, as the sentence that completes the passage on the Cynocephali demonstrates: "Þa syÞÞan geferdon we in Þa westenn India & we Þa Þær noht wunderlices ne mærlices gesawon" ("Then we went into the Indian desert, and we saw nothing marvellous or extraordinary there") (29; trans. Orchard). The Cynocephali are, to Alexander the pagan, symbolically inconsequential. They constitute nothing but a marvelous race, and when their novelty, entertainment value, or military threat has worn off, he and his army go seek the marvelous and extraordinary elsewhere. That Alexander feels the need to note that he did not succeed in this endeavor only emphasizes that marvel-seeking was his purpose to begin with.

The reader may have noted that this last line from the section on the Cynocephali in the *Letter* greatly resembles some excerpts from *Mandeville's Travels.* After describing the physical and behavioral abnormalities of various races, Mandeville excuses himself from further description by explaining "Many oÞer dyuerse folk of dyuerse natures ben Þere in oÞer yles abouten, of the whiche it were to longe to tell & Þerfore I passe ouer schortly" (134–5). Here Mandeville includes no hint of how the reader should take the monstrous inhabitants of the east, nor does he describe them in judgmental or moralistic terms that might give the reader some idea about the symbolic meaning to be attached to them. Like Alexander, he merely passes on because the monsters have served their sensationalist purpose and he has nothing left to say about them. However, as the analysis of symbolic meanings for Mandevillean monsters shows, this non-symbolic method of speaking about monsters constitutes merely one way of speaking among many. Mandeville's Cynocephali, for example, offer both religious and secular meanings, and lack of meaning for a monster in Mandeville may function symbolically itself, as an indication of arbitrariness, since these strange races are merely another kind of human being. So the purpose behind not giving any meaning to a monster in the *Travels* differs from that behind not giving any meaning to a monster in the *Letter.* In addition, whereas one must read the entire *Letter* in order to understand the "moral" being offered, mini-lessons from the *Travels* can be taken out of their larger context and remain comprehensible. The story of the phoenix, for example, from the *Travels,* or even the story of the industrious pygmies, has a self-contained and relevant message for the reader, whereas the *Letter*'s Cynocephali do not.

The contrast between Alexandrian monsters and Mandevillean monsters can help the reader see how tracing the literary uses of monsters can illuminate the changes in thought processes that took place from the Anglo-Saxons to the Late Middle Ages. First one sees in *The Letter of Alexander to Aristotle* and the *Liber Monstrorum* among others a single-minded, focused meaning in which the monsters are a component, but are themselves meaningless outside the larger structure of the work itself . With the twelfth century one sees a radical shift away from thinking in these single-minded terms in the *Bestiary*, whose monsters can simultaneously communicate several different symbolic meanings on both religious and secular plains. In addition, the monsters of the *Bestiary* can be removed from the larger context of the complete work itself without misrepresenting or damaging the message the monster imparts.

Mandeville's Travels goes even further than the *Bestiary* in its production of multiple meanings. A great variety of meanings resides within a single narrative which, unlike the *Bestiary*, is clearly meant to be read in sequence. Even so, the meanings of individual episodes remain intact when removed from the larger project. Such organization reflects a world in which, although the meta-narrative of salvation history still has great influence, other independently produced and independently meaningful systems of signification (commercial, political, secular morality) can operate. Westrem maintains that the *Travels*' popularity "suggests audience receptivity to accounts of a journey neither allegorical nor directed at conventional pilgrimage sites" (76). Higgins also finds the explanation for the *Travels*' success within the symbiotic relationship between the work and its audience. *Mandeville's Travels*

> gives us a fascinating portrait of the lay of the ordinary written landscape—a landscape inhabited and also defined by the ever-growing number of people from various social groups who had access to books, and whose tastes ran to a historically specific mixture of the pious, the informative, and the diverting, as well as the popular and the learned. (268)

The treatment of the monstrous in the *Travels* conforms to Higgins' model, for they are, sometimes simultaneously, pious and secular, informative and diverting, symbolic and arbitrary. In the *Travels* meaning has become fluid and dependent on perspective or situation, rather than fixed as in the *Letter* or the *Liber Monstrorum*. Such fluidity necessitates the kinds of multiple meanings within each monster that one sees so often in *Mandeville's Travels*.

Conclusion

The trajectory of the monstrous from late antiquity through the later Middle Ages appears to be a progressive one. Patristic and Anglo-Saxon monsters, despite what their physical appearance might lead one to think, represent stability and order through their inevitable connection to a Higher Power. This remains true no matter the structure of the work under consideration. The symbolically self-sufficient monsters of the *Physiologus* find stability through scriptural authority, while works that must be taken as a whole, such as the *Liber Monstrorum* and *Alexander the Great's Letter to Aristotle,* ultimately always function as religious lessons. The inevitability of the divine function of monsters demonstrates the "fixity, continuity, and the inherence of semantic and social value" (Bloch 93) Bloch refers to as characteristic of the early medieval mindset. In the twelfth century this gives way, as seen in the *Bestiary,* to a more fluid method of signifying in which new, not necessarily religious meanings of monsters coexist beside the traditional, stable meanings. Even later, *Mandeville's Travels* takes an entirely idiosyncratic approach to monsters and their meanings, denying the creatures any necessary link to morality or spirituality while still allowing for the possibility of such a link. Not only overlap of meaning, as seen in the *Bestiary,* but also apparent contradictions are manifest in the symbolic meanings of Mandeville's monsters. At this point the idea of ontologically determined and fixed meaning has given way, as Bloch puts it, to "a system of value in which worth is created not so much by origin as by relative position with a more fluid whole" (172).

The changes outlined here do indeed make the discourse of the monstrous look like "progress" from a God-centered cosmology to a kind of proto-scientific consideration of the monster on an individual basis. However, having documented the changes that have taken place, I would like to suggest that the elements of the study of medieval monsters that remain stable throughout the millennium under consideration are also significant and suggest that "progressive" does not adequately describe the trajectory in question.

All the monstrous works discussed here share four common elements: the use of the monster as a sign; the consideration of the monster as a literary endeavor; the ultimate function of the monster as a vehicle for human introspection; and the tendency of the monster to remain stubbornly on the periphery. These similarities, as well as the "progressive" differences, must inform any conclusions derived from the monstrous about the medieval mentality.

The monster is always a sign of something else. This occurs most obviously in works such as the *Physiologus* and its offspring, the *Bestiary*, wherein a monster represents a specific virtue or vice or an illustration of a divine mystery. In *Mandeville's Travels* the monster comes to signify all manner of subjects beyond the moral and religious spheres, but its role as a symbol remains consistent. Even in those works wherein the monster appears simply to exist, it is inevitably part of a larger structure of meaning, as in their representation of proof of God's magnificent superabundance for St. Augustine or as elements in the task of determining religious reliability in the *Liber Monstrorum*. The tendency to insist on a symbolic meaning for the monstrous delineates the medieval period from both Antiquity and the Renaissance. Pliny's work testifies as to the fact that the monster as a symbol of divine intent was not uncontested in his age; Foucault's comments on the Renaissance display of exotica are also pertinent here:

> It is often said that the establishment of botanical gardens and zoological collections expressed a new curiosity about exotic plants and animals. In fact, these had already claimed men's interest for a long while. What had changed was the space in which it was possible to see them and from which it was possible to describe them. (Foucault, *The Order of Things* 131)

Whereas the Renaissance set out to arrange exotic animals, i.e., monsters, and everything else "scientifically," according to the material relationships amongst them, the Middle Ages instead described monsters within the "space" of symbolic meaning. In fact, I would venture to say that the medieval monster could not exist without its symbolic significance, and this remains true for every period of the Middle Ages.

Monsters could serve symbolic functions precisely because "[t]here is no difference between the visible marks that God has stamped upon the surface of the earth, so that we may know its inner secrets, and the legible words that the Scriptures . . . have set down in the books preserved for us" (Foucault, *The Order of Things* 33). One consequence of this is the second component all medieval monsters have in common: they are always literary endeavors. One might protest that this is necessarily true because the records we have of their occurrence are contained in books, but their literary participation goes beyond this simple observation. Knowles' summary of the medieval academic point of view, "all arts and sciences can be acquired from books in the cloister" (130), speaks to the intensely literary approach to natural history, and thus to the monstrous, taken by the periods under consideration here. The primary sources bear out this contention. All the monsters observed in this study are in some way literary. Isidore's monsters are explained by an examination of their names; the *Physiologus*' monsters are explicated through scripture; the creatures of the *Bestiary* are allegorical; and Mandeville's monsters, while purporting to be observed and verifiable "facts," result from an intensely literary accumulation and re-writing and not from anything the author might have seen and simply reported. Foucault differentiates the Renaissance from the medieval point of view by noting the former's impulse to "look rather than read, verify rather than comment" (*The Archaeology of Knowledge* 218; trans. Sheridan). The medieval monster is meant to be read, rather than observed, and commented on, that is, interpreted; even when it is "looked at," as in manuscript illustrations, the picture itself is intended for interpretation and not "verification." The medieval monster's undeviating participation in the acts of reading and interpretation makes the monster a distinctly literary endeavor.

The medieval monster also, in its function as an interpreted symbol, is ultimately an exercise in introspection. That is, what the reader learns from the monster is always meant to be incorporated into his/her psyche as an aid to the individual's understanding of the world, of him- or herself, and, on many occasions, of God. In his *De Incarnatione Christi,* Alain de Lille writes:

> Omnis mundi creatura
> Quasi liber, et pictura
> Nobis est, et speculum.
> Nostrae vitae, nostrae mortis,
> Nostri status, nostrae sortis,
> Fidele signaculum. (579)
>
> Every creature in the world is to us like a book and a picture and a mirror. Our lives, our deaths, our situations, our fates are truly signified. (my translation)

That all creatures, including monsters, are "[q]uasi liber" speaks to the literary function mentioned above; that they are also "speculum" indicates that creatures can and should tell the reader something about him- or herself. The repetition of "nostrae/i" leaves no doubt about the real purpose behind the study of "[o]mnis mundi creatura." Clearly, in their religious and moral functions, monsters can help form the reader's interiority, but even Mandeville's monsters can force the reader to reconsider his/her presumptions, values, and categories.

Lastly, I must conclude, in spite of my effort to foreground the monster as my subject, that monsters persist in remaining on the periphery. Even those works that purport to be about monsters, like the *Liber Monstrorum,* are truly about something else, and the monsters contained therein actually point to the "real" subject—religious authority in the case of the *Liber Monstrorum*—instead of telling the reader anything about themselves. The *Wonders of the East,* for example, lists and describes monsters and marvels but then annihilates any pleasure the reader may have taken in their monstrous sensationalism by ending on a clearly religious note. Both alternative endings, the story of Jamnes and Mambres and the tale of the accursed dancers, actually shame the reader for any sensational pleasure s/he may have experienced, decentering the monsters and marvels in the process and replacing them with religious instruction. This process corresponds to the visual depiction of the monster on mappaemundi in which the monstrous races are always confined on the edges of the world with Jerusalem at the center. Even in *Mandeville's Travels,* the monster remains in a servant position to the central subjects of politics, trade, social relations, and religion.

Thus the apparently "progressive" trajectory of the medieval monster is itself contained within a stable, one might even say stagnant, set of presuppositions. What and how the monster may signify changes, but that it must signify is always assumed. The monster may accumulate various and even contradictory meanings along its chronological progression, but these meanings always aim to help construct the reader's interior world in some way. And the monster seems to acquire more freedom of movement, more "agency" in the course of its journey, yet it remains confined to the edges of the world and of literary imagination. Such change within stability seems somehow appropriate to the subject matter, the monster itself being a kind of exercise in contradiction.

Concerning the medieval mindset, the path of the monster indicates a mentality developing from fixed to fluid, perhaps, but also firmly committed to the literary and introspective evaluation of the external world. The discovery of the New World and the scientific developments of the Renaissance will, of course, bring into question and ultimately replace, to a great extent, such a world view, and the monster will eventually cease to be regarded as a serious subject. It will be relabeled as an exotic species or a mere "freak," and will lose much of its power (Wittkower 188–97). But this reconfiguration and what it indicates about the mentality of our "scientific" age is a subject for a different study.

Notes

NOTES TO CHAPTER ONE

1. The long b-version entry on the adamant stone expands greatly on the short y-version entry, and because it represents an "important addition," Curley has "translated [it] and put [it] in square brackets" (Introduction xxxiii). I use here only Curley's translation of the b-version because Carmody has not provided a Latin transcription of the b-version entries for Amos, Adamas, and Margarita, and I have been unable to locate any other Latin reproduction of the b-version of these entries.

NOTES TO CHAPTER TWO

1. While it is not absolutely certain that the author had direct knowledge of Vergil's *Aeneid*, it seems likely given the fact that the *Liber Monstrorum* so vividly reproduces the detail of the Cyclops holding two men in one hand and eating them raw; see Vergil *Aeneid*, III.622–40.
2. Some confusion concerning section divisions and their numbers exists. The section Orchard refers to as 37 is numbered 38 in James. In this analysis, the section numbers will correspond to those of the edition from which the quotation is taken.
3. For a reproduction of this highly detailed and tragically destroyed map, see Woodward 310, fig. 18.19. Woodward notes that in all T-O maps, the T "represented a cross" which "reinforce(s) the symbolization of the Passion of Christ" (334). In addition, the "inclusion of 'Christ in Glory' at the head of several mappaemundi demonstrates the third symbolic stage of Christian history, that of the Last Judgment" (335). For an example, see the reproduction of the Psalter Map, fig. 18.63 (Woodward 350). My point is that the function of monsters corresponds roughly to that of the maps in which they often appear: "The function of medieval mappaemundi was largely exegetic" (Woodward 334).

NOTES TO CHAPTER THREE

1. Hassig suggests these new creatures without explication are also a response to changes in the medieval worldview. The lack of moralization "might be related to the general interest in Aristotle and empirical observation" (173). The appearance of everyday animals may relate to the intrusion of economics into the *Bestiary;* the hare, rabbit and squirrel appeared as their pelts were becoming "increasingly popular for providing fur for garments" (174); new domestic animals also appear in the *Bestiary,* often performing their household or agricultural tasks (174–5).
2. In this case the source is Vergil's *Aeneid* 6.288, 7.785–8; the author seems to use Greek or Roman equally and interchangeably as a term of scorn and doubtful validity.
3. This information comes from the Y version of the *Physiologus* because the B version omits the entry on the viper.
4. There seems to have been a great deal of confusion concerning whether sirens were women-fish or woman-birds. The *Liber Monstrorum* obviously depicts them as half fish ("little sea girl"), whereas the description here implies that they are half bird. However, the illustration accompanying this particular entry has both wings and birds' feet and a fish tail. Many other bestiaries seemed to have suffered from the same kind of confusion, and one, MS Royal 2.B.VII conveniently provides an illustration of one of each kind; see Hassig, figures 108–115.
5. I am reproducing only a translation here because the Latin of the *Cambridge Bestiary* has never been transcribed. The interested reader can find a facsimile of the Latin manuscript in *The Bestiary,* ed. M.R. James (Oxford: Oxford UP, 1928).
6. Scholars generally agree that the idea of empirical observation as a worthy academic activity began with Albert the Great who had the good fortune to be born immediately after the twelfth-century Renaissance (c. 1193); see Scanlan's introduction to *Man and the Beasts: De Animalibus (Books 22–26).* Interestingly, a great body of empirical information about the natural world was available prior to Albert, but it was largely ignored by serious scholars; see Stannard, "Natural History."

NOTES TO CHAPTER FOUR

1. "There are no poor among us; we receive all strangers and pilgrims; thieves and robbers are not found in our land, nor do we have adultery or avarice" (*The Letter of Prester John;* trans. Silverberg).
2. Whereas the rosary *per se* had not taken its full and official form during the lifetime of Odoric or of the *Mandeville* author, the practice of keeping track of one's prayers by "telling" beads "existed long before St. Dominic" (c.

1171–1221), whose followers "did promote its use," according to the *Dictionary of the Middle Ages*' entry on the rosary.

3. Cordier points out in his footnote to this passage that the Latin manuscript reads "si aliquis infidelium," so perhaps "infidel" would be an even better translation than "unbeliever" and more in keeping with Odoric's religious intolerance.
4. Two-hundred years after Mandeville, Montaigne would write, as though it were an original idea, that "each man calls barbarism whatever is not his own practice; for indeed it seems we have no other test of truth and reason than the example and pattern of the opinions and customs of the country we live in. *There* is always the perfect religion, the perfect government, the perfect and accomplished manners in all things" (89; trans. Frame).

Bibliography

Aberdeen Bestiary Project. Ed. Iain Beavan et al. 1996. Aberdeen University Library. 3 Oct. 2000. http://www.clues.abdn.us.uk:8080/besttest/alt/translat.

Alain de Lille. *Alani de Insulis: Opera Omnia.* Ed. J. P. Migne. Patralogia Latina, vol. 210. Paris: Petit-Montrouge, 1855.

Albert the Great. *Man and the Beasts: De Animalibus, Books 22–26.* Trans. and ed. James J. Scanlan. Binghamton: Medieval & Renaissance Texts & Studies, 1987.

Aldhelm. *Aldhelm: The Poetic Works.* Eds. and trans. Michael Lapidge and James L. Rosier. Cambridge: D. S. Brewer, 1985.

Aldhelm. *The Riddles of Aldhelm.* Ed. James Hall Pitman. New Haven: Yale UP, 1925.

Amsler, Mark. *Etymology and Grammatical Discourse in Late Antiquity and the Early Middle Ages.* Studies in the History of the Language Sciences. Philadelphia: John Benjamins Publishing Company, 1989.

Aquinas, Saint Thomas. *Summa Theologiae, vol. I.* Trans. and ed. Thomas Gilby, O. P., et al. Cambridge: Blackfriars, 1964.

ARTFL Project: Multi-Lingual Bibles: Latin Vulgate Bible. Ed. Mark Olsen. N.d. University of Chicago. 20 Sept. 2000 http://www.lib.uchicago.edu/efts/ARTFL/public/bibles/vulgate.search.html.

Augustine, Saint. *The City of God Against the Pagans.* Trans. and ed. by EvaMatthews Sanford and William McAllen Green. Cambridge: Harvard UP, 1965.

Bately, Janet. "Those Books That Are Most Necessary for All Men to Know: The Classics and Late Ninth-Century England, a Reappraisal." *The Classics in the Middle Ages.* Eds. Aldo S. Bernardo and Saul Levin. Medieval & Renaissance Texts & Studies. Binghamton: Center for Medieval and Early Renaissance Studies, 1990. 45–78.

Baxter, Ron. *Bestiaries and Their Users in the Middle Ages.* Stroud, England: Sutton Publishing Ltd., 1998.

Beagon, Mary. *Roman Nature: The Thought of Pliny the Elder.* Oxford: Clarendon Press, 1992.

Beer, Jeanette. "Duel of Bestiaries." *Beasts and Birds of the Middle Ages: The Bestiary and Its Legacy.* Eds. Willene B. Clark and Meradith T. McMunn. Philadelphia: University of Pennsylvania Press, 1989. 96–105.

Beer, Jeanette. Preface. Fournival ix-xxxi.

Beer, Rudiger Robert. *Unicorn: Myth and Reality.* Trans. Charles M. Stern. New York: Mason Charter, 1977.

Bennet, J. W. *The Rediscovery of Sir John Mandeville.* London: Oxford UP, 1954.

Beowulf and the Fight at Finnsburg. 3rd ed. Ed. Fr. Klaeber. Boston: D.C. Heath and Company, 1950.

Bessinger, J. B., ed. *A Concordance to the Anglo-Saxon Poetic Records.* Ithaca and London: Cornell UP, 1978.

The Bestiary. Ed. M. R. James. Oxford: Oxford UP, 1928.

Biggs, Frederick M., and Thomas N. Hall. "Traditions Concerning Jamnes and Mambres in Anglo-Saxon England." *Anglo-Saxon England* 25 (1996): 69–89.

Blackwell Encyclopedia of Anglo-Saxon England. Eds. Michael Lapidge, John Blair, Simon Keynes, and Don Scragg. Oxford: Blackwell Publishers, 1999.

Blaise, Albert, ed. *Lexicon Latinitatis Medii Aevi.* Turnholti: Typographi Brepols, 1975.

Bloch, R. Howard. *Etymologies and Genealogies.* Chicago: University of Chicago Press, 1983.

Boethius. *Boetii: Opera Omnia.* Ed. J. P. Migne. Patrologia Latina, vol. 64. Paris: Petit-Montrouge, 1891.

Brehaut, Ernest. *An Encyclopedist of the Dark Ages: Isidore of Seville.* New York: Columbia UP, 1912. New York: B. Franklin, 1964.

Bynum, Caroline Walker. "Wonder." *The American Historical Review* 102 (February 1997): 1–26.

Campbell, Mary. *The Witness and the Other World: Exotic European Travel Writing, 400–1600.* Ithaca: Cornell UP, 1988.

Carmody, Francis J. Introduction. *Physiologus Latinus Versio Y* 95–134.

Cary, George. *The Medieval Alexander.* Cambridge: Cambridge UP, 1956. New York: Garland Publishing Inc., 1987.

Chibnall, Marjorie. "Pliny's *Natural History* and the Middle Ages." *Empire And Aftermath.* Ed. T. A. Dorey. London and Boston: Routledge & Kegan Paul, 1975. 57–78.

Clark, Willene B., and Meredith T. McMunn, eds. *Beasts and Birds of the Middle Ages: The Bestiary and Its Legacy.* Philadelphia: University of Pennsylvania Press, 1989.

Cordier, Henri. Introduction. Yule 3–35.

Cox, Patricia. "The *Physiologus:* A *Poiesis* of Nature." *Church History* 52 (December 1983): 433–43.

Curley, Michael. Introduction. *Physiologus* ix-xliii.

Curley, Michael. Notes. *Physiologus* 68–92.

Curtius, Quintus. *Quintus Curtius: History of Alexander.* Trans. and ed. John C. Rolfe. Loeb Classical Library. Cambridge: Harvard UP, 1946.

Defarrari, Roy J. *A Latin-English Dictionary of St. Thomas Aquinas.* Boston: St. Paul's Editions, 1960.

Dictionary of Medieval Latin from British Sources. Ed. R. E. Latham. London: Oxford UP, 1975–2002.

Dictionary of the Middle Ages. Ed. Joseph R. Strayer. New York: Scribner's, 1982–89.

Diekstra, F. N. M. "The *Physiologus,* the Bestiaries and Medieval Animal Lore." *Neophilologus* 69 (January 1985): 142–55.

Foucault, Michel. *The Archaeology of Knowledge and the Discourse on Language.* Trans. A. M. Sheridan Smith. New York: Pantheon Books, 1972.

Foucault, Michel. *The Order of Things: An Archaeology of the Human Sciences.* New York: Pantheon Books, 1971. New York: Vintage Books, 1994.

Fournival, Richard de. *Master Richard's Bestiary of Love and Response.* Trans. and ed. by Jeanette Beer. Berkeley and Los Angeles: University of California Press, 1986.

Freeman, Margaret B. *The Unicorn Tapestries.* New York: E. P. Dutton, Inc., 1976.

Friedman, John Block. *The Monstrous Races in Medieval Art and Thought.* Cambridge: Harvard UP, 1982.

———. "Peacocks and Preachers: Analytic Technique in Marcus of Orvieto's *Liber de moralitatibus,* Vatican lat. MS 5935." *Beasts and Birds of the Middle Ages: The Bestiary and Its Legacy.* Eds. Willene B. Clark and Meradith T. McMunn. Philadelphia: University of Pennsylvania Press, 1989. 179–96.

George, Wilma, and Brundson Yapp. *The Naming of the Beasts: Natural History in the Medieval Bestiary.* London: Gerald Duckworth & Co., Ltd., 1991.

Georgianna, Linda. "King Hrethel's Sorrow and the Limits of Heroic Action in *Beowulf.*" *Speculum* 62 (1987): 829–50.

Gerald of Wales. *Giraldi Cambrensis Opera.* Ed. George F. Warner. London: Eyre & Spottiswoode, 1891.

Gosman, Martin. "Marco Polo's Voyages: The Conflict between Confirmation and Observation." *Travel Fact and Travel Fiction.* Ed. Zweder von Martels. Leiden, the Netherlands: E. J. Brill, 1994. 72–84.

Grant, Edward. *Physical Science in the Middle Ages.* Cambridge: Cambridge UP, 1977.

Hamelius, P. Introduction. *Mandeville's Travels.* EETS, o.s., 154. London: Kegan Paul, Trench, Trubner & Co., Ltd., 1919. 1–22.

Hanning, Robert. *The Individual and the Twelfth-Century Romance.* New Haven: Yale UP, 1977.

Harper's Latin Dictionary. Ed. E. A. Andrews. New York: American Book Company, 1907.

Haskins, Charles Homer. *The Renaissance of the Twelfth Century.* Cambridge: Harvard UP, 1927.

Hassig, Debra. *Medieval Bestiaries: Text, Image, Ideology.* Cambridge: Cambridge UP, 1995.

Healy, John F. Introduction. Pliny the Elder *Natural History: a Selection,* ix–xl.

Hetoum of Armenia. *A Lytell Cronycle.* Trans. Richard Pynson. Ed. Glenn Burger. Toronto: University of Toronto Press, 1988.

Higgins, Iain Macleod. *Writing East: The "Travels" of Sir John Mandeville.* Philadelphia: University of Pennsylvania Press, 1997.

Houwen, L. A. J. R. "Flattery and the Mermaid in Chaucer's *Nun's Priest's Tale.*" *Animals and the Symbolic in Mediaeval Art and Literature.* Ed. L. A. J. R. Houwen. Groningen, the Netherlands: Egbert Forsten, 1997. 77–92.

Howard, Donald R. *Writers and Pilgrims: Medieval Pilgrimage Narratives and Their Posterity.* Berkeley: University of California Press, 1980.

Howe, Nicholas. "Aldhelm's *Enigmata* and Isidorian Etymology." *Anglo-Saxon England* 14 (1985): 37–59.

———. *The Old English Catalogue Poems.* Anglistica. Copenhagen: Rosenkilde & Bagger, 1985.

Hugh of Fouilloy. *The Medieval Book of Birds: Hugh of Fouilloy's Aviarium.* Trans. and ed. Willene B. Clark. Binghamton: Medieval & Renaissance Texts & Studies, 1992.

Isidore of Seville. *Isidori Hispalensis Episcopi: Etymologiarum sive originum libri XX.* Ed. W. M. Lindsay. Oxford: Clarendon Press, 1911.

James, M. R., ed. *Marvels of the East: A Full Reproduction of the Three Known Copies.* Oxford: Oxford UP, 1929.

John of Plano Carpini. *Mission to Asia.* Trans. a nun of Stanbrook Abbey. Ed. Christopher Dawson. London: Sheed & Ward, Ltd., 1955. New York: Harper & Row, 1966.

Jolly, Karen. "Father God and Mother Earth: Nature-Mysticism in the Anglo-Saxon World." *The Medieval World of Nature.* Ed. Joyce Salisbury. Garland Medieval Casebooks. New York: Garland Publishing, Inc., 1993. 221–52.

Kempe, Margery. *The Book of Margery Kempe.* Ed. Sanford Brown Meech. EETS, o.s. 212. London: Oxford UP, 1940.

Knowles, David. *The Evolution of Medieval Thought.* 2nd ed. London: Longman Group UK Ltd., 1988.

Laistner, M. L. W. "The Decay of Geographical Knowledge and the Decline of Exploration, A. D. 300–500." *Travel and Travellers of the Middle Ages.* Ed. Arthur Percival Newton. London: Routledge & Kegan Paul, 1926. 19–38.

Lapidge, Michael. "*Beowulf,* Aldhelm, the *Liber Monstrorum,* and Wessex." *Studi Medievali* 23 (1982): 151–92.

Lapidge, Michael, and James L. Rosier. Introduction. *Aldhelm: The Poetic Works.* 1–24.

Lapidge, Michael, and James L. Rosier. Notes. *Aldhelm: The Poetic Works.* 220–68.

Le Goff, Jacques. *The Medieval Imagination.* Trans. Arthur Goldhammer. Chicago: University of Chicago Press, 1988.

Le Goff, Jacques. *Time, Work, and Culture in the Middle Ages.* Trans. Arthur Goldhammer. Chicago: University of Chicago Press, 1980.

Letter of Alexander the Great to Aristotle. Orchard 224–53.

Letter of Prester John. Trans. Robert Silverberg. Silverberg 41–5.

Lewis, C. S. *The Discarded Image.* Cambridge: Cambridge UP, 1964.

Liber Monstrorum. Orchard 254–317.

Locher, A. "The Structure of Pliny the Elder's *Natural History.*" *Science in the Early Roman Empire: Pliny the Elder, His Sources and Influence.* Eds. Roger French and Frank Greenaway. London: Croom Helm, Ltd., 1986. 20–9.

Mandeville's Travels. Ed. P. Hamelius. EETS, o.s., 153. London: Kegan Paul, Trench, Trubner & Co., Ltd., 1919.

Maurus, Rhabanus. *B. Rabani Mauri: Opera Omnia.* Ed. J. P. Migne. Patralogia Latina, vol. 109. Paris: Petit-Montrouge, 1864.

McCulloch, Frances. *Medieval Latin and French Bestiaries.* Studies in the Romance Languages and Literatures. Chapel Hill: University of North Carolina Press, 1960.

McMunn, Meradith T. "Bestiary Influences in Two Thirteenth-Century Romances." *Beasts and Birds of the Middle Ages: The Bestiary and Its Legacy.* Eds. Willene B. Clark and Meradith T. McMunn. Philadelphia: University of Pennsylvania Press, 1989. 134–50.

McNelis, James I. "A Greyhound Should Have 'Eres in Þe Manere of a Serpent': Bestiary Material in the Hunting Manuals *Livre de chasse* and *The Master of Game.*" *Animals and the Symbolic in Mediaeval Art and Literature.* Ed. L. A. J. R. Houwen. Groningen, the Netherlands: Egbert Forsten, 1997. 67–76.

Middle English Dictionary. Ann Arbor: University of Michigan Press, 1952–2001.

Montaigne, Michel de. *Montaigne's Essays and Selected Writings.* Trans. and ed. Donald M. Frame. New York: St. Martin's Press, 1963.

Morson, John. "The English Cistercians and the Bestiary." *Bulletin of the John Rylands Library* 39 (September 1956): 146–70.

Moseley, C. W. R. D., ed. and trans. *The Travels of Sir John Mandeville.* New York: Penguin Books, 1983.

O'Donnell, James J. *Augustine.* Boston: G. K. Hall & Company, 1985.

Odoric of Pordenone. *The Travels of Friar Odoric.* Trans. Henry Yule. Yule 97–277.

Ogilvy, J. D. A. *Books Known to the English, 597–1066.* Cambridge, Massachusetts: The Medieval Academy of America, 1967.

Orchard, Andy. *Pride and Prodigies: Studies in the Monsters of the Beowulf-Manuscript.* Cambridge: D. S. Brewer, 1995.

Orosius. *The Old English Orosius.* Ed. Janet Bately. EETS, s.s. 6. London and New York: Oxford UP, 1980.

Oxford Latin Dictionary. Oxford: Oxford UP, 1968–82.

Physiologus. Trans. and ed. Michael Curley. Austin: University of Texas Press, 1979.

Physiologus Latinus: editions preliminaires versio B. Ed. Frances Carmody. Paris: Librairie E. Droz, 1939.

Physiologus Latinus Versio Y. Ed. Francis Carmody. University of California Publications in Classical Philology. Berkeley: University of California Press, 1941.

Pliny the Elder. *Natural History: a Selection.* Trans. and ed. John F. Healy. New York: Penguin Books, 1991.

———. *Pliny: Natural History.* Trans. H Rackham and D. E. Eichholz. Ed. H. Rackham. Loeb Classical Library. Cambridge and London: Harvard UP, 1938–91.

Rackham, H. Introduction. Pliny the Elder *Pliny: Natural History,* vii-xiv.

Reynolds, L. D., and N. G. Wilson. *Scribes and Scholars: a Guide to the Transmission of Greek and Latin Literature.* 3rd ed. Oxford: Clarendon Press, 1991.

Ross, D. J. A. *Alexander Historiatus: A Guide to Medieval Illustrated Alexander Literature.* London: The Warburg Institute, 1963.

———. *Studies in the Alexander Romance.* London: The Pindar Press, 1985.

Rowland, Beryl. "The Art of Memory and the Bestiary." *Beasts and Birds of the Middle Ages: The Bestiary and Its Legacy.* Eds. Willene B. Clark and Meradith T. McMunn. Philadelphia: University of Pennsylvania Press, 1989. 12–25.

Rypins, Stanley. *Three Old English Prose Texts.* EETS, o.s., 161. London: Oxford UP, 1924.

Salisbury, Joyce. *The Beast Within: Animals in the Middle Ages.* New York: Routledge, 1994.

———, ed. *The Medieval World of Nature.* Garland Medieval Casebooks. New York: Garland Publishing, Inc., 1993.

Scaglione, Aldo. "The Classics in Medieval Education." *The Classics in the Middle Ages.* Eds. Aldo S. Bernardo and Saul Levin. Medieval & Renaissance Texts & Studies. Binghamton: Center for Medieval and Early Renaissance Studies, 1990. 343–62.

Scanlan, James J. Introduction. Albert the Great 1–56.

Seymour, M. C., ed. *Mandeville's Travels.* Oxford: Clarendon Press, 1967.

———. *Sir John Mandeville.* Hants, U. K.: Ashgate Publishing Ltd., 1993.

Silverberg, Robert. *The Realm of Prester John.* Garden City, New York: Doubleday & Company, Inc., 1972.

Sisam, Kenneth. *Studies in the History of Old English Literature.* Oxford: Clarendon Press, 1953.

Spencer, H. Leith. *English Preaching in the Late Middle Ages.* Oxford: Clarendon Press, 1993.

Stannard, Jerry. "Natural History." *Science in the Middle Ages.* Ed. David C. Lindberg. Chicago: Chicago UP, 1978. 429–60.

Thompson, C. J. S. *The Mystery and Lore of Monsters.* London: Williams & Norgate, Ltd., 1930. Barnes & Noble, 1994.

Thurston, Mary Elizabeth. *The Lost History of the Canine Race.* Kansas City: Andrews and McMeel, 1996.

Vance, Eugene. *From Topic to Tale: Logic and Narrativity in the Middle Ages.* Minneapolis: University of Minnesota Press, 1987.

Vergil. *Vergil's Aeneid: Books I-VI.* Ed. Clyde Pharr. New York: D. C. Heath & Company, 1930.

Westrem, Scott. "Two Routes to Pleasant Instruction in Late Fourteenth-Century Literature." *The Work of Dissimilitude: Essays from the Sixth Citadel Conference on Medieval and Renaissance Literature.* Eds. David Allen and Robert White. Cranbury, New Jersey: Associated University Presses, 1992. 67–80.

Whitbread, L. G. "The *Liber Monstrorum* and *Beowulf.*" *Medieval Studies* 36 (1974): 434–71.

White, T. H., trans. and ed. *The Bestiary: a Book of Beasts.* New York: G. P. Putnam's Sons, 1954.

Wigginton, Waller, and Trent Stephens. "The Monsters and Theology of Isidore of Seville, Ulisse Aldrovandi, and Modern Science." *Rendezvous: Journal of Arts and Letters* 25 (Fall 1989): 67–82.

Williams, David. *Deformed Discourse: The Function of the Monster in Medieval Thought and Literature.* Montreal: McGill-Queens University Press, 1996.

Wirtjes, Hanneke, ed. *The Middle English Physiologus.* EETS, o.s., 299. Oxford: Oxford UP, 1991.

Wittkower, Rudolf. "Marvels of the East: A Study in the History of Monsters." *Journal of the Warburg and Courtauld Institute* 5 (1942): 159–97.

Wonders of the East. Orchard 183–203.

Woodward, David. "Medieval *Mappaemundi.*" *The History of Cartography.* Vol. 1. Eds. J. B. Harley and David Woodward. Chicago and London: Chicago UP, 1987.

Wormald, Patrick. "Anglo-Saxon Society and its Literature." *The Cambridge Companion to Old English Literature.* Eds. Malcolm Godden and Michael Lapidge. Cambridge: Cambridge UP, 1991. 1–22.

Yule, Henry, ed. and trans. *Cathay and the Way Thither.* Vol. 2. With an introduction by Henri Cordier. London: The Hakluyt Society, 1913. Nendeln, Liechtenstein: Kraus Reprint Ltd., 1967.

Zacher, Christian. *Curiosity and Pilgrimage.* Baltimore and London: Johns Hopkins University Press, 1976.

Ziolkowski, Jan M. "Literary Genre and Animal Symbolism." *Animals and the Symbolic in Mediaeval Art and Literature.* Ed. L. A. J. R. Houwen. Groningen, the Netherlands: Egbert Forsten, 1997. 1–23.

Index

For Product Safety Concerns and Information please contact our EU representative GPSR@taylorandfrancis.com
Taylor & Francis Verlag GmbH, Kaufingerstraße 24, 80331 München, Germany

www.ingramcontent.com/pod-product-compliance
Lightning Source LLC
Chambersburg PA
CBHW071517100726
47908CB00004B/1195

* 9 7 8 0 4 1 5 7 6 2 7 5 5 *